KILLER COUSINS

OTHER FIVE STAR TITLES
BY JUNE SHAW

Relative Danger

A CEALIE GUNTHER MYSTERY

KILLER COUSINS

JUNE SHAW

FIVE STAR

A part of Gale, Cengage Learning

Detroit • New York • San Francisco • New Haven, Conn • Waterville, Maine • London

GALE
CENGAGE Learning

LIBRARY OF CONGRESS CATALOGING-IN-PUBLICATION DATA

Shaw, June.
  Killer cousins / June Shaw. — 1st ed.
    p. cm.
  ISBN-13: 978-1-59414-730-2 (hardcover : alk. paper)
  ISBN-10: 1-59414-730-2 (hardcover : alk. paper)
    1. Cousins—Fiction. 2. Man-woman relationships—Fiction. 3. Murder—Investigation—Fiction. 4. Gatlinburg (Tenn.)—Fiction.
  I. Title.
  PS3619.H3936K55 2009
  813'.6—dc22   2008039745

First Edition. First Printing: January 2009.
Published in 2009 in conjunction with Tekno Books and Ed Gorman.

Printed in the United States of America
1 2 3 4 5 6 7 12 11 10 09 08

For a wonderful lady, my mom—Nora Shaw

ACKNOWLEDGMENTS

I thank my close family. I can accomplish creatively only with your love and support: Nora Shaw, Bob Breaux, Al, Sharon and Blair Naquin, Dawn Naquin and Allison Fakier, Scott Naquin, Debra, Mike, Dylan and Ryan Blanchard, Nolan, Becky, Parker, Brooke, Caroline and Claire Naquin, Billy and Delta Shaw, Ronnie and Lise Shaw, Lois Naquin, and Janet Shaw. Thanks also to special friends Billy and Deanie Sevin, Chuck and Margaret Giroir, Irma Daigle, Jeannette Nannie, Irma Arceneaux, and the queen and princesses of Dizzy Lizzie's and other Red Hat Society groups. I definitely appreciate my teenage cheerleader, Brandi Clement.

Special thanks to many people who provided much-needed information. Larry Weidel, Public Information Officer with the Lafourche Parish Sheriff's Office; Billy J. Bourg, Chief Investigator for the Lafourche Parish District Attorney's Office; and Susan Greene helped with police procedure. Any mistakes made are my own. Dr. Jody Plaisance and Rite Aid druggists Alfred Bourgeois and Herbert Kraemer led me toward additional knowledge about nicotine's negative effects. Feng Shui consultants Edith Marie Toups and Bella Andre graciously taught me basics about Feng Shui. Lisa Bork helped critique this book, along with early help from Linda Bell and other members of the Mystery Writers Critique Group.

I would be lost without encouragement and friendships from my writers' groups, especially SOLA (the RWA chapter in New

Orleans), Mystery Writers of America, Guppies, and Sisters in Crime.

I'm a former teacher and continue to realize how much the educators I worked with and my students taught me. Thanks to all of you for providing inspiration for my writing. Special thanks to former student Randa Guillot, who now helps in many ways as my hairdresser.

Some courageous individuals won contests for their real names or names of friends to appear in this book, especially since they had no idea what roles they might play. I don't know them, so any resemblance would be coincidental. Molly Mac-Rae was the first. Sue Evans won in an auction and wanted her reader buddies Sue Horowitz and Lois Fields included. Thanks to all of you ladies for letting me use you as characters.

I am forever grateful to the people who helped in my long quest to become a nonsmoker. Wanda Whitney gave me helpful tools through her hypnosis. Belinda Thibodaux, who works at Thibodaux Regional Hospital, was tremendously helpful as group leader for our Stop-Smoking groups and didn't give up, even when it seemed not one of us would ever really quit. And mega thanks to my daughter Dawn for urging me to quit with her on that first day of Lent, even after I stressed, "That's not a good day for me to quit. I'm not quite ready." Thank you, God, for finally making me ready, and for all that is good in my life.

And thanks to Alice Duncan, a fantastic lady and editor who champions my work to publication, and editor Tiffany Schofield, who gives authors tremendous help. Special thanks to John Helfers at Tekno Books for first recognizing the merits of *Killer Cousins*, and everyone at Five Star for doing such a great job.

A huge thank you and hug go out to my readers. I love to hear from you. Please contact me at www.juneshaw.com. Thanks so much.

June

CHAPTER 1

My day would have started much better if I hadn't tripped over a body.

I didn't know what it was yet. I'd flown into Gatlinburg, reached my cousin's house, shoved on the stuck gate of her backyard's wooden fence, and fallen.

"Stevie!" I cried, lying facedown in tall grass. "Ste—vie!"

Her screen door slammed. "Oh, Cealie, it's you! You came!"

She squatted beside me, and I noticed my hand landed in dog doo-doo. I jerked my hand back. I wasn't wearing my bifocals but could tell the poop was dry. Still—I swiped my fingers through the grass.

"You didn't answer your doorbell," I said, checking my hand to make sure it was clean, "so I came back here. I tripped over something."

I moved my legs slowly to make sure my stinging knees weren't broken. So many trees cluttered Stevie's yard, I figured a thick branch had fallen, and it was the object my shins lay across. "I'll help you move that thing out of the way." I pointed back to it.

Stevie didn't speak. I glanced back to see what brought about this bizarre occurrence.

She stooped near me but didn't look at my face. Stevie stared at my feet. My cousin blinked bluish-tan eyes so pale they might have been extensions of her cheekbones. I'd never seen her hair this way, gray and long. Her mouth was open. But this time it

9

said nothing. Her chin appeared stuck against her neck. And that neck, like the rest of her that I could see, had ballooned.

I took my time rising. Until I glanced toward where she stared.

"It's a man!" I yelled, scrambling to my feet. "Stevie, there's a man in your grass."

"I knew it." She looked at my face. "I was afraid something like this would happen."

The man was on his back with his eyes shut. I scooted farther from him. "Who is he?"

"I have no idea."

I eyed him, glad I didn't see blood or gore. I wouldn't do well with blood or gore. He appeared middle aged, maybe a few years younger than I, not bad looking and clean-shaven. Ice-blue shirt. Cell phone on his belt. One side of his shirt pulled up, revealing some skin. The edge of what seemed a bandage stuck on his back. Grass on his shoes. He might have been asleep, except he hadn't moved since I tripped over him.

"Check his pulse," I whispered.

"Uh-uh. You do it."

I tried to conceal my inner cringe. It might be heroic to save a person, but I had little doubt this man was stone cold. I knelt beside him. "Sir, are you okay?"

He didn't even make an eye twitch.

I laid my hand on his shoulder. Rigid. My hands weren't. They shook. "Do you need help?" I touched his neck. Much too still. He smelled of vomit. A bluish color tinted his lips.

"What?" Stevie said.

"He's dead. Call the police."

She made me think of the Ghost of Christmas Past with her arms raised, a caftan floating around her. I didn't imagine she could hustle anymore with her age and size. She'd always been the faster runner, but back then she was tall and thin. She was still tall. The yellow caftan with geometric print didn't conceal her weight, which might have tended toward three hundred pounds. I scrambled to the house behind her.

"There's a dead man in my backyard," she said to whoever answered her phone call. She gave directions and said to come through the wooden fence in back.

She hung up. "They're coming. How about some coffee while we wait?"

"Coffee's good. It might make me quit shaking." There was no logic to my statement, but logical wasn't my first reaction.

"I'll add whiskey."

"Great." I soaped my hands at the sink. "You must have a big dog."

"I don't own a dog."

"There's dog mess in your yard."

"Among other things." She clinked cups and spoons, and a strong whiskey smell overcame the unusual tangy odor in the room. Wind chimes and crystals hung from the ceiling and above the sink. What I surmised were stones, along with glassy items of different shapes, sat on her countertop in various assemblages. They hadn't been here when I last came, years ago, and probably all had a psychic nature. I knew Stevie practiced psychic mumbo jumbo but had never seen it in action.

She glanced through the back door. I did, too, hoping the man was sitting up and brushing off his knees.

No such luck. He lay as still as the small broken branches in her yard.

Stevie gulped from the whiskey bottle. She plunked down the bottle and carried two mugs, handing me one. We swigged our spiked coffee, which sent a nice burn down my throat. I hoped it would numb me so I'd quit shaking. I hoped the police would arrive soon and tell us the man was just ill.

Now, as always, I found it difficult to focus on Stevie's eyes. Their translucent irises made me stare at their pinprick black centers. My view expanded to her entire face. It had aged, grown fuller and softened, remaining attractive.

"Who is that man outside? And why did he die in your yard?" I asked.

Stevie's spooky eyes widened. Sirens screamed behind her house. "Let's get out there," she said.

Uniformed police officers and some people in regular clothes bustled in the back gate. A few knelt, checking the man. Others focused on the gate and various parts of the yard. A slightly built man without a uniform headed for Stevie and me.

"I'm Detective Renwick," he said. He was slightly taller than my five feet two inches with gray threading his black hair. "And you are?" He eyed us.

"Stevie Midnight. I live here. And this is my cousin, Cealie Gunther. She found that man."

Oh great, Stevie, this is your dead person. Why aim the investigator at me? I gave a tight smile to Stevie and a sweet one to Renwick.

"Do you live here, Ms. Gunther?" he asked, not returning my smile.

"No, sir. I just arrived from the airport. I flew in to visit."

He shoved dark glasses atop his head. "You only came to visit her?"

His gaze sought my attention. All the commotion behind him made it difficult to stay connected. People measured the man, inspected the gate, snapped pictures. My eyes burned, stomach knotted.

"Sir?" I said, realizing Renwick waited for an answer. "Yes, I wanted to visit my cousin."

The whole truth was that I'd detoured here because Stevie kept sending E-mails saying she was in danger and needed help. That she would die if I didn't come here and visit with her. She'd scared me for nothing at first, then later convinced me she needed saving. Stevie used to make me cry when we were kids. And why she thought I could protect her now was way beyond my understanding. I owned a copyediting agency. Neither my store managers nor I were detectives.

If Stevie wanted police help now, she'd tell him. Renwick turned from the study of my face to hers. Then back to mine. Maybe searching for resemblance.

"We don't look much alike," I said. "She's older. Her side of the family has paler eyes. And they're taller."

"Everything Cealie said is true," Stevie said. "Except I'm not that much older. Just a couple of months." She gave me a so-there nod.

"Yes, ma'am," he said, writing on a pad. "Did either of you see what happened back here? Or hear anything unusual?"

"No, sorry," Stevie said, and I looked at her, curious.

"You, ma'am?" he asked me. I told him what happened when I arrived. "We'll have to check your rental car," he said, and I nodded.

"My car is through that door in the garage," Stevie told the detective.

"Is Stevie your given name?" he asked.

"Yes, given to me by my mother." She grinned with her joke. "And my father gave me my last name. I never married."

"Your parents seemed to like similar first names." He nodded at each of us.

"Oh yes. Stevie. Cealie." She gave me the first smile she'd offered since I arrived. "Our mothers were sisters. They both wrote great poetry. I can show you some of Mother's if you'd like."

"Not today," Renwick said. "Does anyone live with you?"

Her expression crimped, like she was embarrassed. "No, there's only me."

"I'd like to come in," Renwick said.

"Wonderful. I have fresh coffee. I'll put on a little more, and all your friends back here can have some, too."

Good grief. Did she need company that badly?

"No coffee, but I'd like to look around."

"Come and look away." She rushed through the door ahead of him. I kept quiet and followed.

In the kitchen Stevie fixed more coffee, seemingly oblivious to the detective. I watched his face when he spied all of her psychic paraphernalia. Renwick sniffed the air, pungent with aromas that might have come from lit candles or netherworld objects. He wrote on his pad.

He moved to other parts of the house, inspecting. I slid non-chalantly behind him, keeping a few feet between us. My shins started to ache. Renwick paused at the doorway of the third bedroom. I saw the bed was gone from it. What resembled a small altar was set up near the far wall. A wide circle of squat, lit candles sat on the carpet. Renwick shook his head.

The phone shrilled in the kitchen, making him glance back. He spied me in the hall.

I gave him my innocent-grandma smile. "I'll go get that," I said, pointing.

My cousin answered the phone. Her caller's voice boomed, "Stevie, there are cop cars all around your house!" The woman sounded young. "Oh, some of them are coming over here. I'll get back to you."

Disconnecting, Stevie noticed me. "My neighbor," she explained.

"She has a loud voice."

"Especially when she's excited." Stevie nodded to the detective returning from the hall. "The coffee's poured."

"I'd like to ask a few more questions," Renwick said.

I glanced through the screen door while he took a chair at the table. Chills spiked up my spine. Yellow tape spread outside

14

the open gate. More people gathered. Men positioned a gurney near the man on the grass.

"Do you know who he is?" I asked. "Or what killed him? Did he die of natural causes?"

"We'll let you know. Do you visit here often?"

"It's been a while, probably before Stevie's hair turned gray."

"And what color is *yours* now?" she shot back.

"I haven't had the courage to find out lately. But this shade's natural burnt sienna."

"Good shade. But your roots—"

"Okay," our questioner said, gaze leveled at me, "so you flew in today for a visit with your cousin here?"

"Oh, no," Stevie said. "Cealie probably never would have come if I hadn't told her I was in danger and needed help."

Renwick's eyebrows scrunched up. "What danger? You were threatened?"

"Absolutely, the signs are everywhere. My tarot cards. The warnings in my candles and crystals."

"*What?* You got me here because of stupid candles and cards?" I said and mentally slapped myself. I'd made last-minute changes in my flight to Acapulco. I came and got involved in Stevie's situation—just because she'd foreseen difficulty in chunks of *glass?*

Our investigator wrote. Stevie obviously noticed his eye rolls. "My gift of foretelling has helped lots of people," she snapped at him. "Even the police."

He raised an eyebrow. "How did you do that?"

"I helped your department locate a young woman's body. I told you all where to look in the woods."

"When was that?"

"About eight years ago."

"Before my time, ma'am." He faced me. "If you arrived from the airport, why did you come through the back gate instead of

15

the front door?"

"I rang the doorbell a while, but Stevie didn't answer. I thought she might be out back, so I drove around there." I faced Stevie. "Where were you when I rang the bell?"

Immediately I wished I hadn't asked. She probably hadn't been taking a shower, since her long hair wasn't damp. And it didn't look like she'd just blown it dry and styled it. In fact Stevie's hair, for the first time I'd ever seen, had no style at all.

She gave me an angry glance. "I was meditating."

"You can meditate so hard a doorbell won't disturb you?" I asked, then slapped my hand over my mouth. My tongue often worked before my thoughts. Sure, I'd like to learn to meditate. But my question in front of this policeman made it sound like I didn't believe her.

"I could meditate even if the walls came crashing down around me," she said.

The note-taker wrote. I stood beside the counter, fiddling with the newspaper folded there. I curled its corners, then smoothed what I'd curled. An ad in the corner sped up my heartbeats. *Please join us for our grand opening. Cajun Delights specializes in seafood and Cajun dishes.*

The restaurant would belong to my ex-lover, Gil Thurman. Intimate parts of my torso woke up.

I tugged at the neckline of my naturally wrinkled periwinkle pantsuit and gave an innocent closemouthed smile to the officer staring at me. I certainly didn't want to think about sex now, and couldn't believe my thoughts had strayed there. Probably my mind needed to escape this whole surreal experience and return me to a more pleasant place.

I let go of my clothes and the officer turned back to Stevie, who was answering his questions. My fingers slid over the ad. Okay, I had given in to my urges concerning Gil a few days ago. But then I'd promised myself and told him—I never would again. Lusting for Gil always made my mind quit working. With my mind disabled, I'd never get on with my current life's mission.

I now discovered Stevie's kitchen had heated.

Detective Renwick stood. "That's all for now. We'll probably want to talk to you again. I'll ask both of you not to leave town."

"But I wasn't planning to stay long," I shot back.

He pulled his dark glasses down over his eyes. "Is there any reason you can't stay?"

Only that I'd never really liked Stevie much. Recently she'd made me needlessly fear for my grandchild Kat when I visited Kat and my son Roger in Chicago. Stevie had always been ditzy and since she'd grown, considered herself rather psychic, and that made me really uncomfortable. She used to pull my hair when we were kids and kept her hair short so I couldn't pull it.

I smiled at the cop. "I just made a quick stopover on my way to Mexico."

"We want you to extend your stay in our area a little while. You'll be free to go once we determine exactly what happened here."

Stevie walked him to the back door. She turned and stared at me.

I could reach up and yank her hair now. But its gray color and thin texture destroyed my desire. Her eyes drowned me in their omniscient stare, making me decide she might discern every thought germinating in my brain.

I didn't really believe she could but wiped my mind clean, just in case.

"I don't think the man died of natural causes," she said. "I think somebody killed him."

She had ways of knowing things. She'd gotten me here under false pretense. And now I couldn't leave until a stranger's death was resolved?

I'd get right to work to discover why he died. Then I would take the next flight out of town.

CHAPTER 2

Stevie splashed more coffee into her mug. "Want a refill?" she asked me.

"No way." Too many jitters already from caffeine and a dead man. My shins ached. I imagined his unmoving legs beneath them. Something else bothered me. "What's wrong with you today? You've hardly smiled at all."

Sure, a corpse lay in her yard, but even that would never have worried Stevie enough to keep her smile away. I was ordinarily cheerful, too, but her smiles usually lasted for days. She often laughed like a hyena that couldn't catch its breath, and I always feared I'd have to resuscitate her. "You seem so tense," I said. "All of your movements look nervous."

She dropped to a chair at her table. Lifted the corners of her lips. Pressed her arms against her sides. "This okay?"

"That smile's not real. What's the problem?"

She opened her mouth. *Rap-rap-rap* sounded from the front door, and two sets of quick footsteps approached.

A sliver of a woman darted in. "The cops came and questioned me." Her voice was the one I'd heard booming over the phone earlier. I had imagined her to be a larger person. A strong gust could blow her away. She stopped, a mop-headed girl of about three at her side. "Oh, you have company. I thought everybody left," the young woman said.

"The investigators are outside," Stevie replied. She gave the child a smile that lit even her eyes. "Cherish, come give Aunt

19

Stevie a big hug." Stevie wasn't really the child's aunt.

Cherish crossed her arms. "I wanted to keep watching *Scooby-Doo*."

"You can watch it in my room." Stevie ran with the child toward the bedrooms and let loose her annoying cackle. The girl's mom grinned at me and blew a pink bubble with her gum. Cartoon characters screamed. Stevie returned. "That's my favorite cousin, Cealie Gunther," she said.

The bubble backed into the woman's mouth. "Stevie told me a bunch of stuff about you. I live next door. I'm April McGee."

Her comment surprised me. Stevie and I had very little contact in years and weren't ever close. "Nice to meet you," I said.

"How did that man die?" April asked Stevie.

"Maybe he just walked in my yard and had a stroke or a heart attack."

"You think so?" April shoved aside a section of her silky all-one-length black hair that dropped over part of her baby blue eyes.

Stevie spread her hands. "Who knows?"

"But why would a stranger pick your yard to come into to die?" I asked.

"Maybe he walked by and started to feel bad. He could have wanted to use a phone to call someone."

April nodded. "Sounds logical." She plopped her capri-clad seat down on a chair.

"But," I said, "he had a cell phone clipped to his belt."

"Oh." April zipped her head around toward Stevie, who thrummed blunt fingernails on the table.

"I can't explain everything." Stevie shoved up to her feet. "How can I know why a stranger chose my gate to come through when he was ready to die?"

From the TV in her bedroom, a character called for Scooby

Doo. Stevie glanced there, looking even more annoyed.

Uneasy, I nudged the newspaper closer. Most ads in this section glared for notice. Not Cajun Delights.

Recently, when we were near Chicago, Gil told me he'd be coming to this area to open another restaurant. I wasn't sure when. But if he came around this town now, I'd avoid him.

I *would.*

Stevie opened the refrigerator. She grabbed a canned diet lime drink for April. Then sat, looking calmer, and sipped her coffee.

April swallowed lime drink over the gum in her mouth. "Cops came and asked me things, mainly if I knew that dead man or saw anything strange at your place. I didn't." She grinned. "Cherish used the potty again all by herself."

Stevie laughed. My interest drifted. I'd fought the attraction to Gil, but then a few days ago, gave in.

But no more. I tightly cloaked myself inside my mantra: *I am woman! I can do anything—alone!* I needed to avoid Gil so that I could rediscover myself.

Still, I recalled our sweet lovemaking. Satisfactory. No, much more than that. With my body spooned against Gil's, I'd felt like I was in the most natural place in the world. And thinking about Gil comforted me more than considering what was outside or in here.

Women's voices swirled around me. I peered at Stevie and her neighbor, still discussing Cherish and laughing.

I smiled as though I were invested in their stories. My imaginings drifted to a sweeter scene involving Gil and me twisted together.

April raised a question that snagged my attention. "What if somebody came in your backyard and killed him?"

"Who?" Stevie asked, snapping to her feet. She topped her coffee mug from the decanter and grabbed another diet lime drink for April. "Who knows who could have passed my house or followed that man to murder him?"

April popped her bubble gum. "I do."

"You do?" Stevie and I asked together.

"Uh-huh, and I told the cops." She yanked the gum from her mouth, set it on the table, and cracked open her second lime drink. She swallowed some. "I was swinging on my back porch, catching up on *The Soap Opera Digest* while Cherish played in her sandbox in the yard. I glanced up every time somebody passed. I saw who came behind our houses."

"Tell us," I said, ready to solve the mystery. The people who loved that poor man needed to know what caused his death so they could have closure.

Stevie looked like a tent standing beside her miniscule neighbor. "Who'd you see pass by?"

"Those two women who walk together all the time."

"The ones with white hair?" Stevie asked, and April nodded. "They didn't kill anyone. Who else?"

"The mailman."

Stevie responded with an annoyed sound rolling through her throat.

"And then," April said, returning the used gum to her mouth, "there were those other guys."

"What guys?" I asked.

"It's over!" Cherish dashed in. "Mamma, I wanna go home."

Stevie grabbed Cherish and cuddled the child on her lap. "Was your show good?"

Kinky brown curls wobbled with her nods. "I wanna see it again."

Stevie's nose scrunched, and her cackles followed. "I don't have a tape of the movie, but I'll try to buy one for you."

"Okay." Cherish slid down. "Let's go, Mamma."

"All right." April held her hand.

I stood in their path. "But who else came around these houses today?"

Bubble gum popped, making me jump. "That guy who walks his dog and the one who checks our gas meters." April tugged Cherish's hand. "Tell Aunt Stevie and her cousin bye-bye."

Cherish gave us a hand flip.

"Come back and see me," Stevie said, walking them to the back door.

"You haven't smoked yet?" April asked, and Stevie shook her head. "Good for you." April looked through the glass on the door. "Oh, they're still here. Come on, baby, we need to go through the front."

She and Cherish let themselves out, while I determined what had seemed especially unusual. Stevie hadn't smoked!

I hadn't even seen signs of her ashtrays. Normally ashtrays cluttered the house and held mountains of smashed butts that made the place smell like a barroom.

"You quit," I said, smiling. "When?"

Stevie stared out at all the people still milling back there, her hands shaky against the screen door. "Today."

"Maybe today's not the best day to try to quit," I said.

No wonder she seemed so uptight. Nicotine withdrawals. And the death. That dead man had parents, grandparents, friends, maybe children. And now something or someone had snuffed out his life. Heat built up behind my eyes.

"No time is best to quit." Stevie's cloudy gaze told of her longing for the nicotine that had been her best friend and enemy for at least three decades.

"But with what happened today, couldn't you smoke only a few and then totally quit another time?" I suggested.

She gazed across the top of my head. "You don't know anything about giving up smoking. Today's the day my group chose to quit." Her strange eyes fixed on glittery objects dangling above her window.

"Oh, you have a support group. Good." I had no idea how to stop a person from smoking besides saying don't do it.

"We met last night and said we wouldn't smoke today. We'll meet again tonight."

"Do you think any of the people April mentioned could have killed that man?"

"Probably not."

My anger sprang up. I shoved my fists on my hips and spoke with attitude. "So you really made me come over here because you imagined scary things in a stupid deck of cards and some candles?"

Her forehead creased. She looked scared. "Cealie, I really think someone's out to get me. I—" She flung her hands over her chest and looked pale.

"Are you okay?"

She lowered her hands. "I'm just . . . really glad you're here. And I'm not ready to tell the police anything else now."

I rubbed her arm. "Then here's what I think we should do. Let's go on your back porch, watch who passes by, and possibly come up with an idea. Lots of murderers return to check their victims, sometimes because they're proud."

"You really think someone killed him?" she asked, voice soft.

"Who knows? But we'd better go and see what we can find out. First I need my things out of my rental car, especially my new friend, Minnie. She's a cactus." I grinned, content with all the plant knowledge I'd recently acquired. What I'd learned brought Minnie back from the verge of death. Of course my lack of knowledge had created that verge and at the same time learned that I could never teach . . .

I'd never kept any type of plant alive before I chose Minnie, and felt pleased with myself for at least learning to care for a cactus. I'd learned about the numerous types of cacti and that I could never teach in a public high school today unless I was allowed to carry something to use to defend myself.

We looked out the back door, where people still milled. The detective who questioned us was searching behind bushes near the porch.

"Detective Renwick," Stevie said, "did y'all find anything?"

"Nothing definite yet."

We went through the hall toward the front door. This time I paid more attention since I wasn't following police. The old house held a mainly comfortable feel. It sported earth tones with an oak floor and walls painted an unusual shade blending yellows with the green of spring leaves. Her living room held sofas and chairs in midnight blue and black yet felt airy because of lots of glass. The extra large windows, set of stemmed glassware on a glass serving tray, and artwork in shapeless watery colors added to the spacious feel.

"Pretty room," I mentioned as we walked out.

"It's my career area," she said. I looked at her curiously. She explained, "Feng Shui."

I nodded. I'd heard of the ancient Chinese art of arranging people's homes to enhance their lives. If that's what she'd done, good for her.

Stevie crossed her porch, and I again noted the round crystal hanging on a red string about eight inches from the porch's ceiling. Probably more Feng Shui beliefs. She took off down the steps and reached the sidewalk ahead of me. The sidewalk sloped in front of the house next door. "That's where April lives," she said as we walked near. The unassuming brick house resembled Stevie's—tan brick with green shutters and a front porch. April lived at the corner with a tall wooden fence behind it like Stevie's. Because they resided on the side of a rocky mountain, there were no neighbors in back, only a wide section of grass and then a road winding up the incline.

"How could April see who was on the street back there?" I asked.

"The land slopes so much, we can see most of it from our back porches."

We rounded the corner, and I admired the view of lush mountains. Intruding on the scene's quiet, Stevie kept snapping her fingers. She huffed while she walked. Yes, it was definitely time for her to give up the smokes.

"Weird car," she said when we reached my PT Cruiser that I'd parked on the grass next to the road behind her house. We eyed the police units still parked near, their yellow tape crossing her gate. We looked away.

"That's the beauty of renting from a new car lot. You get so many choices," I said, admiring my Cruiser's brown side panels. I noted the grass was cut back here, much different from the tall grass I'd discovered in my cousin's yard.

I popped the doors and the hatchback. "We're here," I told Minnie, removing her from the cup holder in front.

Stevie yanked up my suitcase and satchel.

"This is my sidekick." I proudly held out my little cactus. Minnie's triangular green stem stood straight again, one of my major achievements. And all of the poufs on her pink head appeared healthy. "She was grafted to look this nice."

Stevie's eyebrows wrinkled as she skimmed me and my plant. I tried to take my luggage, but she kept a firm grip, maybe needing to keep her hands busy. We backtracked along the sidewalk without speaking. I listened for cops' voices, but instead heard April.

"Cherish!" she yelled. "Get back in here! I can't come out there now."

"Aw," the child griped. Their door slammed, probably Cherish going back in.

"April seems especially protective," I said. "Their yard is

fenced, but she won't let the girl play out there without her."

"An unexplained death just took place next door," Stevie snapped.

"But April was watching every person that passed behind their fence even before she knew about the body."

The hard set of Stevie's jaw let me know I shouldn't ask more. The pang of nicotine withdrawal was probably striking.

In her house Stevie brought my luggage down the hall. I set Minnie on a countertop near the kitchen window. "You'll get some sunshine here. Don't be bothered by all the strange stuff. You can look at the pretty colors and glittering objects."

Minnie seemed to lean toward me, and if it were possible for a cactus to grin, I was certain she did. I'd learned that talking to plants was a good thing.

Stevie reappeared. "You're all set in the guest bedroom."

I hoped that wasn't the one with the candles and altar. "So now we'll go and look for a killer?"

"Right after I straighten up in here." She set the used mugs in the sink and tossed April's empty cans and the newspaper in the trash. "Oh, this looked interesting," she said, retrieving the paper. "A Cajun restaurant opened. Maybe we can check it out later."

I replied with a noncommittal grin. Stevie didn't know anything about its owner. I knew so much about Gil. His deep-throated laughter. And hunky body.

Heat rushed through me.

Nope, if Gil was around town, I definitely needed to avoid him.

"Let's go look for a killer, if there was one," I said, concerned about the man who died. That was also the major way to avoid temptation. Catch the bad guy or gal, then hop on the next jet to Acapulco, where I was headed before I detoured to see about Stevie.

"Of course he could have died of natural causes." She put away condensed milk and a canister marked *Sugar*. No wonder her coffee tasted so good. And no wonder she'd puffed up so much. So would I if I kept drinking coffee she fixed. I wasn't trim now and feared that adding many more pounds might make me resemble a box that a stove came in.

Stevie washed the mugs. I zapped a damp towel across the table and stove, noting a mirror on the rear of the stove and facing the kitchen. "There." I set my towel beside hers. "Now we can go."

She grabbed a dry towel, dried the surfaces, and put everything away.

All of this was her usual practice? Or aftereffects from having no nicotine since last night?

Out on the back porch, we sat on cushioned rockers. Police still inspected the gate and parts of the yard. They looked at us. I nodded at them, then stared at the section of sloping road visible beyond the fence. The dead man was gone. I was shaky inside.

"See if anyone out there looks like a killer," Stevie said, her fingernails going *click-click-click* against her chair arm.

Our position gave us a limited view of the road. I stood to see out there better.

A couple of cars and trucks passed. Birds screeched. A boy laughed. Brakes hissed on a heavy vehicle, then it accelerated. "Sounds like a garbage truck," I said. "But it seems late for garbage pickup."

"Maybe their truck broke down."

"Maybe." I listened to the repeated hiss and pickup with forward motion. A school bus might make similar noise, but it seemed way too late for one to be dropping off kids. "But," I said, "what if it's late because the people on it stopped to kill someone before getting garbage?"

Stevie stared at me. Took quivery breaths. Turned away.

"Right," I said. "A garbage truck would be the perfect body-disposal vehicle, so why would people on it want to drop the body off in your yard?"

She shuddered. "You are so weird."

"*I'm* weird?"

People in her yard stared at me.

I huffed a little and decided to let it go. "Who knows about all the people we see often, maybe those who pass our houses every day?" I asked Stevie more pleasantly. "Some of them walk or run. Vehicles drive around us all the time, and we hardly pay attention."

Blunt fingernails increased their annoying clatter.

"And," I said, turning to see the white truck braking and men from it picking up trash down the road, "we don't care who comes in our yards presumably to check our meters or make deliveries. But because people inspect our meters or deliver to our houses, does that mean we can trust them? That they aren't killers?"

"Nobody guarantees it."

"And even if someone wears a uniform or drives a labeled vehicle, that person isn't necessarily a representative of the place. Or the people we shop from could be killers."

"Grmm." Stevie's throat sound was an agreement, mulling, or desire for a cigarette.

Detective Renwick approached. "We're leaving for now. We'd like that police tape to stay up until our investigation is finished."

"Can you tell us anything now?" I asked.

"Not yet. Let us know if you think of anything else." Renwick followed the other officers out the gate. Their cars started and drove off. All grew quiet.

I crossed my arms. Stevie crossed hers. I felt my elastic waistband to make sure my cell phone was still hooked to my slacks under my shirt, in case I needed it. We watched for suspicious-looking people.

Few cars passed. Two white-headed women the same height ambled alongside the road. A large man in a black cap and gray jogging clothes strolled past. He stared at Stevie's fence and then us. He gave a whistle, and a brown Lab ran close to him.

The pulse in my head beat stronger. I slid my eyes toward Stevie. She stared grim faced at the road with what seemed unfocused vision. Of course with her luminescent eyes, who could tell? Did she know that man who'd walked past? Or was she worrying about the dead one? Had that Lab come into this yard—maybe with his owner? Had my fingers lain in that Lab's poop?

I smelled my hand, glad not to find lingering poop odor.

Shivers accompanied the bumps sprouting across my arms. The evening deepened shadows in trees surrounding us. Stevie appeared in a trance. She sat rock still except for her tapping fingertips.

"Did you think of anything?" I asked her.

"No. But it's almost time for my meeting. We need to get dinner."

We went in and she fixed more coffee, thrusting condensed milk and sugar into her mug. "Want some?"

I shook my head. "Maybe it was just his time to die."

Her intense look gave me the heebie-jeebies. She leaned against the counter, her angry eyes taking in Minnie beside her wide hand. I imagined Stevie dropping that hand on my plant. She could mash Minnie with no problem.

"I hope you don't mind if I leave my cactus there," I said, shifting closer.

"Don't mind at all." Stevie filled a cup with water and dumped it on Minnie.

"Oh no. A cactus doesn't need much water." I grabbed Minnie's pot and moved it farther from the sink. "I watered her too much at first but then learned better."

Stevie didn't seem impressed by my knowledge. "We need to eat." She swigged her coffee and washed everything before I could get in a good blink. I wasn't going to dry only those things, but she did, and then set them in place. "You want leftovers or to go and try that new place?"

New chills skittered through me. Leftover whatever Stevie's fridge held—or mouthwatering cuisine at the place that might also hold Gil Thurman?

Uh-uh, nada, I told my sexual yearnings. I tried to summon enthusiasm. "Leftovers would be great."

Stevie heated casseroles in the microwave.

Her creamed spinach tasted especially good. So did the lasagna and garlic bread.

"This is all wonderful," I said, finally setting down my fork, "but I think my clothes just shrank three sizes."

She heaped another spoonful of lasagna onto her plate and grabbed more bread, her eyes fluttering downward like someone who might be embarrassed. "I've gotten bigger since you last saw me." Her gaze met mine. "But it's because I have to take medicine. For my arthritis." She raised a slightly bent finger.

"Medicine can be heck," I said, but couldn't help thinking of the gazillion fat grams in this meal and all of her mugs of coffee.

She brought out pralines for dessert—pralines! I had to eat one and a half while she gobbled three between washing dishes. I dried things, and she put them away. "Don't you ever use your dishwasher?" I asked, tiring of this housework I always carefully avoided. "Or maybe we could stop somewhere, and I'll pick up lovely throw-away dishes. They're my favorites."

"Let's go to my meeting. I need support."

We rode in her Jeep Cherokee. She zipped through skinny

dark roads that snaked down the mountainside, making me glad she was driving. "I'm so proud of you for quitting smoking," I said.

Her lips pressed together. Veins in her neck protruded. Her knuckles whitened while her hands tightened on the wheel. She passed a truck, barely squeezing through the curve, then headlights of a larger truck came toward us. I held my breath. She veered toward the shoulder, the mountainside plunging beside us.

Not soon enough we were on level ground. I started to breathe normally when she nosed into a spot near a half dozen other cars. A pole lamp lit this small patch of concrete nestled between trees near what looked like a small park.

"This is it." Stevie shoved out of her car.

We walked on a path between trees made visible only by a couple of lamps. A few men and women walked ahead of us into a small redbrick building. Our shoes clicked on the sidewalk, making some in the group turn toward us.

"Oh, Stevie," the shortest woman said, "do you know what happened today to one of our Quitters' members?"

"What?" Stevie asked, as we reached her near the door.

The short woman may have been in her early forties. Her face appeared pale, her figure shapely. "Somebody found him dead in a person's yard."

My heart leaped into my throat. My head swiveled toward Stevie.

She had lied to the police and to me. She *did* know the dead man.

CHAPTER 3

We swept into the dark building with Stevie's group. Lights flickered on.

"You see what happens?" the second woman ahead of us said. She was large with brassy red hair and too-snug stretchy jeans and spoke to no one in particular. "You quit smoking to improve your health—and something else kills you."

"Exactly," the shapely woman said. She and most of the others dropped to folding chairs arranged in a semicircle. Their gazes slid to me and away from me. I sat beside Stevie on the single empty metal chair.

"So you'd just as soon keep smoking. Is that it?" This from the man who'd let us in. Probably mid-fifties. Lanky with pink cheeks and thin midnight black hair that looked dyed, he stood in front of the group. "If a smoker dies from another cause, does that give you an excuse to keep lighting up?"

"Any excuse seems good at this point." The speaker sat at the far end of the group, his three-pronged walking cane nearby. Tight faced, he pumped his heel, making his knee bounce. "I'm dying for a cigarette."

The group leader faced him. "And one cigarette might literally kill you. Outside a few minutes ago, you told me you'd quit last night. And if you smoked one, you'd want more. Then more. And before you know it, you'd be right back to where you were yesterday, coughing your lungs out."

"Ugggh." I covered my mouth with my hand. All eyes trained

33

on me. "Sorry. That wasn't a pleasant image."

Faces in the room all looked tense.

"Are you a smoker?" the leader asked me. "It's late for you to be joining our sessions."

"I only tried smoking twice but got weak and coughed so much I gave up. In fact both times I was with Stevie, in the cemetery near her house."

"Appropriate place," the last man said. With extra-wide shoulders and a baby-smooth complexion, he wore cappuccino-colored linen slacks with a piece of grass sticking out of its cuff. The pattern of his dark brown rayon shirt resembled squids.

"Everyone," Stevie said, "this is my cousin Cealie Gunther. She's visiting me."

The shapely woman gave me a warm smile—the camaraderie of short people. No one else appeared happy that I was here.

"Hi," I told the group. "Good luck with your goal. I empathize. Quitting smoking isn't easy."

"You can say that again," the taller woman said, others nodding.

"And that's the reason we're here." On an easel the leader set a poster with only a title: THE QUITTERS GROUP.

I didn't think that an appropriate name, and knew an apostrophe should have been behind the second word. I also didn't know any of these people's names.

The leader's mouth opened to speak. I interjected, "Excuse me. You all know who I am now, but I don't know you. Not fair, is it?"

Tha-rump tha-rump came from Stevie's fingertips on her shoulder bag on her lap.

The leader gave me a pinched expression. "I'm Ish Muller." His brief nod allowed me to glimpse his premature bald spot.

"Father Paul Edward," the man with the cane said. He wore street clothes.

"Kern Parfait," said the man wearing squids.

"Hey. I'm Fawn." The small woman waved.

I grinned, then looked at the larger woman who seemed unnerved by my stare. She swerved her eyes away. "Jenna." She swallowed her last name.

"Now," Ish said, regaining everyone's focus, "tell us how you all made out. Did everyone quit last night?"

Shaky heads with gloomy eyes nodded.

"Good. Now let's hear what the last twenty-four hours were like for you," Ish said.

"I yelled at my husband and almost killed both my kids." Fawn held up a red-striped straw. "But sucking on this kept me from hurting anyone." She sucked on the straw, removed it, and exhaled.

"Anything that helps. What else? Anybody?" Ish said.

"I kept busy with my work," Father said.

"I took lots of deep breaths." Stevie, at my side, surprised me with her quiet tone. And I hadn't noticed her doing deep breathing at home. Of course I arrived after a man died there. "And meditation helped," she added.

That's what she'd said she was doing when I rang her front doorbell. She'd also said she didn't know the dead man, but now I'd discovered he belonged to this group. What else wasn't she telling me?

And why weren't any of them concerned about their fellow member's demise?

The group peered at Jenna. Her cheeks flushed. She kept her head down.

Finally she looked up. "All right, I admit it. I had one today. But it was just one. And mid-afternoon. I couldn't stand it anymore."

"That's okay." Fawn patted Jenna's arm. "You won't do it again, right?"

Jenna hunched forward, hands twisting in her lap. Everyone focused on her. She looked so dejected under such scrutiny that I had to turn my eyes away. No one should have to squirm and sit in other people's judgment while trying to stop a habit.

After long moments, during which I imagined she nodded, Ish again spoke. "So—you'll all continue to need help. Here is today's material. Does everyone have a pencil or pen?"

He passed out papers to all except me. I watched Stevie print her name in tall letters. Her paper contained lines for complete sentences or paragraphs. It also held cartoons of smiling people. I guessed those happy people had quit smoking.

I leaned near her. "You didn't tell me the man who died came to these sessions."

"I didn't know." A grimace froze on her face.

"He was in this small group, and you didn't know he was here?" I indicated the people following Ish's instructions for writing. "How could you miss anybody in here?"

My voice probably carried. Ish gave me a pained expression.

"Sorry to interrupt you," I said.

"I never saw the man before," my cousin told me. "If he was here, I didn't see him."

"Who?" Fawn leaned forward.

"Yes, may I ask who you're talking about?" Ish didn't hide his annoyance.

I wasn't about to tell them their fellow stop-smoker died in Stevie's yard.

But Stevie did. "The man you were talking about when we came in," she announced. "He was discovered dead in someone's yard today. That yard was mine."

"Oh." Fawn pressed back in her chair.

"Your yard?" the priest said.

Jenna's face blanched.

Ish came to Stevie. "Pierce Trottier died at your place?"

36

"I guess so, if that was his name."

"I'm sorry a friend of yours died today," I said to everyone. They probably would not like to know I fell across their friend. I didn't like it, either. Suddenly, I felt him pressed against my shins.

"How could you have not known him?" Ish asked Stevie.

"I *didn't* know him. When did he come here? I never saw him in any of our sessions."

"I want a cigarette!" Jenna said. "I'm sorry, I'm going to have one."

"No, don't!" Fawn produced a straw from her purse. "Have a straw instead."

Jenna swept past her out the door.

"Now you see?" The priest glared at Stevie. "You're making her smoke again."

"I'm not making anybody smoke. And I didn't know that man." Stevie got up to her feet. "I'm leaving. Are you coming?" she asked me.

"Of course." I felt like her supporter, but wasn't even sure I agreed with her. Was she lying to all of us? "Nice meeting you all," I said.

"Don't forget your material." Ish intercepted Stevie. "Read these. They'll help you."

I stood behind my cousin and couldn't see her face, but determined flames could've flared out her nostrils. She yanked the papers from his hands and stormed out.

The moment I walked outside, I smelled smoke. I spied a tiny red glow behind bushes. "See you later," I called to the person I figured was Jenna.

No response. The red glow moved deeper behind the bushes.

I snapped on my seatbelt a second before Stevie peeled into the street, her foot never seeming to touch the brakes, even at corners.

"Well that was nice," I said. Her face turned to me, her expression curious. "The meeting," I explained. "Lots of interesting people."

Her throat made a gritty sound. She stared at the road, her hand dipping into the large purse at her side. She dug around.

I hoped she wouldn't pull out a cigarette, but knew she could do worse.

Stevie withdrew a Tootsie Pop. "Want one?"

I hadn't eaten a chocolate Tootsie Pop in more years than I wanted to count. It enticed me, but my waistband still felt too tight. "Maybe later."

She stuck hers in her mouth. Within moments, she appeared soothed.

At least that new bulge in her cheek and white stick dangling from her mouth gave her a semblance of the Stevie I'd known. The lively jokester had been her image, even until a few weeks ago, when we'd spoken on the phone. Something in the recent past had caused her personality to twist one hundred-eighty degrees.

Had the transformation come about last night, when nicotine started leaching from her system? Or did this sudden change come about because a man died, a man she claimed she hadn't known?

She found me staring at her. "Want one now?" she asked, hand heading for her purse.

I wanted both her hands clasping the steering wheel as she zigzagged up the mountainside. "No candy, thanks." I faced the road, hoping she'd do the same.

She did, and in no time we reached her house. She parked in the attached garage, got out, and slammed the door. She left the papers Ish gave her on the seat.

I grabbed them, noticed the pristine appearance of her garage, and followed her inside.

The door led to the kitchen. She stood leaning back against the table, waiting for me. "I didn't know him," she reiterated.

"I believe you." Instinctively, I used fingernails from my left hand to pinch my right palm. A technique for tempering my lie? Or habit to try to convince myself I'd told the truth? At the moment I couldn't tell.

"Do you want something to eat?" Stevie asked.

"I'm still full." And my stomach was doing a twitchy dance from the ride.

"I'll just have a snack." She retrieved Devilish Chocolates, ripped the bag open, and held it toward me. I shook my head with much effort, and she gobbled the entire contents.

So much for putting all blame for her blossoming figure on medicine. She raised her hand to toss the crumpled bag to a wastebasket.

"You did a good thing today," I said.

Color drained from her face. "Huh?" Stevie's arm jerked, letting the trash go. The wadded bag struck the cabinet and bounced to the floor.

"That was a positive step you took." I tossed her bag in the wastebasket. "Quitting smoking."

"Oh yes, that."

"Did you do anything else special today? Anything out of the ordinary?"

Her gaze skittered everywhere around the room but toward my face. She heaved a sigh. "Just gave a strawberry sticker to one of my students. Lacy. It's her birthday." A glimmer of a smile flashed. "I gave her a big squeeze."

Not too big, I hoped, looking at Stevie's size and considering her tiny first-grade students.

I mentally slapped the side of my head. No matter how hard I tried, I'd never been able to rid myself of those rapidly surfacing judgments.

"I know you enjoy your students."

"They keep me happy," Stevie said, and told of incidents with some of the children.

I considered telling about the fearsome teens I'd recently encountered in my granddaughter Kat's high school, but decided not to disrupt her cheerful mood.

"I'll go to bed now," I said.

"Your things are in the guest bedroom. Let me know if you need anything else."

I was satisfied that my bedroom appeared normal. No candles, altars, or stones. The room had a pleasant airy feel. Sheer blue curtains. Purple, red, and green blended surprisingly well on the bedspread with lots of throw pillows in those colors.

Stevie had set my luggage on one section of a king-size bed. She'd turned down the covers on the opposite side.

I dressed in a lightweight gown and left my suitcase where it was since I didn't move much while I slept.

I slid into the bed's turned-back section and considered the day. My flight change to here. Finding a body, which seemed too horrible to think about. Stevie's mega change in size and habits. Her group members. And the cushiony feel of Gil's shoulders. Within minutes, I slept.

A while later I awoke, wishing I'd emptied my bladder before going to bed. A sound had awakened me. Did it come from my window?

I shrank beneath the covers. Listened.

After long minutes, with no sound repeating, I decided what I'd heard must have come from a dream. I traipsed down the dark hall to the bathroom.

A voice uttered strange sounds. A pungent aroma swelled in the hallway. From the open doorway of the extra bedroom came an unusual shifting glow.

I drew back. What made that noise? And the radiance?

I waited. Took a breath. Peeked through the slim opening of the door.

Stevie lay on the carpet. Wearing a white gauzy gown, she prostrated herself in the center of a circle of lit candles. Their flames danced. But no fan stirred the air to give them movement. My cousin was humming. No, no rhythm came from the sounds in her throat. With nuances of their own, they sounded like utterances that still remained trapped deep within her body.

Trembling inside, I tiptoed away, leaving Stevie to say her prayers or make amends or whatever she was doing with possible otherworld spirits. My main concern was that later during the night, those spirits wouldn't come to investigate me.

I needed to learn who this person was that I thought I'd known all my life. And hurry away from her.

CHAPTER 4

The second half of the night brought little sleep. Suppose Stevie dozed off on that floor, and the candles set the house on fire? What could I learn about the man who died outside, the one whose legs left an imprinted feel against my shins?

I dragged myself from the bed, then remembered the noise that seemed to come from the window. I dashed there and yanked the curtains aside.

Sunlight brightened most of the yard and the part of April's house that I could see. Her house was fairly close, her curtains apparently sheer. Trees and shrubs made shadows on the tall grass. No tree or shrub grew close to my room. The wooden fence stood about five feet toward the back, partitioning the backyard but not this part of the house containing my bedroom. Anyone could have walked from the street in front and come near my window.

Oh, come on, Cealie, who'd want to peek at you in bed?

I shook my head to get rid of ridiculous thoughts and walked to the bright kitchen, wondering what Stevie I might find today.

She seemed especially cheerful. "Hey-Cea-lie," she said like three chirps. She flitted around the stove, which gave off tempting sausage smells. She wore a long-sleeved muumuu, similar to what she wore yesterday but with geometric shapes in different colors. "I slept great. How about you?"

"I went to sleep right away." Without mentioning the restless balance of my night, I considered what she ordinarily did in the wee hours. "Did you go and work out at your gym at two a.m.?" I dropped to a chair and wondered if she'd volunteer an explanation about the candlelit ceremony.

She set a filled mug in front of me. "Not last night. I hope you like your coffee."

Rich and creamy. "This is good."

Stevie cackled. "Your breakfast is ready." Before I could say I usually ate later, she set sausages, an omelet, and buttered toast in front of me.

Who could resist? Not *moi*.

"There's nothing in the paper about that man who died here," she said and rushed out of the room. I was eating my last bite when she returned. Her expression looked guarded, indicating she didn't want to discuss that man anymore.

I stared at all the dirty dishes and pots. "Why don't we go shopping now?" I said. "I'd like to get pretty paper plates and toss-away cutlery. And we'll find some nice casserole dishes to use in the microwave."

"We can shop if you'd like, but I love my silver and dishes. They're like part of my family."

Family. The blessed people we run to. Or away from. I'd resumed my journey to relinquish the need to cling to family members when I stopped here. Then Stevie made me want to avoid relatives even more. Of course this morning, she was making me feel almost at home.

"Okay, you wash, I'll dry," I said. We did our tasks rapidly and this time I knew where to pick up most dishes. "Now let's not have anymore cooking, except in there." I pointed to her microwave.

"But for lunch," she said, "I planned on making you shrimp fettuccini."

Yum.

I shifted my butt. Feared it would spread more and wobble

behind me by the time I left.

"What about the police?" I asked. "How about calling to see if they've learned anything about Pierce Trottier?"

Her demeanor closed. Constant movement shut down. Smile disappeared.

"Don't you want to know what happened?" I asked.

"Of course." She grabbed the phone and called. Asked questions and soon hung up. "They can't tell us anything yet."

Her hands swept around in jittery motions. Her expression was tense. Probably now, after a meal, she wanted a cigarette.

I retrieved the material I'd carried in from her car. "You might look over these papers. Ish said they'd help, I guess to get rid of desires."

My mind replayed a quick flash of my own desires. They involved Gil. I'd entertained them right before I'd fallen asleep. Probably another reason I slept so well for a while.

Stevie eyed the papers I held. "Ish can say anything he wants. He doesn't know."

I laid the papers aside. "Where's a phone book?" I asked, and she pointed to a drawer. I grabbed the book. Looked up *Trottier, Pierce*. No name even came close.

I didn't want to stay near Stevie with her vacillating emotions any longer than I needed to. I prodded my mind about what I might do. "I'm going to make a call," I said. "I'll use my cell phone."

"You can use mine right there."

"Thanks, but I'm calling out of state. I have unlimited hours."

My excuse worked. I rushed to my bedroom. Shut the door, connected with a gynecologist's office in New England. "I need to speak to Dr. Marie," I told the receptionist. "I'm her patient Cealie Gunther. I'm in Gatlinburg now."

"She's with patients. I'll give her the message. She'll probably return your call right before we close at noon. Saturday hours," she said.

Clatters of pots told me Stevie was already cooking.

"Isn't it early to fix lunch?" I asked, reentering the kitchen.

She plunked pots on the stove, reached in overhead cabinets for bowls, grabbed ingredients from the fridge and pantry. "Not for me."

Without enthusiasm, I said, "Can I help?"

"I'd rather be alone when I cook."

"Oh well then." I walked near Minnie cactus and winked. She'd understand my good luck. "I'll go and take a shower," I told Stevie.

"Let me know if you need anything."

I gathered my clothes and hoped I wouldn't find anything weird behind the shower curtain with its odd symbols similar to the ones on Stevie's caftan.

To my relief, I discovered only soap, shampoo, and conditioner. I took a quick shower and ran my fingers through my waves so they'd dry on their own. I dressed and then stopped in the hall. The door to the room I'd seen Stevie in last night was shut. Candle scents lingered. Were the candles still lit? In their midst, would some item sit, possibly a burnt offering? A stuffed doll resembling the man I'd found outside?

Come on, you don't really believe Stevie would harm anyone.

But she'd been in that trancelike state during the night. I loved my cousin, although I hadn't always liked her. I knew she wouldn't hurt another person when she was alert. Who knew what might happen when she went into that otherworldly state?

Clack-clack-clack sounded from the kitchen. A metal spoon hit the sides of a pot being stirred.

I grabbed the doorknob to the psychic room.

Found the door was locked.

Surprised to find my hand sweaty, I noted my heart pumping

faster. What was my cousin hiding in that room?

"Finding what you want?" she asked right behind me.

Glad my hand had slipped off that forbidden doorknob, I turned. She towered above me in our narrow space. "Finding . . . ?" I asked.

"Towels. Soap." She chuckled. "Oh Cealie, you look like you've seen a ghost."

I moved ahead of her toward the kitchen. "That's silly. I'm sure there are no ghosts in this house." I glanced back. "Right?"

Her laughter, dotted with gasps, gave me little reassurance that there weren't.

Enticing aromas swelled in her kitchen. She'd already said she didn't want my help there. "Suppose I go check out the people who pass by? Maybe we can find a killer," I said.

"Help yourself." She took food out of the fridge.

I grabbed my cell phone and went toward the back door. A sudden image slammed into mind—suppose Stevie was the person who was supposed to be lying facedown in her grass? What if *she* was the intended victim? "I don't guess you ever come through the back gate? I imagine you always park in your garage."

"I do." She dumped things into a pot. "But sometimes when I'm visiting April and we're in her backyard, I'll come around through my gate in back."

"You don't keep your gate locked?"

"Usually, but sometimes I'm on the porch and hear her and Cherish, so I walk over. I leave the gate open to come back."

"Ah." I walked outside. A chill remained in the midmorning air. I shivered, especially when I saw the grass where a man's body had lain. I looked away and surveyed the yard.

Trees clustered. Bushes filled many other spaces. I stooped behind an extra large bush. A person could have hidden here in waiting. For whom? The man we found? How would anyone know he'd come back here?

Suppose a person had hidden, actually wanting Stevie to come through that gate?

I stared at the house. Through the open door I could see Stevie fluttering around the florescent-lit kitchen.

The gate was shut now. I walked a distance from the fence and eyed various sections of it, trying to see through slits between boards. By focusing, I noticed vehicular motion on the street behind only one patch of the fence, a three-foot section to my right. The other boards were set too tightly for me to notice anything.

What if a killer waited here for Stevie to come back from April's yard? Would he know her from anyone else? Had he noticed a person reaching the gate, seen it open, and then—

Pop sounded from the fence. I shrieked and ducked. A gunshot?

"Hey, the gate's locked. How about letting me in?" April's voice was followed by another *pop* I now recognized as her smacking bubble gum.

I struggled with the bolt. "Good morning, April. Hi, Cherish."

The child passed by without looking at me. April paused.

"The gate's not always locked?" I asked her.

"Not when Stevie knows we'll be coming over."

"Right. And what about the yellow tape out there?"

"We ducked under it." A pink bubble expanded and backed into her mouth. "Did y'all find out anything from the cops?"

I shook my head, glanced to see Cherish beating on the screen door. Stevie happily let her inside. April went to the house.

I left the gate open a bit and set up my chair on the porch where I could see the road.

Fewer cars and trucks passed than yesterday, maybe because it was a weekend. Probably not one killer among them. But who knew? A yellow dog trotted alongside the road. I mused over last night's events. Stevie acted so strangely in that extra bedroom which she'd since locked. She hadn't wanted to tell me about it. I considered all the people from her group. I'd read many mystery novels. Often a culprit was someone the victim knew well.

Laughter resounded from Stevie's house. April's shrill tone. I peered inside the kitchen. April stood at the stove, staring into the pot Stevie was stirring. No sign of Cherish. She'd probably insisted on cartoons, and Stevie probably turned them on.

Da-dunk da-dunk da-dunk played from my waist. "The Mexican Hat Dance" on my cell phone. Not feeling like dancing, I just answered.

"How's my friend Cealie?" Dr. Marie asked. "Are you having a problem?"

"Yes, but not physical. Can you tell me how you could kill a person without leaving any wounds?"

Her bubbly laughter resounded. "Did you want to do away with anyone in particular?"

Stevie's raucous hilarity came from the kitchen, the same guffawing she'd often do right after she made me cry.

"I might, but I'd never get away with it. You know me and my big mouth. I'd blab." Dr. Marie chuckled, and I stepped away from the porch. I walked farther into the yard and explained to my gynecologist in Cape Cod what happened here yesterday. "I'd like to know your ideas," I said.

"Are you sure there weren't any wounds?"

"No. I just didn't see any."

"He certainly could have died from natural causes, even though you said he looked younger than you."

That thought didn't make me feel much better. It made me tell myself I needed to start exercising and watching my diet. Starting fairly soon.

"But," she said, "it's certainly possible that someone killed him without leaving wounds. The most likely way might be various poisons that could be slipped into his food or drink."

"I thought so. And even some poisons that could be gotten legally, right?"

"Absolutely. Or maybe too much of a certain prescription. Do you know if he was taking any medications?"

"I know nothing about him, except he supposedly attended a small stop-smoking group that my cousin also belonged to. And I tripped over him. He was dead at the time. And he smelled of vomit."

"Some people get nauseated and vomit when they have a heart attack. Many poisons also cause that. I'm sure the medical examiner will discover what killed him, and you'll find out. Let me know how that goes, will you?"

"I will." Something I hadn't wanted to consider popped up. I felt foolish saying it. "Dr. Marie, curses couldn't possibly kill a person, right? You know, like voodoo or having a psychic cast a spell?"

She chuckled. "Many people, even in the medical community, believe that's possible."

"But some people believe anything."

"True."

I spoke more quietly. "My legs . . . I still feel his legs against mine. The part of my shins that lay across him. It's like he's part of me. I can't shake that feeling."

She didn't say anything. Softly exhaled. "It'll go away. Maybe not until after someone discovers how he died. I hope that happens soon."

"Me, too." I took a breath, needing a lighter mood. "Another annoying thing took place with that incident. My hand landed in dog poop." I heard her giggle and then added, "At least it was dry poop, probably from a medium-sized dog. Where that came from is another mystery."

"Sounds like there are many mysteries to solve, Cealie. I'm sure everything will work out."

"Thanks. I'll see you in the fall."

"I'll look forward to your visit."

We hung up. Now I had a new consideration. Had Pierce Trottier been on medication?

"Lunch is ready," Stevie yelled, but I could have sworn we'd eaten breakfast a few minutes ago. Stevie stuck her head out the screen door. Her eyes sparkled. Surely they could keep someone mesmerized.

That's stupid, Cealie. Stop it! "Coming," I said, aware of goose flesh sprouting on my arms.

No, my cousin couldn't be a killer. She might be annoying and mentally off a little, but a blood relative of mine wouldn't harbor any killer genes.

But surely genes didn't pass on to create murderers. Maybe instincts?

I shook my head, trying to toss out the concept that my cousin would kill, if only by accident. A spell gone awry.

Someone else killed that man, if he was murdered. Who knew what prescriptions he might be on? Stevie swore she hadn't known him, but others in her stop-smoking group did. Maybe if I went to another meeting, I could learn more.

"Cea-lie!" my unsettling cousin screamed from the porch.

I remembered the gate and went to lock it. A robust man came walking close. Without looking at Stevie's gate, he appeared to be heading straight for it. He was reaching the cops' yellow tape when he glanced up and saw me. A hulking person, he wore a navy sweat suit. His shaved head leaned forward on a thick neck, and dark eyes met my stare.

I opened my mouth to say something—what? Hi? Or scream for him to get away?

But he swiveled around and strode on. Following close on his heels was a mid-sized brown Lab.

The dog made me realize this was the same man who'd come close before. He wore a cap then but not this time. And he'd been heading for this yard.

Maybe this was our killer. I rushed inside to tell Stevie.

CHAPTER 5

"Where's April?" I entered Stevie's kitchen and wanted to tell her what happened but not in front of her neighbor.

"She and Cherish left." Stevie set silverware at our places.

"A man with a dog just came toward your gate. But he saw me and hurried off."

Her face tightened. She gave a one-shouldered shrug and poured our drinks. "We'll go out to eat tonight." She served two mounds of buttery cheese-saturated fettuccini on her plate. "We'll try that new Cajun place."

My hand jerked. I forced it calm. "Maybe we could go someplace else."

"You don't like Cajun?"

Yep, food and men. One particular Cajun man. "Well . . . yes, I do."

I did not like the prospect of running into Gil. I'd resisted the temptation of going to bed with him back in Chicago, at least for a while. And darn it, I didn't want Stevie to know anything about him and me. Just because we were related by blood didn't mean we had to be close. And she didn't need to know about my personal life. As soon as Pierce Trottier's death was solved, I would leave. I doubted I would connect with Stevie much again.

And I wasn't sure I could resist Gil's attraction.

Yes, of course I could. I breathed deeply, cloaking myself in my mantra: *I am woman. I can do anything—alone!*

That was the problem with Gil. He confused me. The man always made me temporarily forget my life's current mission, rediscovering myself. I'd married Freddie and been happy as his wife for many years, then felt lost after he died. I didn't know myself anymore. I became half of a couple, a broken half that could no longer function, even in the copyediting business he and I had struggled to build. Then the magazine article "Change Your Inner Underwear" made me determine the need to change mine. I tossed bulky bras and bought sexy ones, and took off to rediscover what I was like. Then I met Gil, who almost made me forget my quest. But I couldn't become half a couple again. Not so soon.

I can avoid Gil this time. Yes, I can!

I'd dumped too much fettuccini on my plate. I added a slab of garlic bread.

"Stevie," I said, "why did you really want me to come? I heard you tell the detectives you feared danger from what you saw in your cards and whatnot. But why contact me for help?" I smirked. "If you remember when we were kids, I'm not very good in a fight."

Buttery cheese coated her lips. She swiped a napkin across them. Her gaze drifted across the room. It appeared to focus on stones on a side table. She then stared at glittery objects catching sunlight above the sink. Her eyes shifted toward me. "I was told you could help."

"Who told you that?"

Her throat made a garbled sound. Her gaze swerved back to those strange items. She looked apprehensive. Maybe she only wanted a cigarette.

I'd become apprehensive, too. "Stevie—who?"

She stared at my eyes. Didn't speak. Didn't blink.

Oh my gosh, Dr. Marie warned that people my age might die of natural causes. And now I imagined Stevie's mind possibly slipping. Could she forget so quickly?

I wouldn't ask which of those objects had told her, or whether she believed some spirit from the past mentioned my name. The concept was way too spooky. Of course I didn't believe any of that hooey stuff, but having strange objects around made me shift in my seat.

"Great garlic bread," I said. "And you make wonderful fettuccini." I'd planned to eat only part of the pile on my plate but slurped the last noodle.

"Have some more." She heaped some onto her plate and ate it with more crusty bread.

"I couldn't," I said but dished out more. I took another half slice of bread.

By the time I rose, I felt my waistline swollen. My butt felt like a small blimp bouncing behind me. I loosened the button on my slacks. Assisting with the cleanup, I looked forward even more to moving on. Some people actually enjoyed doing dishes. And cooking. At least that's what I'd heard. And Stevie, making sounds similar to humming, looked pleased while she zipped through dishwashing. I, however, took much longer to dry all of our used items and put them away.

I passed near Minnie and winked. Even though she was a cactus, she seemed like a friend and might recall how little I liked these housekeeping chores.

"What'll we do now?" I asked. "Sit outside to try to see a killer? Go to the police station and rush whoever's trying to learn how the man died?"

Her gaze trained on mysterious objects around the room. "I'm going to meditate."

Hmm, she'd go in that room, light candles, and lie before whomever she considered the teller of secrets. What if she also tried to make me utter strange sounds to that person or spirit?

Chills skittered down my back. I could normally fend for

myself—say *no* and mean it—but Stevie was much stronger than I was.

She shifted closer, her weird eyes trained on me. She could grab me in a stronghold and dump me in the center of her candles.

A doorbell rang. "Now what?" Stevie headed for the front of the house, and I mentally thanked whoever stood outside.

Stevie's voice sounded surprised but not pleased. Another woman spoke with cheer. Light footsteps accompanied Stevie's toward the kitchen.

A woman holding a striped straw appeared at the door. Fawn, from the quit-smoking group. "Hi," she told me. Without invitation, she plopped down at the table. "I'm sorry Stevie got upset at the meeting. I want her to come back tomorrow. You come, too." She aimed her straw at me.

"It's up to her." I nodded toward my cousin, who avoided this person.

At the counter Stevie stacked together everything necessary to make and serve coffee.

I sat with company. "Fawn, Stevie never met Pierce Trottier." I scanned Stevie for her reaction—her head jerked toward us, eyes narrowed—and then I faced the small woman. "Did you know him?"

"Of course. You'd never want to meet a better man than Pierce."

"Really?"

"He was studying to be a minister."

"Minister? But he wasn't a young man. Didn't he already have a job?"

She quit sucking air through her straw. "He was an accountant, but he felt a higher calling."

My admiration for the man soared.

"And you really didn't know him?" Fawn asked Stevie.

"No. I never saw him at a meeting." She sat, her fierce stare daring either of us to call her a liar.

Fawn inhaled through her straw. She moved the straw aside and blew out. "God, I want to smoke. Especially with coffee."

"I know what you mean." Stevie's nostrils widened. She breathed in a ragged deep breath, then opened her mouth and blew.

These women must miss having their nicotine as much as I would miss my caffeine if I could never have it anymore. "Can't you have one cigarette?" I asked them. "Or limit yourselves to two or three a day?"

The straw fluttered. "We've all tried cutting back. We're like alcoholics, unable to have just one. But we'll get through this, right, Stevie?"

Stevie's expression wasn't as assured as Fawn's. They both gulped from their coffee mugs as though the contents could relieve their apparent pain.

Fawn puffed on her straw. "And," she said to me, "did you know Pierce was engaged?"

"Oh, his poor fiancée. Had he ever been married?"

She shrugged and flicked imaginary ashes off her straw. "You need to come back to our meetings, Stevie. I know you got angry last night, but you have to realize giving up those nasty damn cigarettes alters our moods. Withdrawal can make us act like people we really aren't."

Maybe that is what happened to my cousin, why she acts so differently from the Stevie I've known.

Fawn aimed the straw at her. "We might have to reconsider our actions and realize weird ones might come from missing that killer from our midst."

I blinked extra hard. "What killer?"

"Nicotine. And tars and carbon monoxide and other poisons."

I'd hoped she would name a person, and our quest to locate

a murderer would be over.

Stevie narrowed her eyes. I couldn't tell if she agreed or was getting ready to punch Fawn. Or me? Both? Fawn said they might do strange things.

Come on, detectives and medical examiner, my mind screamed while I forced a tight-lipped smile at Stevie. *Y'all find out why that man died. Then let me move on. I didn't create these women's demons. Why am I stuck in the midst of their battle with them?*

Fawn drained her mug. "You probably walked out of our meeting because your system is changing. Actually, your body's healing. You're getting healthier, Stevie. So am I." She sucked that damned straw. Loudly exhaled. Smiled at my hostess, whose shoulders flattened and grew broader. I envisioned a bull, ready to charge.

Stevie spread her hands on the table. Pressing them down, she shoved herself up. Stared at Fawn. "I'll think about what you said."

So would I. Regarding both uptight women, I thought if cigarettes could cause those emotional problems, besides all the obvious health concerns everyone spoke about, the places that made the horrible things should be shut down immediately.

"I need to go," Fawn said, Stevie's demeanor obviously giving her that message. "I hope we'll see you tomorrow night. You, too, Cealie."

My grin was noncommittal. Didn't want her to know I was thinking I hoped to be on a jet by then, looking forward to people bartering with me on a moonlit beach in Acapulco.

Stevie saw Fawn out the front door. Stevie's footsteps came toward the kitchen. She didn't come into the room.

I washed our dishes. Stevie still hadn't returned. I dried our things and put everything away. I rolled my eyes at Minnie the cactus. "Strange goings-on, right? But don't worry. We'll leave soon." The main reason I'd thought of traveling to Mexico now was to look for other types of cacti that grew there.

I placed Minnie's pot farther away from the sink to protect her from accidental dumps of water. Then walked down the hall.

"Stevie?" I glanced through open doors. Didn't see or hear her. The door to the mystic room was shut. I stood outside it. "Stevie?"

Everything stayed quiet.

I smelled burning candles. Heard murmuring inside the room. I placed my ear against the door.

Breathing? Maybe mine. No other sounds besides quiet.

She was probably in that room. I was tempted to knock or try the knob, but she'd said she was going to meditate. Having a person knocking on your door while you meditated probably wouldn't help. And with her avoiding cigarettes, she needed all the help she could get.

But what if it was a cigarette I smelled? Suppose she went in that room to light up?

Well, that was her business, not mine. I had my own life to lead and problems to solve. She had hers. She was probably doing that the best way she could.

Entering the room I slept in, I phoned a couple of friends and family members. I spoke to my son, Tommy, in Alaska, hung up, then considered what I should do. Stevie still hadn't come out of her room.

My scan through my bedroom let me glance in the dresser's mirror. Then I knew. My large eyes looked brown and clear, my slim nose with no shine. But my hair. Still burnt sienna—except for the two inches of gray at the roots. Maybe my hair could use a touch-up. Besides, hairdressers talked a lot and knew things about many people. Maybe I'd be lucky and find someone who might help my hair and also my cause to find out why a man died.

Getting the phone book, I called a few hairdressers. Most took clients by appointment only. For others, I told Stevie's address and asked if they were far away. The hairdresser who said her shop was closest and could take me soon was the person whose address and directions I wrote.

"Stevie, I'm going to the Beauty First shop," I said through the still-closed hall door. A rumbling sound seemed to emanate from some abstract source.

I hustled away from the house. Easily following the directions, I drove only a few streets over.

Beauty First was painted bright pink on a red sign. Gingerbread trim on the building. I was surprised to see only one car in the parking lot. Surely other women wanted to put beauty first, especially early on a Saturday afternoon.

"I need a little touch-up on my roots," I told Audrey Ray, the shop's owner. Her hair was jet black, teased in a sort of beehive. She wore electric blue eye shadow. Gooey blue-black mascara glittered along her lashes. Her lipstick was magenta. Her cheeks were pink circles of blush, adding to my feeling that maybe I should have chosen another salon.

She had me sit in front of a huge mirror. The nostril-stinging odor of solution for perms made me happy. Some customers must come here. Audrey Ray had an instrumental CD playing softly.

"Um," she said, pulling my waves until they stood out from my head like wings. In the mirror surrounded by too-bright lights, I watched her grimace.

"My color's natural," I told her. "Natural burnt sienna. There's a pinch of gray at the roots because my previous hairdresser put that in." I grinned at her reflection. Wished she'd take the joke and smile back. "Why are you getting those scissors?"

"Your ends need a nip. And you need a lot more than a touch-up."

"No, I don't." I reached my hand up to block her scissors. Too late. She'd already nipped the hair near my face. Possibly she was right. I drew my hand away. "Maybe a little."

Her reflection grinned. Her hands swept over my waves, nipping tips. "I don't have that color. You'll need to pick another one."

I hadn't planned to change color yet, but maybe this was a good time. "Let me see what you have."

"Here's a few shades. Oh, and I sell lipstick that changes color. That's what I'm wearing."

She handed me samples of miniature ponytails in different colors. I mused, grinning while I recalled the last idea I'd had for a new color. I pointed to it.

"Perfect." She parted my hair and spread in her mixture. "Now you can stay there while we wait, unless I get a walk-in who needs that chair." She washed her items in a sink. I peered in the mirror circled by globe lights.

When did those sags develop under my eyes? And the crowfeet near them had lengthened since I last looked. Ugh, that lumpiness under my chin? Surely from Stevie's sugared coffee and fatty meals.

I eyed my neck. Tight skin had always clung there.

I jumped from the chair as though it were a hot seat. No benefit to studying a maturing woman in a well-lit mirror.

Audrey Ray moved behind a beaded curtain in a small room. A microwave *bing*ed. "Would you like hot mint tea?"

"Sure, thanks," I said, and she fixed me some. I told her how much I loved the scenic landscape here, and she expressed how much she appreciated nature's gift. She'd divorced twice. I mentioned my husband Freddie dying a couple of years ago and then hinted at why I was especially glad she was freshening up my hair color. "My cousin and I might eat at a restaurant tonight. They serve Cajun dishes."

"I love that new place. Wonderful food and such funny jokes."

"Right. And when you went, was the owner there? A distinguished-looking man, about my age? His name is Gil Thurman."

She stared at my face. I feared she was picking out each sag and cavernous line, and deciding I was much older than Gil. "Not that I noticed."

"Oh." I was done with anticipating Gil's presence.

"You won't be too long. Come on, I'll sweep up and then rinse you."

She swept hair around the chair I'd sat in. Surely not all mine. Too much gray.

I looked out of her window and took momentary pleasure in the rolling landscape. I wanted to ask about the dead man but wasn't sure what to say, especially since nothing was in the newspaper yet. A teenager pumped his bike up the road. A small car slowed. The woman driving it glanced at the shop and sped on. She'd probably read the sign *We take walk-ins.* Did anyone besides me walk in? I'd been inside a while and no one else called or came. I feared the worst when my hair was done.

And I couldn't think of any way to ask a tactful question so sank right in. "Do y'all have many accountants around here?"

"I guess as many as in other places. You need one?"

"Possibly. Do you know any good ones?"

"Not right off." She waved her hand to indicate I should follow to the sink. I did, and she rinsed my hair. "One of my customers is marrying a guy who does accounting. She says he's real good. Of course I wouldn't know if she means with taxes and stuff, if you know what I mean."

"I know. Would you know the man's name?"

"Sure, Kelly's going to marry Pierce Trottier. She talks about it all the time. You can sit up now."

"Trottier," I said like I'd never heard the name, but my neck muscles tightened. "Would his firm be in the phone book?"

"I guess. But if you want, I can call Kelly. She's not teaching today so she might be home."

"That's okay. I can look it up when I'm ready." Anxiety spiked up my scalp. What if Audrey Ray called his fiancée now? The woman would probably be bawling and telling the whole story of what happened. And that I'd tripped over him? Would his fiancée know my name?

I imagined she would. The police might even tell her more than they'd tell us. I groaned. I surely didn't want Audrey Ray telling her I was sitting here, asking questions about him. I couldn't imagine how that might hurt the woman who loved him.

My hairdresser snapped the black cape off me. I resumed my place on the chair in front of the lights. She draped a towel on my shoulders. With her blow dryer, she blasted hot air across my head. "They're getting married next month."

"They were?"

She flicked off her blow dryer. "What do you mean *were?* Did you hear that they broke up?"

"I mean . . . *are, were*—they're both just verbs, about the same, right?"

She stared at my reflection. Couldn't possibly know I owned a copyediting agency, and we proofread for grammar errors.

"You had me worried. Kelly's been a customer for years. She's the sweetest person and adores Pierce. I'd sure hate to see them break up right before the wedding."

Heat blasted my head as she blew my hair up, out and over. I wondered about the man who died. Why had he? And what about the poor woman he was ready to marry?

I gazed at the gold-flecked counter, imagining Kelly's horror yesterday when she learned her fiancé died. I imagined his parents, if they were still alive, hearing that their son wasn't. My heart couldn't take in such pain.

"There." Audrey Ray's dryer went silent. "How's that?"

I wiped my blurred, damp eyes and looked in the mirror.

Big hair. Much bigger than usual. But not too bad.

"You gave it a nice shape," I said, the second thing I noticed. Kind of puffy, yet somewhat inspired. Little flips here and there, drawing the eye away from my wrinkles. And even those wrinkles showed less. Or maybe my eye grew accustomed to my bright image. And strawberry? Yep, it sure was. Nature's Strawberry Highlights turned my hair into the color of a ripe strawberry. It resembled a large one.

"You want to try some lipstick?" she asked.

I didn't. I paid Audrey Ray, adding a nice tip, and left her shop.

I didn't look forward to finding Stevie locked inside that strange bedroom. If she was still in there, how would I get her out? She hadn't even answered when I knocked on the door twice and called her name before I left.

Was she meditating?

Tension tightened my spine as I drove nearer her place. With her shifting moods, who knew what kind of disposition I'd find her in?

Reaching her street, I felt my anxiety soar.

Two police cars were parked in front of Stevie's house.

Chapter 6

I stopped behind the squad cars and bolted into my cousin's house. "Stevie, what's wrong?"

No answer.

I dashed down the hall. Saw lights on in my bedroom.

"That's her!" Stevie's voice carried.

She and the police were going through my things. I knew because Stevie held my newest pastel yellow bra. A female deputy stopped rooting through dresser drawers. A young man in uniform didn't stop fingering my outfits hanging in the closet.

"Where have you been?" Detective Renwick barked at me.

"Cealie, what happened to you?" Stevie grabbed me in a hug that snapped my breath. She stared at my head. "And what in the world happened to your hair?"

I sat on the bed. They'd even pulled back the covers, maybe checking for stray hair? Surely this must be part of the investigation for the dead man since I was the one who'd fallen on him.

"Let's see," I said, and all of them gathered round. I recounted my last hours, giving a detailed description of my experience at Beauty First. "And then I drove here."

Everybody's shoulders lowered. Expressions faded, from intense to "who cares?" Most of the cops backed away from me.

"That's it? You only went to have your hair done?" Renwick lifted his gaze to my coiffeur.

I patted down the top a wee bit. "Was that a problem? Y'all

don't let a stranger get her hair fixed? Did somebody report me?"

Stevie's hands fluttered around her sides. "Me. I called and told them you were missing."

"Missing?"

"You just disappeared, and I thought whoever killed the man in my yard got you."

Renwick stuck his pad in his pocket. "The only reason we came, with you seemingly missing for less than a day, was because someone died here. Your cousin made us believe something bad also happened to you."

"How nice of you to check up on me." I patted his shoulder. "But if I ever have a problem, I have a cell phone. I'll be sure to call you if I need help."

All the cops turned to leave, except the young man who dug through my closet. He returned to it, stared inside, and fingered my low-cut, chamois-colored sweater that was hanging next to my short leather skirt. "Nice outfit," he said, and for an instant, I imagined him wearing it. Maybe because of his shapely eyebrows. Possibly from his stance—one hand on his slim hip. I envisioned him wearing a push-up bra with my slut outfit he kept admiring.

"Why didn't you tell me you were leaving?" Stevie grimaced at me in the hall while the others went out. "I got so worried."

"I knocked on that door." I pointed to the one open now, emitting the smell of extinguished candles. "I told you where I was going and called your name twice, but you never answered."

Her expression blanked. "You did? I was consulting . . ." She stared at the space beside me. Shut her mouth.

Obviously she wasn't going to tell me with whom or what she'd spoken in that room. I wasn't sure I wanted to know. Or possibly my cousin had a mental problem. Unless I could help,

I'd just as soon not know about it. She seemed to function well enough.

I moved farther from the candle room. It started to give off strange vibes. Or maybe I imagined them. "You sure have nice police in Gatlinburg. They'll come to see about you right away."

Stevie trailed me to the kitchen. Under the bright fluorescent lights, she stood peering down at my hair.

"The hairdresser gave me a little touch-up," I said, hinting for a compliment. "This shade's natural. Nature's strawberry highlights."

"Let's go eat," she said.

"Already? Are you sure you want to eat again so soon?"

She grabbed her purse.

Stevie knew where to locate Cajun Delights restaurant. She wound her Jeep down the road, this time slowly enough for me to enjoy watching the water trickle along the mountain's rocky side. We traveled near a bubbly tree-lined creek. I opened my window to hear water lapping against rocks, deciding tranquility tapes must have been made from such a place.

If I hadn't found a dead person and if we weren't headed to my former lover's restaurant, I would have experienced perfect peace. My driver, annoying as she'd been, kept her thoughts to herself.

She turned to a street with lush trees at the base of a mountain. The few commercial buildings blended with nature. My heart struck harder when Stevie pulled into a parking lot filled with cars and trucks. The tall wooden sign out front said *Cajun Delights,* its cayenne-red letters on a worn green finish unmistakable. The cypress exterior was gray. "Seems like lots of people heard about this place opening," she said, "or the food is extra good."

"It is," I replied. Stevie glanced at me, and I had to think of a different response. "I mean, I like Cajun cooking. Cajuns prepare good food."

She parked. I didn't think she guessed I'd eaten in similar restaurants that Gil opened in other cities. No need for her to know about what had once been between us.

"Attractive," she said. We walked near the aerated pond holding fish and ducks. People watched them from a wooden bridge. "This place has a comfortable feel."

I didn't trust my voice, so I said nothing. We stepped onto the porch where families sat on swings. Some strolled beneath the roof's tin overhang. *Welcome to Cajun Delights. We're glad you're here.* Those words on a small sign posted on the leaded glass door sent my pulse into overdrive.

Gil might be inside.

Maybe he wasn't.

Who knew where he might be at this moment? I struggled to get my ideas straight, but hormones raced. Darn, I wasn't a teenager. Gil probably stayed back around Chicago. Of course he'd told me he was flying out this way soon. How soon? I fought with my thoughts in an attempt to straighten them out, but couldn't. "Dammit," I blurted.

Stevie glanced at me. I almost fibbed and said I'd stubbed my toe. Instead I tightened my lips and gave her a half smirk.

A man entering ahead of us peered back. I felt I should apologize for my language once I saw he wore a minister's white banded collar with a black shirt. He looked at me but not Stevie, and turned around to follow a pair of sultry young women through the doorway. He walked with a limp.

"He looks familiar," I told Stevie and then remembered. "Isn't he Father Paul Edward from your stop-smoking group?"

She pulled back and spoke softly, "I hope he doesn't spot me. I'll want to see how he does without smoking after he eats."

"Is that a difficult time to do without a smoke?" I asked, having forgotten Stevie and those others must be going through withdrawal pains.

"It's when you want a cigarette the worst. After eating—and sex." At my startled expression, she said, "At least that's what people tell me, you know, about sex. They say a smoke's especially good then."

I'd never known Stevie to have sexual encounters. It surprised me to hear her mention them.

What surprised me most was those shapely young women Father Paul Edward seemed to be with. And his walk. One of his legs dragged and its foot dipped. He used a three-pronged cane.

"Does he really have trouble walking?" I asked Stevie.

"Mmm, smell that," she said.

The food did smell scrumptious as we entered Gil's restaurant. Tantalizing scents of fried seafood mingled with the smell of tangy crab boil used to pepper up the large red-shelled crabs I spied on waiters' trays. Smiling customers ate at tables with black-and-white cloths holding tempting dishes. Every chair appeared filled, yet a hostess escorted us to a table near a far wall.

We sat near the knotty pine wall. I scanned the framed pictures of swamp scenes. Across the room I spied Father Paul Edward laughing with the women seated beside him.

I glanced around at all the faces, looking for Gil. Disappointment dropped in when I didn't find him.

"I want a seafood platter," Stevie told our waiter. "A large one."

Without opening my menu, I asked, "Would you have boiled crayfish?"

"Sorry," he said, "we haven't gotten any yet."

More disappointment. I sighed. "Then I'd like shrimp stew and lima beans. A cup of shrimp and corn soup as an appetizer, please."

"How did you know they'd have dishes like that?" Stevie asked me.

"Lucky guess."

She eyed the entrées and appetizers people surrounding us ate. "This does seem like a nice place. And all of the food looks great."

I made noncommittal sounds. "Nice music."

"Yes, that's good, too."

We turned toward a small platform holding a trio playing soft jazz. Right beyond them stood the most striking woman. Probably in her early thirties, she wore a magenta suit and similar makeup that showed off a willowy figure. Shoulder-length blond hair flipped in a fashionable style and surrounded a beauty-queen face pinched up in a scowl. She stared at her watch.

The musicians quit playing. The beauty queen turned to a man with extra-short hair who rushed to the platform. The cute man didn't look at home stuffed into his tweed sports coat.

"Good evening," he said into the mike, "and welcome. We hope you'll enjoy your experience at Cajun Delights and come back again soon."

Customers applauded. The man said, "I'd like to introduce our lovely daytime manager to you, Babs Jacobs." He pointed to the woman, her scowl replaced by a bright smile while we all clapped. "And I'll be overseeing things here in the evening," the man onstage said. "So if anything's wrong with your meals, you can take it out on me, Jake Bryant."

I chuckled with others at his self-deprecating humor. I liked this young man.

He continued, "We wish the owner could be here."

Yes, we do wish that.

"But he's out of town. Come back again, and you'll be sure to meet him," Jake said.

The fluttering in my chest signaled my wanting to see the

owner, yet I knew I shouldn't.

Stevie spread butter on crackers we'd been served. She ate them, seemingly unaware of my anxiety.

I glanced toward the side to try to break up my thoughts. Father Paul Edward was laughing. So were the women at his table. Did that man of the cloth—apparently also a man of the world—know much about the man who died in Stevie's yard?

"Right now we'll have our joke contest," Jake Bryant said. He flung out his hands. He didn't wear a wedding band. "Please come up and share a favorite joke with us. They have to be clean. Cajun jokes are especially encouraged, if anyone knows any."

Now, during the grand-opening, joke contests would be held every evening. Later they'd take place at a variety of times. Contest winners would be chosen by customers and receive their meals on the house.

"I wish I knew some jokes to tell," Stevie said.

I did. I'd heard many at Gil's restaurants but could never imagine, as Gil sometimes suggested, that I'd ever get onstage to tell one.

The waiter served our appetizers. Stevie attacked her fried onion rings, and I dug into my corn soup. The shrimp were chewy, the creamy base well seasoned.

One brave soul took to the stage. The small middle-aged man began his joke.

Almost as loud as his voice through the mike, a woman's angry tone could be heard.

The complaints came from Babs Jacobs. She stood near Jake Bryant, pointing her finger at him. This was her left hand. I noted her fingers also without rings.

"What is her problem?" I asked.

Babs must have realized how loudly she spoke. She lowered her voice.

Stevie swallowed an onion, her gaze aimed at Babs. "She can't see well enough to drive in the dark. Jake came in late to take Babs's place."

I set my spoon down. "How do you know that?"

My cousin's eyes did their mystic-thing—gazing as though not seeing, at least not through their pupils. "I read her vibes."

Okay, this psychic seeing of hers spooked me.

Customers clapped as the jokester left the stage. Another man took his place. My interest held on the two managers, farther aside from the stage now and still talking. Babs continued to look annoyed. She held up her wrist and appeared to show Jake her watch. And then she stomped off.

"I think you're right about her. I have problems driving at night, too," I told Stevie. "So can you tell anything about *his* problem?"

"He likes her, but doesn't think he stands a chance with her."

"Amazing. How do you know that?"

She rolled her eyes toward Jake. "I saw the way he looked at her."

"Oh." So much for her intuitive knowledge. I checked Jake out and could see the way he peered soulfully at Babs's trim departing figure. If he really did want to date her, I hoped he would give himself a chance and ask her.

If I stayed around town long enough, maybe I could make sure they got together.

People applauded for the joke-teller. No one else went on stage. Jake looked first resigned and then happy as he hopped up to the mike. "We'd like for all of you to decide on the winner," he said.

Audience applause chose the first contestant. I watched Jake leaving the spotlight. His smiling face became serious. Of course Stevie could read signs such as a man wanting interest from a woman. I could also read that body language.

The trio resumed their music, and our entrées arrived. Stevie praised her fried oysters, fish, and shrimp, and the stuffed crabs and gumbo. Her meal looked appetizing, and mine tasted scrumptious. I tore into the stew. People everywhere smiled and ate. Father Paul Edward came toward our table, but didn't glance at us. Cheerily following the pretty ladies, he leaned slightly on his cane, his foot drooping.

I'd seen a movie in which a killer faked a clubfoot. When Father reached my side, I had to squash an instinct to yank his cane away, then watch to see if he'd keep going without a foot problem.

Stop it, Cealie.

He walked off with the women, and I gave myself a mental head slap for my wicked thoughts.

"Well, he's not smoking," Stevie said. "At least not on a cigarette."

"Ooh, you wicked person," I said and gave her a good-girl hand slap.

"Of course, people can't smoke in restaurants anymore," she said, "but I looked for a cigarette-pack bulge in his pocket. None. No cigarette in his hand, either, ready to light up when he got outside."

"What would he be doing with those ladies?" I asked, watching them sashay on spiked heels, their hips rolling.

"They look like ladies of the evening. Maybe he wants to take them both into the evening at home and see what happens."

"Stevie, you really are wicked. I like that." I felt comforted by seeing this playful part of her I'd enjoyed when we were kids.

"They sure ate fast. I guess they were in a hurry," she said.

I finished my meal, sorry I'd have to leave Gil's place, sorry he wasn't here. Cajun Delights was a terrific restaurant, but without him lacked the spark I'd come to love.

"That was good." Stevie wiped her mouth with her napkin.

"Mmm, and that looks even better." She stared at the entrance. The old Stevie was back, it seemed, since now she sounded like that young teen girl, who along with me, ogled older teen boys.

I looked where she did, ready to make a smart comment.

And faced Gil Thurman.

CHAPTER 7

Gil stood six foot three, with a well-muscled chest and broad shoulders beneath a white shirt and navy sports coat. A pinch of dark chest hair was visible where his shirt opened at the collar. His jeans were pale blue, hiding soft briefs probably the same shade.

Intimate parts of my body reacted.

I struggled to close my mouth.

My peripheral vision let me spy Stevie staring at my face. Maybe wondering why I didn't speak. Or possibly I was drooling.

I ignored her, focusing completely on Gil.

His thick, steel-gray hair had grown a little near the temples, where a sprinkling of hair had turned silver. His eyes were deep gray. It took only a moment for them to survey his restaurant. His gaze met mine. A smile lit Gil's face. He strode toward me.

I met him halfway across the room. We hugged. He was also glad to see me. Very glad, I could tell as we hugged tighter.

"What a surprise," Jake Bryant announced in the mike. "Here he is, everyone. The man who gives us Cajun Delights, Mr. Gil Thurman."

I pulled away from Gil.

He grabbed my waist and drew me partway in front of him. I smiled at everyone staring at us and clapping. I gave them a wave. I wasn't sure what Gil was doing behind me. I was pretty sure he wasn't waving. He probably awarded them his great smile. I liked the feel of him clinging to my waist.

"Would you like to come up here and speak to your guests?" Jake asked him.

I shifted aside so Gil could pass to the bandstand while people clapped.

"Stay here," he said in a deep-throated whisper. He gripped me tighter and kept me in front of him.

I didn't mind. Mmm, warm and comfy snug against him.

"We're happy you're all here," Gil said in a loud tone, and I kept smiling at all the people. "We hope you enjoy your experience. Please let anyone on our staff know if there's anything at all we can do for you."

I raised my hand like I was telling them 'bye. And then Gil's large hand tightened on my waist, nudging. We moved to a recessed area, away from everyone.

"Hello. How are you?" he said to me, his head leaning down. His lips that I knew to remain warm moved toward mine.

Heat flooded my body.

"So you know each other," my cousin said.

I jerked away from Gil. "Stevie," I said in a high-pitched tone. "Oh, this is the restaurant's owner, Gil. Mr. Gil Thurman."

Her eyebrows drew toward each other. "From what I just saw, I don't think you ordinarily call him *Mister*. But I'm happy to meet you, Mr. Thurman." She accepted his handshake.

"Don't you call me *Mister*, either," he said. "I'm Gil. And your name, lovely lady, is . . . ?"

Color flooded Stevie's cheeks. She giggled. "Stevie Midnight."

"She's my first cousin," I said.

"I'm sure Cealie's told me about you. But with the years creeping up, I forget. Please excuse me," Gil told her.

"No way are years creeping up on you," Stevie replied. She kept grinning at him like a flirtatious thing was going on at her end. Then she addressed me, "But I doubt if cousin Cealie mentioned me. I sometimes think she'd like to forget I exist."

"Don't be ridiculous." I gave her hand a friendly squeeze and smiled at Gil. "She's one of my favorite relatives."

I let go of Stevie's hand and discreetly pinched my right palm. Hoped my lie wasn't a big one.

"Come join us at our table," Stevie told him, still wearing that silly expression. Her eyes actually sparkled. Her cheeks stayed rosy.

No, don't join us. What would Gil and I say in front of you?

"Thank you. I will." Gil swung an arm out, letting us lead the way.

"But we were almost through eating," I said.

Gil saw my smile vanish. He looked amused. He widened his smile at me, probably looking forward to seeing me squirm while I tried to explain our relationship to my cousin.

She stepped out ahead of him. I walked behind Stevie toward the table where we'd sat. Gil touched my lower back. His hand remained, its heat shooting pleasant chills to significant parts of my body.

"Here we are," Stevie said, reaching our table. "Oh, everything's gone."

Gil no longer touched me. He looked unhappy. "I'm sorry that happened." He stepped toward our waiter.

"But we were finished with everything," I said.

He spoke to the waiter for only a second.

Jake Bryant came rushing to Gil. "We need to talk."

Gil nodded. He smiled at our waiter, who hurried away. Then Gil came to us. "I'm sorry I won't be able to join you." He glanced at Stevie. His gaze held on mine. "I'll look forward to seeing you another time. Soon."

"So nice to meet you," Stevie said, accepting his handshake. "You certainly will see us again real soon."

Gil gave my shoulder a light squeeze. And then he was gone. Then I breathed.

"Oh. My. God." Stevie leaned toward me. "That man is gorgeous."

My throat stayed tight. I nodded.

"So tell me how you know him. Oh, Cealie, you have a real hunk there."

I shook my head, finally loosening my throat so words could seep out. "No, he's not mine. Not my hunk." I shook my head.

"Then tell me how he can be mine."

Okay, I didn't really want to renew my relationship with Gil. But I sure didn't think my cousin should try to hop in where I left off with him.

"He's a grown man. He can be with whoever he chooses," I snapped.

"Whomever," she said, correcting me.

"Yes."

"You own a copyediting agency and don't know that?"

"Of course I know it, but the word sounds pretentious. I don't say *whomever* unless I need proper grammar. I don't try to sound proper with you."

"Whatever."

"Whomever," I said.

Soon I could hear Gil's voice. I quit talking and listened. He stood a few feet away from us, past tables filled with customers, and I could hear his annoyed tone with Jake. So unlike Gil to raise his voice.

A distance beyond them, I was surprised to see Father Paul Edward and his female escorts still here. They sat on stools at the bar, all laughing. And was that orangey drink liquor in the priest's tall glass?

"She's not!" Jake Bryant told Gil. His angry voice made customers at nearby tables stare at them. So did we.

Gil touched Jake's arm and tilted his head toward the rear of the building. They walked off, toward what would be the main office. There, Gil would let Jake share all of his complaints without other people listening.

"At least we know what that's about." Stevie made her fingernails tap dance on a black square of our tablecloth.

"I don't even know who he's talking about, so how could I know the problem?"

"I'll guarantee you, he's talking about Babs."

"How would you know that?"

"Uhhh." Stevie touched her temple.

I had no idea whether this meant she figured out their problem, or she was psychic and guiding spirits told her. Or maybe she had a headache.

"We should go," I said, catching the eye of our waiter. He headed in our direction, his cart filled with meals. "Can I have our check please?" I asked.

"It's taken care of." He set shrimp and corn soup in front of me and added a plate of shrimp stew and lima beans.

"I'm sorry, you've made a mistake." I set the soup back on his tray.

He returned the bowl in front of me. "I did, ma'am, and I'm sorry. I shouldn't have taken your dishes away without finding out if you were finished eating."

"That's no problem. We were done. Thanks, but we don't want this."

"Speak for yourself." Stevie grinned at the seafood platter placed in front of her.

Our waiter gave us fresh iced tea. He set a strawberry daiquiri next to my glass. "Can I get you something from the bar, ma'am?" he asked Stevie.

"I hardly ever drink," she said, which surprised me. She'd yanked whiskey out of her kitchen cabinet to dump in our coffee after I tripped over her visitor. Now she eyed my glass holding the red drink. "But I'll have one of those."

"Right away." He walked off, and Stevie seemed to be eyeing his butt.

"Did you lose something back there?" I asked.

"He probably goes to college, and he used *can* instead of *may* to ask me about a drink. I'm a teacher. Maybe I should correct him," she said and grinned. "I could give him lessons. Private ones. Free."

I forced a grin to meet hers. I'd never known Stevie to come on to a guy. I hoped going after real young ones wasn't a new thing for her now that she'd aged. Of course she'd never had a guy of any age that I'd known of. I never thought she was really interested.

Now as I picked at my food and she tore into hers, I considered the concept unthinkable. How could any woman not want to have a man around?

I ate limas and shook my head. No, I didn't want one, at least not now. Maybe one day I'd want to settle down again. And then if Gil was still available, I'd surely seek him.

Sighing, I stabbed a shrimp from my stew. I needed my mantra. I pictured draping myself with it: *I am woman! I can do anything. Alone.*

"Yum," Stevie said. "Try one of my stuffed crabs."

"I couldn't fit anything else in here." I patted my belly and with the opposite hand grabbed a silver shell off her plate. Crabmeat cooked with the Cajun trinity of onions, bell pepper, and garlic filled the tin. Topped with crunchy browned breadcrumbs. I wolfed it down with no problem.

"And here's a shrimp." Stevie handed me a fried one.

I chewed and pointed to my plate, letting her know she could have some of my dish.

If her fork came toward my plate, I missed it. I stared at the place where Gil had gone, hoping he'd come back. I watched, disappointment sinking in, and turned toward the bar.

Yep, the priest from Stevie's stop-smoking group was still there. I knew I shouldn't butt in but determined I would, especially now.

Instead of having two women with him at the bar, Father Paul Edward now had four.

CHAPTER 8

"I didn't think I'd eat all that," Stevie said after our second plates were almost empty. We still sat at our table, sipping frozen strawberry daiquiris.

"I'm guilty of gluttony," I said. "I'm going straight to hell."

"Maybe." She sipped her drink. "And maybe me, too."

Considering damnation made me glance again toward the bar. I'd already looked for Gil and hadn't seen him again, but Father and his four women still chuckled and drank back there. I felt like I'd need a wheelbarrow to tug me off with everything I ate and wasn't too interested in going to see about the preacher and his women friends.

But I was Cealie. *You like to butt in,* Gil sometimes told me, which I knew wasn't true. *You like to control,* he'd also said, giving me the urge to map out his future with him alone and missing vital male parts of his anatomy.

I slipped a large tip under my plate. "Father Paul Edward is still here with those women. Let's go find out what's going on."

"Maybe we shouldn't." Stevie leaned sideways for a better look at the bar. "Is he holding cigarettes?"

"Let's get closer to see."

"Maybe he's holding some out of habit," she said, "and getting ready to light up once he gets outside."

I steamed ahead toward the collared priest. A woman on a bar stool next to him watched me and whispered in his ear. One by one, all in the group eyed us.

81

"Stevie, how nice to see you," Father said. He nodded to me. "And your friend."

"I met you at your meeting. I'm her cousin, Cealie Gunther." I put out my hand.

His grip surprised me with its strength. "Nice restaurant, isn't it?" he said.

"It's a great place," Stevie answered.

"Who are your friends?" I did a backward sweep of my hand, indicating all four women.

Stevie clutched my arm. "Cea-lie," she warned through clenched teeth near my ear.

I tugged my arm free.

The priest pointed to the woman on his right. "This is Lark."

Lark flashed me a big smile. I gave a huge one in return. She turned her smile at Stevie, long, sleek bottle-blond hair slipping over her shoulder.

"And that's her sister, Clark." The priest tipped his head toward an identical woman, and Clark nodded.

"Kind of like Clark Kent," I said. "Clever. Only you're not a man."

She shoved up her boobs so they popped halfway above her dress. "Not hardly."

The priest swiveled toward the women seated to his left. These were the two he'd come in with. They looked even more high-end maintenance than the others. Both wore platinum blond hair to their waists and slinky red dresses. Killer bodies. The bling-bling at their ears and necks appeared to be diamonds. "This is Sue Horowitz," Father said of the one nearest him, "and her cousin, Lois Fields."

"Hi, ladies," I said, and they flipped their heads in small nods. "Y'all look like you could be sisters," I added, and both gave me big grins.

Stevie was probably about to get mad at me. I wanted to

know what a priest was doing out with four sexy women and couldn't figure any way to find out except to ask him.

Stevie moved close and nudged my back. She cut me a watch-your-step look.

Tough.

I shifted closer to the man so I couldn't see her. "Father, I'd like to ask you something."

Stevie's raspy cough was a threatening bark.

Barking noises repeated, but she wasn't creating them. This came from Jake Bryant, clearing his throat at the mike. The musicians stopped playing.

What now? I'd never seen a manager speak more than once in an evening. I craned my neck to see him across the dining room but had to move farther into it to clearly see the stage.

"We have a special treat tonight," Jake said. "We're having a *second* joke contest."

He piqued my curiosity to the max. This was something new for one of Gil's restaurants.

Jake wore an extra-bright smile, which I determined was forced. He put out a hand in showmanship. "If anyone tells a Boudreaux and Thibodaux joke, you'll receive a nice gift certificate to return here as our guest."

"How nice?" a man shouted, making customers laugh.

"Will a hundred dollars do?" Jake asked.

A young woman dashed to the mike. Jake stepped away. I looked around for Gil. Didn't see him. I watched the woman telling her joke.

"One day Boudreaux called Thibodaux and asked what he was doing. 'I got me a job at an airport. Wait, hold on. Yeah, flight 3672, you can come in Runway One from the west. Oops, here's another call. Hello. Sure, flight 219, come on down Runway One from the east. That's fine.' Thibodaux hung up from the pilots.

" 'Hey, buddy,' Boudreaux told him, 'I just heard you telling one plane to come in the runway from one side and another plane to land in the same place from the opposite end. That could be real dangerous.'

" 'Aw, that's true. Hold on a minute,' Thibodaux said. He got the pilots from both planes on the line again and told them, 'Y'all be careful now.' "

Customers chuckled and applauded. They peered around, waiting for the next person to get onstage. I checked out people at the bar.

Father Paul Edward and his friends were gone.

"What's the problem?" Stevie asked.

I pointed to the empty bar stools. "Did you see them leave?"

"Some of us don't watch people every minute to find out what they're doing."

I guessed she meant I shouldn't spy on them. "So," I said, "did he pull out a cigarette to smoke outside?"

"Not once." She twiddled her fingers. "But I'd sure like to."

I hated to tempt her but really wanted information. "Maybe he's smoking out there now."

"Let's hurry and go see."

Darn, I did want to check out what the priest and his lady friends might be doing. But if I left now, I'd miss the rest of the joke contest. And Boudreaux and Thibodaux jokes were my absolute favorites. Those two surnames were common down in Cajun country, where Gil's mother came from, and many good-natured folks in their area loved to share these stories, joking about themselves.

Stevie and I headed for the exit.

"No one else knows a Boudreaux and Thibodaux joke?" Jake asked at the mike. "Then we'll give the gift certificate to the young woman who entertained us."

The jokester ran up for her prize. "Congratulations," Jake

said. "I hope more of you will learn some of those jokes because you never know when we'll have the contests. We'll definitely have them when a certain person is here."

I reached the doorway but looked back, heat striking my face. Jake was staring at me.

"What's the deal?" Stevie asked with the door open.

"Deal?" I tried to sound innocent. "Come on, let's go." I went out.

"That manager was talking about you."

"Don't be silly." I made a big show of inhaling through my nostrils to get her interest elsewhere. "Smell that? Somebody's been smoking right here."

She studied the ground. "I don't see any butts."

"Maybe there are ashtrays on the side of the restaurant."

She stared at my face.

"I just said there *might* be."

"Somebody did smoke close to the door," she said. "But it must have been somebody lighting up, not putting out."

I nodded, then pointed ahead. She moved on, and I walked behind, hoping she wouldn't turn around. I couldn't keep my smile away any longer.

Gil must have told his manager to have that second joke contest for me. I floated to the car, my thoughts soaring.

No, no, no. I don't care what Gil does!

Woman here—who can do anything—and without a man. Remember that, Cealie.

Gil hadn't been around again, and I was disappointed. I tried to convince myself it was only because I missed visiting an old friend. But I didn't believe it for a second. Gil was hunky. He turned me on.

I needed to stay away from him. Then I could do my own thing. I'd keep discovering what that thing was.

Who knew? Maybe I loved to cook.

"What?" Stevie spun toward me. "Why are you laughing?"

"I just thought of the funniest thing."

"Tell me. No, then you might lose your punch. Wait and say it the next time we're here and there's a joke contest."

Great suggestion. If I ever got on stage and said I loved to cook, Gil might roll off his chair, laughing.

Stevie walked past the parking lots. She peeked behind the building where trees stood near a connecting wooden fence. The parking lot was well lit, but not the rear of the restaurant.

"What are you doing?" I asked.

"Sniffing. Looking." We returned to her car and got in. Stevie pulled out into light evening traffic.

"You were looking for the priest. Why would he be with all those women? It's not like they're his church's Altar Society."

"I have no idea. I don't stick my nostrils into other people's business."

"And I do?"

She cut me a look.

Okay, maybe I did like to snoop into some things people did, especially if they were strange. Especially if they affected me.

Both shins bothered me at the same time. I bent and massaged them. They didn't really hurt. It felt more like pressure, something shoving against them.

A rigid dead man.

I saw him in my mind's eye as clearly as when I stood next to him on the tall grass. Brown hair, nice middle-aged face, a small wad resembling gum between his lips.

I hadn't really thought of any gum on his lips before but now realized some was there. He had smelled of vomit.

I stared at my shins. Were those indentations, especially on my right leg? I turned my legs sideways for a different view.

The streets were dark, with only an occasional streetlight flashing by. At this angle, both my legs appeared indented. My heartbeat sped. Would my legs stay this way? I imagined cold, stiff male legs pressing against them.

"Do you see something interesting?" Stevie asked, tone annoyed.

I shifted my legs. Kicked a small package out from beneath the seat. I leaned to push it back. Seeing what it was, I grabbed the pack. "Cigarettes? I thought you quit."

"I did. I only kept them for any emergency." She reached for the unopened package.

I pulled it farther away. "What emergency? Wanting a smoke?"

"Just give them to me."

"You don't need to keep temptation."

She stretched toward my side. I lowered my window. I didn't normally litter, but this was an emergency. Getting rid of poisonous things that tempted her felt like a dire need. I held the pack higher.

She lunged.

It appeared she came all the way across the front seat, although I doubt that was possible since she was strapped in.

"Watch out!" I screamed.

Bumps erupted beneath us. The car swerved. Stevie's hand slapped mine.

Her Jeep jerked and stopped.

My heart stuck in my throat. I pried my eyes open.

A pine tree stretched in front of Stevie's grill. At least we hadn't hit hard enough to make her airbags pop open. She leaned back, eyes shut.

"You okay?" I asked.

Her chest rose with her deep inhale. "Yeah. You?"

"I'm good."

"Great." She cranked the motor, and it started. She backed slowly from the tree and over the curb. We lurched forward.

No cars had come near that I noticed. Nobody stopped to

see if we were okay, so I didn't think anyone had seen us get into the near-tragic accident.

I remembered the cigarettes. I wasn't holding the pack. Didn't see them on the floor.

Stevie, even right after this stressful situation, appeared more at ease than fifteen minutes ago. I didn't search under her seat or check her bra, both places she could have stashed the smokes. I did believe she yanked the pack from my hand when we lost control, but I hadn't actually seen it. I could confront her about dangers of smoking and the danger she'd just put us through, but would she care? Didn't she already know?

What I knew was I needed to leave this place soon. I'd let her do whatever she wanted. She was a big girl. I gave myself a mental head slap for considering the meaning that came to mind. My cousin was *old* enough to take care of herself and live as she wanted. If she wanted nicotine so much she was willing to let it kill her, that was her choice!

Darn it, Cealie, where did that thought come from? I absolutely did not want her destroying herself anymore. If I could do anything to stop her while I was here, I would.

She remoted her garage open and drove inside. The door shut behind us. We slipped out of the Jeep.

Da-dunt, da-dunt, da-dunt.

Stevie cut me a glance as I kicked my feet to "The Mexican Hat Dance" and grabbed my phone from my purse. "Hello, Cealie here."

"Yes, I know."

Gil's baritone voice made my feet stop. My legs weak.

"You okay?" Stevie reached the door for her kitchen but eyed me as I slumped against the garage wall.

"I'm fine." I waved to shoo her away.

"Yes, you are," Gil said. "But you don't normally brag."

I laughed at him and grinned at Stevie, who kept staring.

Then she went in the kitchen and shut the door.

"You probably know this, but I was talking to my cousin," I told Gil.

"I remembered you'd mentioned her once, although she didn't look too much like you described her."

"She's changed an awful lot since the last time I saw her. I guess I have, too."

"Your hair changed quite a bit since I saw you, which wasn't long ago. But it sure feels like it was." I heard what I figured was a smile when he spoke about my hair. And then the last part sounded like he missed me. I didn't want to miss him.

"So," I said playfully, "you liked my hair?"

"It's different, just like you."

"I'll take that as a compliment."

"Good. I'm sorry we had a little problem tonight."

"I wanted to tell you our waiter didn't make a mistake. Stevie and I had finished eating almost every morsel on our plates."

"I know."

"You do? Then why did you send out more food?"

"I wanted to keep my most important customer around as long as I could."

I blushed—all the way down past my belly button.

Down, Cealie. Leave him alone. You're woman. He's just a man . . .

"I never know how long my best customer will stay. I try to keep her as long as possible before she disappears."

I was flattered. Confused. I wanted Gil—no question about that. But I also wanted freedom. I needed to travel, to see all the places I wanted to go and do the things I might enjoy during my lifetime. I had only one life to live and no idea how much time remained in it. I couldn't be tied down right now.

End of thoughts of making love with Gil.

"It was time for us to go," I said.

"I see." Disappointment tinted his tone. "I hope you'll come back soon. Unless you want me to come there. I'm free now."

"Sorry, it's a little late. Maybe we'll eat there again before . . ."

"Before I leave town?" he said.

"Or I do."

"I get it. Cealie's going through her avoid-Gil time again."

"No, it's . . . a lot more complicated than that."

"I'm a simple man. If you want to see me again, I hope I'll be here."

"Right. Well, we'll probably see each other again real soon."

"I hope so. Good night, Cealie."

"Good night."

What did he mean, he hoped he'd be here? In Gatlinburg? Or available for me?

I went into the house pouting, glad I didn't see Stevie. The door to her weird room was shut. Also the door to her bedroom. I could get to bed without having to speak to her.

Going in my bedroom, I shut the door and changed into my nightgown. I chose to wear my sheer red gown with spaghetti straps. Just because.

I headed for my space in bed, deciding I'd only frustrate myself by dressing like this tonight. Especially after my near argument with Gil. Especially after realizing I may have just been responsible for finishing all of my sexual encounters with him.

I was letting out a sound similar to a growl when I headed to bed. My toe struck my shoe. I picked up my shoes and carried them to the closet, shoving aside a stack of sweaters on the floor. A magazine fell out from between them. I picked it up. Maybe I could read some of it instead of the latest cookbook I'd bought to put me to sleep.

Mmm, a guy on a beach graced the cover. I'd never seen this magazine. *Tightened Buns.* What a title. The nice-chested guy was way too young. But maybe he'd brought his dad.

I flipped the page, carrying the magazine to my bed.

Nope, Daddy wasn't on page two. But maybe farther along.

Men showed off their buns. Most had arm and leg muscles resembling ropes. I thought they looked too knotty. I thought—*My cousin buys these things?*

I put on my bifocals. Some of the guys faced the camera in little jock-strap thingies. And Stevie bought this?

Shocked, I studied the magazine to learn more about my relative. She might really need help if this was what she was reading.

I also wanted to get to sleep. I shut the cover and closed my eyes.

Thought of Gil. Envisioned tight buns. Pictured his.

I recalled times we'd been together, me feeling his buns. Him feeling mine. Him tossing my nightgown to the floor. I smiled, the happy thoughts of me and him joined together not about to let me drift into sleep.

I awoke during the night, surprised to realize I'd slept. The happy scenes returned, Gil and me, sometimes naked. Sometimes not. We made each other happy in various ways.

You do not want to make him happy, I told myself. *And you don't want him doing that for you.*

I shoved myself up. What, was I stupid? Why wouldn't I want to be happy?

I do. But not now. Not in that way.

Gil knew what he wanted from his life. Not me. All I wanted from the life I'd had going was a permanent relationship with my husband, Freddy. Then that stroke stole him from me. Immediately, I was no longer a complete person.

Then who was I? Where was the Cealie I'd known, the confident woman who struggled for years with her husband to eventually create a smashingly successful business?

I was learning to be more than half a couple again. I couldn't need support from a man to be the person I was meant to be. I couldn't do that again! I'd seen countless self-confident women who didn't lean on a man. I was on my way to rediscovering Cealie.

Sure, I'd like to travel with Gil. But he'd been almost everywhere, and now his travels were mainly to cities where he opened restaurants.

No problem with that. But suppose he wanted to go to a Cajun Delights grand opening in Boise—right when I yearned for Amsterdam? Or koala bears and kangaroos in their natural habitat?

Or maybe I wanted to become a deep-sea fisherman, and he wouldn't want to leave shore. I didn't want to fish at the moment—but *what if?* I needed my life open to possibilities.

So Gil? Yes, he was extremely important. But so was my feeling of self-worth and discovery of self-knowledge.

Glad to discover I'd been able to sleep after entertaining visions of Gil naked, I slid out of bed for the bathroom. I stepped into the dark hall, dreading what I'd find. Stevie, again locked in that room, chanting?

Or maybe she'd left. The Stevie I knew had jumped out of bed at two a.m. and gone to work out at a gym four nights a week. Afterward she'd shower and sleep for a couple of hours before getting up for work.

Thinking about her schedule wore me out. I considered the schedule and was sure that with Stevie's size, she didn't jump out of anywhere anymore.

I gave my cheek a light pat for my wayward thoughts.

Reaching the extra bedroom, I found the door locked. No light across its bottom. Still, she could be in there with candles lit. I sniffed the door. No candle smells. I pressed my ear against the door, listening.

No sound except my breathing. I breathed quieter and listened. Silence. Maybe she'd fallen asleep with the candles lit. I sniffed against the door. And heard crunching.

"Are you catching a cold?" Stevie asked.

I whipped around. She wasn't in the hall but sat across in the dark at her dining-room table. A small rectangle of light came from her laptop computer.

"I'm okay," I said, walking closer. "What are you doing this late? School work?"

"No, we're almost finished for the year. Most of my school work is done." She sighed. Ate a chocolate-chip cookie and held out the bag. I shook my head. "This is only entertainment. Trying to find answers to what bugs me. And maybe find a man." She gave me a weak grin.

Stevie wanted a man?

"What does bug you?" I asked instead of the question about a man.

"Lots of things. Foremost is who or what killed Pierce Trottier."

"Right. What are you learning?"

"I did an online search for his name."

"Great idea. What did you find?"

"Only this." She handed me a printout. The only mention of his name was to advertise his accounting firm in Tuscaloosa, Alabama, unless that was some other Pierce Trottier.

"Did he live there before he came here?"

"How would I know? I told you, I didn't know the man."

"And I believe you." Was that true? Just in case, I slid my left hand into my right palm and pinched, reminding myself to stick to the truth. "Did you find out anything else?"

She shook her head.

"Maybe we can discover whether anyone connected to him

lived in Tuscaloosa before coming here."

"How are we supposed to know any people connected to him?"

"Good point." We did, of course, know those who'd wanted to quit smoking with him. But since Stevie so vehemently denied ever seeing him with them, I chose not to bring up the subject.

Her IN-box list was onscreen. The subjects were mainly political views from unreliable sources and offers to match her with men. She was about to click on *Free Cartoons*. "These might make me laugh."

"I don't think so." I pointed to the sender—neatopornflicks.

"Oops, hadn't noticed that point." She looked seriously at the others. Eat pizza and lose weight. Lose thirty pounds this week. Better yourself. Someone wants to meet you. Help, my children and I need money. Be happy now.

She wasn't deleting any of them. I couldn't imagine she was seriously entertaining info from these places. "You know this isn't the way to happiness or to help people or meet a guy, if that's what you want."

She stared at me.

"This is mostly spam. Why don't you get it blocked?"

She snapped her mailbox off the screen and shut her laptop.

"You didn't have to do that. I didn't know if you realized you could stop that junk from coming in your IN box." Did I really need to apologize?

"I am an intelligent person. I'm a teacher," she said, like her profession made her brilliant.

"Do whatever you want." I went to the bathroom.

Going back to my room, I noticed no light from the dining room. Only a glow beneath the shut door to Stevie's bedroom.

What *was* her problem? Did she really want to read all that junk from obscure sites which probably weren't reliable?

And what did I know? Maybe those twenty or more sites

were exactly what she needed.

What I needed was to get away from her. First, however, I or someone else had to discover how Pierce Trottier died. I'd get on that task again first thing in the morning.

My second thought might have been wise, maybe not. I scribbled a note and left it on the kitchen table.

What would Stevie think when she read my note suggesting that if she still worked out at a gym, I didn't want to stop her from going? I offered to work out with her.

Lying in bed, I shook my head. There was no way I really wanted to work out. She surely didn't anymore. I fell asleep, imagining my waistline and behind spreading wider with each meal I ate here.

In the morning I thought better of what I'd done last night. If Stevie hadn't read the note yet, I'd throw it away.

Reaching the kitchen, I smiled, seeing a single page on the table.

Only one word was printed on this page. *OKAY.*

Uggh, she'd taken me seriously.

"Stevie," I said, walking through the house. Her bedroom door was open, her bed made, bathroom door open. Door to the spare bedroom locked. No smell or sound suggested she was inside. Her car was gone.

It was Sunday, not a workday for her, and she'd left me without a word. Well yes, she did leave one word, but that was the wrong one. I guessed I'd ticked her off with my comments about her spam and sent her away, maybe for the day.

Pierce Trottier may have lived in Tuscaloosa, Alabama, I remembered. Today's newspaper might have his obituary. I grabbed the paper from the countertop and checked. I wanted to learn about his family. I felt connected to the man and wanted to attend his services to pay my respects.

A short list. He wasn't on it.

I flipped through pages, hoping I wouldn't find any article about an out-of-towner falling on him.

Grateful, I didn't find one. Stevie gave me a printout with information about him last night. Trottier's name was unusual. It would seem odd for two men with that name to be doing the same line of work. The printout didn't give a phone number for Accounting by Pierce, Pierce Trottier owner.

I grabbed my cell phone and called Information. Asked for Tuscaloosa, Accounting by Pierce. The number was no longer in service.

I asked for Trottier, Pierce. Nothing listed.

Not ready to give up, I pressed *0* and spoke to a real person.

"Sorry, there's no listing for Accounting by Pierce or the name Pierce Trottier," she said.

"Can you tell me when the accounting firm's phone number shut down?"

"Sorry, I don't have that information."

"How about Trottier with any other first name?"

No luck there, either. I wasn't sure what else to do now except eat breakfast. I checked the pantry. Powdered donuts. Sugar-coated Pop-Tarts and cereal. Sugar for the coffee.

I looked in the fridge. Texas-size biscuits with butter flakes. Condensed milk. My mind's eye saw my waistline expanding as wide as my behind.

I ate one slice of toast with a pat of butter and drank a half cup of milk. Even so, I felt my hips carrying two extra pounds as I passed the forbidden room. I returned to its door. Still locked. I sniffed. No lit-candle odor. I checked walls for fire extinguishers and found only a couple. That wouldn't do. I tossed on clothes and drove to a nearby mart.

I bought five smoke alarms. Two large fire extinguishers. I piled stacks of paper plates, cups, napkins, and throwaway cutlery in my buggy. Then added food. I grabbed fresh peaches and apples and pears. Going for grapes, I spied a woman who looked familiar. Attractive. Dressed well and slender with fashionable blond hair. I picked up a package of green grapes. She was choosing purple ones.

"Hi, I've met you," I said, "but can't figure out where."

She stared at my face a full minute. "I'm sorry. I don't remember."

"I'm Cealie Gunther, visiting in town with my cousin Stevie Midnight." Maybe she knew Stevie. I tried to recall our connection. "Oh, you were at Cajun Delights. You're the daytime manager, aren't you?"

"Yes. Babs Jacobs. Hi." She gave me her slim hand.

"So we didn't meet. I just saw you around the stage." I remembered all of the circumstances. She wasn't smiling then. Her replacement, Jake, probably arrived late. Stevie guessed Babs was scared to drive at night. Stevie and I both guessed Jake liked her and was too shy or didn't think he stood a chance with her. "That nice evening manager told all of us your name. Who is he?" I pretended I was thinking.

"Jake Bryant. He is pretty nice."

I watched her expression while she mentioned him. She seemed to be speaking about a co-worker, not a love interest.

Maybe I could change that.

"He appeared to be a real pleasant guy," I said with more enthusiasm than I actually felt. I took a mental scroll of what I knew about Jake and came up short. Oh yes, so was he. And stubby. But I did believe he was a good person. He'd joked about himself, which made me like him.

That, and he managed my hunky ex-lover's restaurant.

So did she. But her smile didn't grow any wider. I glanced at her hand to double-check for a ring. None on any fingers.

"How's your boss?" I had to ask. She cocked her head and

looked at me quizzically. "You know. Gil Thurman," I said.

"Oh, him." Her lips spread into a wide, bright smile. "He owns the place but doesn't tell us what to do or anything."

I skimmed her face. She looked barely over thirty.

"You must know your business real well for him to trust you to run the restaurant," I said.

"Why? Did he say anything about me? You really know him?" Concern replaced her happy expression.

I wouldn't tell her how intimately I knew the man she worked for.

"I met him." *And often massaged the small strawberry birthmark on his right hip.*

"You have a slight Southern accent," Babs told me.

"So do you," I said.

She smiled at our common connection. "I need to move. I go to work in a little while." She picked up a package of purple grapes.

"You think the purple ones are better than green?"

"These have been a lot sweeter."

"I'll try purple." I swapped my green grapes. "In case Gil is there, would you tell him we met, and I said hi?"

"I will. Nice meeting you, Ms. Gunther."

A thought made me want to call her back and tell her something positive about Jake that might make her consider him as a love interest. But I watched her and decided that would be out of line. I didn't really know the man. And I couldn't think of anything clever to say.

I shoved my buggy toward the checkout, considering things I might tell her if we met at the front of the store. *Give the man a chance. Check out his buns. He might be really hot.*

But then I was tugging at my clothes like they were uncomfortable and determined I was considering myself and Gil. Yes, he was really hot. And I'd often checked out his buns. Very nice.

And I was confused and angry about my thoughts. I used to believe by the time a woman reached a certain age, she would be done with indecision. I found that not true, at least for me. I wanted Gil.

But didn't want commitment right now.

A woman behind me giggled.

"I'm sorry," she said as I turned. She was maybe forty, with a man probably her husband, pushing a buggy. "You just looked so funny. Nodding real hard. Then shaking your head like you were telling somebody no."

I stared at her.

"Oh, I'm really sorry," she said and rushed her mate toward a checkout farther from me. She lowered her voice, but I heard what she said. "That poor woman. Probably has a tic, and I had to go and point out how she kept shaking her head."

"See? I told you you talk too much," her mate warned her.

I stood in the first line, making certain I didn't move my head or allow another single thought of Gil to enter it.

CHAPTER 9

I drove to Stevie's house, deciding I wouldn't become a matchmaker with Babs and Jake. Even though at first they seemed a good match, I wasn't sure now. I wasn't sure if I really thought they'd go well together, or if I'd wanted an excuse to keep going to Cajun Delights. Now my mind was made up. I was keeping my nose far away from their business. And Gil's restaurant.

With my purse on my shoulder, I hauled my filled bags toward the kitchen. Noise from the rear section of the house stopped me. Voices.

I set my bags on the floor. Who was in the house? What should I do?

Before I could get too frightened, one voice spoke louder. Stevie's. I hadn't thought she'd be home. "So that'll be fine," she said.

"Are you sure?" The second speaker was April, I could tell once I carried my bags into the kitchen. Stevie was speaking on the phone with her. I couldn't hear every word April said but could hear her loud voice.

I gave Stevie a sarcastic smile. Why had she left me? Where had she gone? Why had she made me believe she was leaving me all alone today?

She frowned at the bags I set on the table. "I'm sure. See you later." She hung up and stared at me.

"I thought you'd be gone all day," I said, somewhat deject-edly.

"To mass?"

I noticed her clothes. A little nicer than the loose long dresses she wore to school. Her shapeless outfit looked less like nightclothes and more like something she'd wear during the day. "I didn't realize you had mass today."

"I didn't ask you since you were never a churchgoer."

"I was when I was young."

"Your momma made you go then. That was a long time ago."

Was she purposely stressing my age? As if I wasn't months younger than she? Or did she think I looked older than she did now?

"You didn't need to buy groceries. I have food."

Yes, and it's rich enough to make me double my size.

"Most of what I bought isn't to eat." I pulled out smoke detectors. "I didn't see many of these."

She grimaced. "I'm going to change clothes." She stomped out of the room.

I removed everything from the bags, angrier by the minute. Leaving it all on the table, I marched over to Minnie. "Do you see what she's like? My cousin is so frustrating!"

"Like you aren't?" Stevie was back in the room.

"You were going to change," I said, like she was the one who'd been caught doing the wrong thing.

"I changed my mind. We might go out to eat today." She came across the kitchen so quickly she might have been much younger. "You know what? You think I'm stupid for having candles and stones and chimes. But guess what? I am not the woman in this family who thinks a cactus is a person." She poked her finger at Minnie.

"I know she isn't a person." I pulled Minnie's pot farther away from Stevie's finger. "She's a plant, and a nice one. And

101

talking to plants is supposed to be good for them. It helps them grow."

"Who says?"

"Experts. I read different sources after I almost killed her, and that's one of the things growers urged. Many plants thrive when people talk to them, exactly like babies need to be held."

Stevie grabbed Minnie's pot and brought it close to her face. "Hi. I'm your momma's cousin. How are you? I'm fine today. I went to church and ate breakfast and went to the bathroom."

She set the pot down. Turned to me. "Does she look any better than before I told her my business?"

I clenched my teeth. Huffed through my nostrils. "That's ridiculous," I said. "A plant won't brighten up the minute somebody speaks to it." And then I wondered. "I guess it's the combination of how you care for a living thing."

Stevie grabbed Minnie. "I forgot to tell you I also talked on the phone. And ate two chocolate Pop-Tarts." She set Minnie down. Eyed me like she wondered what I'd do about it.

"What is your problem?" I asked.

She slammed her fists on the counter. "I want a cigarette!"

"Is that all?"

"*All?* Do you have any idea how hard it is to do without something you crave all the time? *Do you?*"

I've desired things—boiled crayfish, sex, chocolate—but not all the time. "I never experienced what you're going through."

"I need nicotine, Cealie. I need it!"

"No, you don't. Just let out tension. Scream whenever you want to smoke."

"*Heee-lp! I want to smoke!*"

"Not like that. Don't yell *help.*"

She looked even more frustrated. "Then what?"

This quitting smoking was more frustrating than I imagined. "Throw something."

She grabbed Minnie's pot.

"Not this." I took it away.

She scanned the kitchen. Stared at the butcher block of knives.

"Let's go in your bedroom," I said.

She slunk there with me. I went to the opposite side of her king-size bed. I felt we were waiting for Valentine's Day with her room done up in pink, red, and white. Lots of decorative pillows in those colors.

I pointed to them. "You can throw pillows."

She stared at the bed. Her shoulders rose with her huge inhales and apparent indecision. Stevie picked up a pillow. Tossed it on the bed. She lifted another. Did the same. "This isn't much fun."

"Throw 'em at me."

She tossed a round pink pillow across the bed. Then threw a square red one. "I still want to smoke."

I threw the square one back at her. "Tough. You can't, and that's that."

She threw it back. "Who says?"

I chunked it harder. "Me."

She flung it again. "You? You can't tell me what to do."

"Yes, I can." I tossed.

"I could sit on you and squash you." She pummeled me with three pillows.

"That hurts." I slammed them back.

"They always liked you best." Stevie rammed me with every pillow from her bed.

"Who?" I shielded my face with my arm. Then grabbed pillows and threw.

"Grandpa Midnight. And Ms. Rodrigue." She viciously threw them back. Those tightly sewn pillow corners hurt like the devil. Our pillow war didn't slow down.

"Ms. Rodrigue, our neighbor?" She'd lived between Stevie's family and mine during the year we resided in the same city. Then Stevie's family left town. I had mixed feelings about that. She and I often played well together. At other times she was mean.

Stevie slammed me with a hard white pillow I blocked with my forearm. "She always gave you the most candy."

"Really?" Most days when I'd walked home from the bus stop, the widow was sitting on her front porch. I'd tell her hey, and she'd hold up a bag of the chocolates we called silver bells. Some people believed she was murdered.

"She said she gave you more since you were so small, which never made any sense to me." Stevie walked around the foot of her bed while she spoke. She tossed a hard pillow at my face.

I grabbed it. "I never heard that. It's stupid. And not my fault." I hit her arm with the pillow.

She yanked more pillows off the bed, slamming me with them as she stepped closer. "And Grandpa Midnight always wanted to hold *you*."

I shielded my face with my arms. "You never wanted to sit on his knee."

" 'Cause he stunk. He smoked big fat cigars that made his teeth brown and his breath stink."

"So you're mad at me?"

She was right in front of me, red faced, glaring down. She held a red pillow high, like she was ready to slam me. And then her eyes went unfocused. She appeared deep in thought.

Stevie's eyes refocused on me. She snickered. So did I. She giggled. I did, too.

We fell against each other, hugging and laughing.

She and I laughed and hugged and then stared at each other and giggled. Then we hugged again.

After a while we stood holding each other. We seemed to realize at the same time that this felt a little awkward and pulled apart. A quiet moment ensued. "We need to find out why a man died here," I said.

Steve nodded. "Do you want to hear one of Mamma's best poems?" she asked.

"Absolutely."

Stevie went to her dresser, opened a drawer, and grabbed papers. She carried them as if she was holding a precious item.

She laid them on her bed. Brushing at her eye, she lifted the top sheet. "This is her favorite." She stood erect, cleared her throat, and read, " 'Fears. This is my worst—Stevie will leave me.' "

I watched. Waited. She lowered her head, looking solemn. She peered at me.

"That was nice," I said. "Cute."

"Cute? My mother's poem is cute?"

"Sure, I like it, and I get it. She hated knowing one day you'd leave her."

Stevie nodded, smiling now, like it was a wonderful thing that I could comprehend what her mother's poem meant.

"Now I'll tell my mother's. This is short, too." I stared off, my inner view showing me my mother's constant smiling pink face. Her arms out to hug me. "An angel touched my life the day my daughter sprang into this world. I knew I was blessed."

Stevie was quiet. "That's pretty good."

"You didn't like it? She was talking about me, you know?"

"I know it, Cealie. Isn't everything about you?"

"No. What are you talking about?"

"You went and tattled when I was only playing around with your ponytail that day, and I got punished. And Mamma always made me let you go first whenever we played games."

"Because I'm younger."

She shoved fists on her hips. "Don't give me that crap

anymore, cousin. I'm not a whole lot older. I just looked it 'cause I was always bigger."

"Taller," I corrected. "There was a time when you were really thin."

"So I'm not now? Is that what you're saying?"

"Girl, neither of us is thin anymore. There was just a time when you were skinny."

"And you think your body was perfect?" She shoved my arm.

"I've never been close to perfect. What's really bothering you, Stevie?"

"You!"

The phone rang. She slapped my arm and went for the phone on her nightstand.

I stood, stunned. Moments ago my cousin and I laughed and hugged. But then we got back to the place where we'd usually stayed—far apart. Only this time, I actually felt threatened. Did she know her strength? Had she meant to harm me? Would she try something again?

The high-pitched voice from the receiver left little doubt as to the identity of her caller. I left the room, not caring to stay around Stevie anymore.

After her reaction to me, I didn't want to be near her at all. I grabbed my purse, jotted a note saying I was going shopping for a few hours, and left it on the kitchen table. I glanced at Minnie and considered taking her with me. But that would be silly. She'd probably die from heat in the parked car. And Stevie surely wasn't a vengeful person.

She didn't want to hurt me, I told myself, hurrying from the house and rubbing my arm that ached where she'd hit me. Bruises were forming.

I drove off, apprehension making my scalp tingle. Why had she been so aggressive? When could I leave town?

I considered what to do, then determined I'd start checking

out people from the stop-smoking group. They were the only ones I knew with some attachment to Pierce Trottier.

First, I needed to settle down after that fight. Food would bring comfort, but I wasn't too hungry. Maybe a little gumbo. I aimed for Cajun Delights. Besides, I told myself as a convincing argument, the priest and his lady friends might be there. I could question them.

Many cars filled the parking lot. I parked and walked on the wooden bridge, pausing to watch fish and ducks. A brisk breeze refreshed my skin. Birds sang from a tree. Losing myself in nature, I then sauntered to the restaurant, realizing how meditation might ease a person's spirit.

Maybe Stevie really could lose herself in thought so much she wasn't aware of anything else, even the doorbell I'd rung when I first arrived. I would need to practice being one with my surroundings.

Touching the restaurant's cypress exterior, I eyed cheerful families swinging underneath the tin overhang. Laughter and chatter abounded, along with tempting aromas when the door opened. I walked inside and glanced at the table reserved for Gil.

Drats. Empty.

But maybe he was here. A young woman seated me. I asked for tea and gumbo, then scanned faces.

No priest with his girlie friends. And no Gil that I could see. But Babs was near.

"Oh, hello," she said, walking beside my table.

"Hey, Babs. Have you seen your boss?"

She shook her head. Beyond her, I recognized the brassy red hair of a woman entering the restaurant. A straight view let me notice her stretch jeans were way too tight. She was a member of the stop-smoking group. And she came in alone.

I went to her. "Hi, I met you when I was with my cousin, Stevie. I'm Cealie Gunther."

"Hey. I'm Jenna." She looked away. I recalled she hadn't met my gaze at the meeting. And she'd walked out to smoke.

She kept her gaze away, looking apprehensive.

"Your group's leader seems to stress out on how well his students achieve," I said to get her reaction and learn whether she'd quit smoking yet.

She faced me. "Ish? He's got nerve. The man never smoked once, and he's trying to tell *us* what to do."

"He never smoked? You're kidding?"

She wagged her finger. "Not even one cigarette."

"That would be like me wanting to teach a class like that. How can someone who never smoked tell others how bad it is?"

"Exactly." Jenna's nod revealed her hair's black roots.

"I'm sitting alone," I said, wanting to learn more. "How about joining me?"

"No thanks." She stomped off toward an empty booth.

My seafood gumbo was to die for. Thick gravy chock-full of shrimp, lump crabmeat, and oysters. Seasoned to perfection. I ate French bread and potato salad and then remembered I hadn't been especially hungry. Still no sign of Gil, so I left.

I was glad I'd learned a pinch of news from Jenna. It didn't seem like much, but it was something. I would check out more people from The Quitters Group and also try to amend my cousin's aggressive behavior. Maybe I could help her calm down, I thought as I saw a mom-and-pop drugstore.

I parked and went in. I asked a clerk where to find aids to help people quit smoking. She sent me toward the druggist.

I angled toward the rear of the store. Along the way I spied straws and grabbed three packs. Maybe pretending to smoke straws would help Stevie like they helped Fawn.

I trotted to the rear of the store and found Father Paul Edward and the twins. They were studying racks of condoms.

CHAPTER 10

The twins, Lark and Clark, crowded beside Father Paul Edward in their spiky heels and slinky dresses. He lifted a condom pack, and all of them laughed.

"Umk." The sound leapt out of my throat before I could stop it.

The group turned to me.

"Hi, y'all," I said.

"Hey," the women replied in unison. The priest stared at me the way people do when they're trying to place someone.

"You have a great confessional," I said, and his expression relaxed. He nodded.

I rushed to the next aisle. If the priest thought I'd been to confession to him, so what? Probably he was mentally scrolling to recall what horrible things I'd told him. If I were Catholic and *did* go to his church, I could go in his little confessional and tell him plenty. Gluttony and judging people might top my list.

Could a confessor help rid me of faults I'd like to shed? Possibly, but those cubbyholes might make me claustrophobic. Nowadays why not have drive-up confessionals for people in a rush? They could put up signs: Toot and tell, or go to hell.

I giggled, then mentally stomped my wayward thoughts about that priest. Maybe he was with those women who appeared to be hookers, and all of them appeared to be buying condoms. So what? That didn't mean they *were* hookers or were buying and planning to use the things. Possibly they were only checking out current styles.

"I know where I spoke to you," the priest said, and I spun around. He came down the aisle, hobbling with his cane, one foot dipping. The twins sashayed at his sides.

"You do?" I said.

"Yes, with your cousin at our quitters' meeting." He grinned. I didn't know why.

"Oh, right, I do believe I met you there." I did a quick mental scroll to determine whether I was actually fibbing to a priest. Decided I was innocent.

His friends smiled, like this knowledge made them extremely happy.

Father smiled wider, shaking his head. "That Ish," he said.

I had no idea why he'd consider Ish funny. "So he really wasn't a smoker?"

"Nope, never smoked." Father laughed. "Strange, isn't it?"

The twins grinned as if we told funny jokes.

"That's incredible," I told Father. "That would be like me standing in front of your group telling you that you should quit the habit because I heard it's bad for you."

The smile wiped off his face, replaced by a scowl. "Maybe you could do that."

The girls also scowled at me.

"Ladies, ready?" Father asked, done with our discussion.

They nodded in unison, and all went toward the front of the store.

What was that all about? What would make this priest consider their stern group leader so amusing?

Unable to answer that question, I found stacks of patches and gum and lozenges that helped people stop smoking close to the white-haired druggist filling a prescription.

"Do they put all these stop-smoking things right here so you can guard them?" I asked him.

"Pretty much. Nicotine is a dangerous substance."

"These things contain nicotine?"

"A little. It's much less than you're getting in a cigarette. What would you like?"

Hmm, what might Stevie use? Different boxes held all kinds of items. "I might take one of each."

"I wouldn't advise that. You can't use more than one of these products at a time."

"Why not? It seems it would help much more if a person has a double dose of products, maybe wear a patch and chew the gum."

"No way. And don't smoke while you're using them, either. That could speed up your heart too much, which could especially be a problem if you already have heart problems."

"My heart's great, and I don't smoke. I want to help my cousin with tension while she quits."

"There are pills to help with tension. She'd need a prescription."

I didn't think I could convince Stevie to get a prescription from her doctor. I wasn't sure which of these nonprescription items might be best. "I'll study these to decide what to get her."

"All right. But she should be the one to choose."

"She'd prefer to be surprised."

With closer scrutiny, I discovered some of the quit-smoking items were for people who smoked before breakfast. Others were for those who smoked a small number of daily cigarettes. Different milligrams and packs for the same item supposedly helped those who smoked a lot. Stevie didn't smoke any cigarettes anymore, that I knew of, so I decided not to get those items.

Of course she might sneak some smokes when I didn't see her. The odor of smoke had come from the room she kept locked. Suppose she kept going into that room to hide from me to smoke.

What would I care? I asked myself, then decided I did care. Smoking could kill her. I didn't want that.

Selecting a product to help her was a much harder task than I'd anticipated. I considered the gum. People either chewed gum or didn't. I'd seen April chewing but not Stevie.

Lozenges seemed the simplest way to quit. When the urge to smoke hit, just suck on a mint.

Inspecting a package, I discovered these didn't have spearmint or peppermint flavors. These lozenges might sting when first placed on the tongue. The user was advised to keep one in her cheek, not suck on it. This seemed too much work. I set the box back into place.

Patches? These packs, like all of the other items, displayed milligrams, seven, fourteen, or twenty-one. *Use one patch each day,* the instructions said, also warning the user not to smoke while using the patch.

I walked to the druggist. "What would happen if a person used two of these? And smoked while wearing them?

He looked annoyed. Maybe I'd made him lose count of pills.

"Nicotine is a poison. Would you want a double dose?" He stared like I was really stupid. "It's probably best if you let your cousin pick whatever she'd prefer."

"But she might choose nothing."

He shook his head. "Most of us wish we could get people we love to quit smoking. But that's not a choice we can make for them."

"I want to help," I explained.

"Which is great. You might have noticed lots of those packages suggest users also get into a support group."

"She is in one."

"Great. That's the best thing for her. And if she wants some type of stop-smoking aid, we can help find one that suits her. Or her doctor might suggest something newer, like laser treatment."

"You've really helped," I said, pleased that he had become nice again.

"My mother died of lung cancer. I wished I could have helped her."

"I'm sorry," I said. Right before leaving, I decided to get the lozenges. I left the drugstore filled with knowledge, my compassion growing. I sympathized with the druggist. Then reminded myself I needed to stop judging people.

I thought of the priest who'd also been inside the drugstore, the two women joining him. Ladies of the evening?

I chose to think not. They were only his friends. Everyone needed friends.

Driving away, I grinned, wondering how friendly he became with them.

I considered the other man we'd mentioned from their stop-smoking group. Ish Muller had never smoked. Could he really help others?

He'd seemed the most sinister of the group. Maybe he had some other connection to the man who died? I'd try to find out.

I needed to focus on what to do now and wasn't ready to return to Stevie's house.

The sun was sinking. Water bubbled in a brook along the scenic route. I pulled over and sat on a wide, cool rock. In no time, tranquility set in.

I envisioned myself in a long, white, gauzy dress, prostate in the midst of candles in the locked room. Nope, I'd fall asleep, and the candles might catch the house on fire. Forget meditating with her candles.

The druggist had mentioned a new laser treatment. If Stevie

didn't agree to try it, maybe I could catch her motionless on her stomach in that room and zap her with a laser.

I smirked, needing to come up with much better ideas.

I hated to leave this spot, but darkness was setting in. Peace settled inside me like a much-needed rest.

Back at Stevie's, I didn't see her inside. I rushed to the kitchen and set the lozenges at her place on the table.

I heard the hall toilet flush. A moment later, Stevie appeared.

She glanced at me. We both said nothing. I couldn't read her mood but decided she must still be angry with me. I didn't want her to throw anything.

She stepped across the room and grabbed Minnie. My instinct was to yank my cactus out of her hands before she broke it. She shoved her face close to my plant. "I just pooped."

A snort escaped my throat.

"I think your friend smiled," she told me.

"Probably so," I said, and both of us grinned.

She moved through the kitchen, her gaze swinging to the table. She stared at the lozenges.

"I bought them for you."

She picked up the box, perused its rear, set it down. Stared at me, stone-faced.

Rap-rap-rap sounded from the front door. Stevie strode there, leaving me to wonder how she felt about my gift.

Shoes clomped on the wooden floor, followed by a loud voice, giving me little doubt about our visitors.

"Hey," April said when I went into the living room, where they'd stopped. "Cherish wanted to come show Aunt Stevie her new toy."

"Ooh, what did you get?" Stevie stooped near the child.

"This." Beaming, Cherish held up a toy cash register. Corners of it were faded, paper parts of it torn.

"Neat," Stevie said. "Show me how it works."

"We can't stay long," April said.

"Here's a dollar for an ice cream." Stevie handed Cherish pretend money. "I'd like chocolate please and a nickel back."

The girl cranked the handle. Her toy went *ding*, and plastic coins rolled out. She gave one to Stevie.

"Thanks. This cash register is like the one our stop-smoking leader brought to our meeting the first night."

"Ish?" I said, finding it hard to imagine him with any toy.

"Yes. He had us drop coins in it and imagine all the money we'd be saving after we stopped smoking."

April tilted her head. "Ish? I saw him."

"That's such an unusual name," I said. "I'd never heard anything like that."

"It got my attention." April faced her child. "Come on. I need to get to work."

Stevie kissed Cherish's cheek. "I love your new toy." She looked at April. "Where did you meet Ish?"

"We didn't meet. I was coming out of the finance company a few weeks ago, and they called his name at the window of an accounting office across the hall."

I stepped into April's path toward the front door. "Really? What finance company do you use?"

"Cealie!" My cousin's raised eyebrows assured me I was out of line asking her neighbor such a question.

"It's none of my business," I told April, "and you don't have to tell me. But the man who died out there was an accountant. Maybe the one near your finance company knew something about him."

April tucked her chin. Cherish whined, "I wanna go see Scooby."

I could have Scoobied her.

April seemed annoyed. "Ish's name was called at the office

that belonged to Pierce Trottier." She rushed to the front door with her child.

I stared at Stevie. "Did Ish tell you Pierce Trottier was his accountant?"

"He didn't mention it."

We remained quiet. I mulled over a new idea and figured she did the same.

"Maybe there was a lot more connection between your group leader and the dead man than we could have imagined," I said. "Stevie, let's go visit Ish."

She appeared to ponder that thought.

"I'll give him a really good reason for why we're there," I said with enthusiasm, although I had no idea what I might say to him. "I'll be discreet."

"I'm with you." She yanked a phone book out of a drawer and located his address.

Darkness draped the roads we traversed. After a few miles on a straight shoot, we swirled up a steep hill. Treetops clumped, creating a canopy, blotting any brightness from the moon. Stevie drove around the narrow road that swirled in front of cabins, some well lit, others dark as the night.

We stayed quiet for most of the ride. My heart pounded. "Should we call the police?"

She glanced at me. "Are you kidding? You don't think Ish killed him, do you?"

"Maybe."

"I am not going over there with the idea that he's a killer." She tapped the brakes. "Is that the kind of question you plan to ask him? We'll go home right now."

"Uh-uh, no way. I wouldn't ask him that."

Since she glanced at my hands, I didn't pinch my right palm. Maybe she knew about my doing that. Possibly I had pinched my palm when I fibbed ever since I was a child.

"Cealie, just because Ish was a client, why would you think he killed Pierce?"

"Your man Ish didn't seem too friendly." And my trepidation grew the closer we got to his place.

"So he won't get a hospitality trophy. Darn it, you're getting judgmental in your old age."

"*Old age?*" Anger replaced my apprehension.

"Don't get your girdle all bunched up."

"I do not wear a girdle!"

Facing forward, she tapped my arm. "I think it's the next cabin."

The scene ahead made my childish bickering instinct fall away.

Sheltered by towering trees, an eye-catching log cabin squatted on the mountain's ledge. Its rustic porch graced the entire front and jutted over the edge of the valley. This cabin appeared rustic, yet new. Its wooden exterior and porch provided the pastoral feel. Wood that looked varnished made the cabin seem new, as did the bright chandelier hanging inside huge triangular windows. The windows peaked at the pointed roof, which appeared to aim for the sky.

Stevie parked in the driveway behind a BMW. She set the brakes on her Jeep. As we got out, I grabbed my cell phone out of my purse and kept it in my hand, just in case. My cousin knew the man who owned this place a lot better than I did and might trust him. I didn't have to.

The air felt cooler so high up. The scent of pine trees hung in the air, along with the odor of something burning.

A small barbecue pit on the porch held embers. Two squirrels chased each other up a tree. I ambled from the driveway, admiring the cabin. At the far end of the porch sat a screened-in area near doors of what was probably the master bedroom. The screened area probably held a large hot tub.

This was the kind of place I could settle in forever, especially during fall when the leaves displayed their new colors.

I stood admiring the view as long as possible. Feet crunched against twigs nearby. I glanced back, expecting a person. Saw no one.

"It's probably only a small black bear," Stevie said.

I scrambled to the porch. Hearing her laughter, I decided she'd been kidding. But I knew some bears lived out here.

She paused with me before knocking or ringing a bell, and I figured she was also taking in the picturesque cottage. The large triangular window drew the eye to its apex, where brightly varnished wood beams perfectly scored the scene with thick vertical and thinner horizontal lines.

Something appeared out of place in those planed lines. Near the top of the window, something was hanging.

I glanced at the door. Looked up higher once again.

Parting one of those perfect glass rectangles was a dangling object.

A person.

"Stevie!" I screamed, grabbing her arm.

"What? Be quiet. I thought we'd surprise him. That hurts." She yanked her arm away. Then her gaze followed where my finger aimed. "Dammit, Cealie. Not another dead man."

I forced my finger to keep still enough to punch 9-1-1 on my phone.

Stevie's arm shook against mine. "Oh, no. It's Ish."

CHAPTER 11

Sirens screamed, their lights flashing across the black mountainside as police cars sped up the slope. Stevie and I watched from Ish's front porch. I forced myself to avoid staring at Ish's body hanging from his home's rafters. My stomach balled into a knot.

Another dead person around me?

I hadn't cared for the man but felt awful to find him dead.

Police cars hurtled closer. The first one pulled up. Its front door flew open, and a female police officer rushed out.

"Where's the body?" she asked.

"Up there. It's Ish Muller," I said, pointing.

Near us, the cabin's front door flew open.

Ish Muller stomped out on his porch. "What's going on here?"

Stevie and I stared at each other.

More policemen and women rushed near with emergency workers and a gurney.

"Oh my God, Stevie," I said and leaned close to her. "If Ish isn't hanging up there, it means he killed that man."

Police officers rushed from their cars. Detective Renwick marched to the front of the others. Happy to see him, I nodded.

"What the hell is going on!" Ish yelled.

"I'm Detective Renwick. Do you live here?"

"I do."

"We need to go inside, sir."

"Why is that?"

"There's a body hanging inside your house." Still eyeballing Ish, Renwick pointed toward the huge window's apex.

Ish snorted. "*That* body?"

"Yes, that one!" I said and nudged past the detective and Ish. I stepped into the den.

"Where are you going?" Ish snapped at me. He stepped inside, others following.

"There it is!" I pointed to the dangling body.

Everyone stared at a rope attached to a ceiling beam. Hanging from the rope was what I did not expect to see. A life-sized inflatable doll.

"Oops," I said and stepped closer to get a better angle.

The doll was female. Full lips with red lipstick and wide powder-blue eyes with thick eyelashes. Her pantsuit appeared more manly than feminine. The suit was what had led me to believe it was a man up there. A rope circled the doll's neck like a hangman's noose.

Most of us stared at the doll. At each other. At the doll. At Ish.

Detective Renwick turned harsh eyes toward me.

I shrugged. "It sure looked like I saw a dead person."

"You're getting experience with that," he said.

I puffed up my chest. "Are you insinuating something?"

"Not at all."

Ish stepped closer to us. "If you're all finished checking out my *body*, you can leave my home."

"We will," the detective said.

Ish gave my cousin extra-mean eyes. "It appears you're connected with having this circus come to my home." He swung those mean eyes toward me, making sure I knew I was included in his statement.

"I'm really sorry," Stevie told him.

The front door remained open. People in uniform crammed

together there, craning their necks to see the doll.

They moved away as the detective stepped toward the door. He turned to Ish. "I can understand why Mrs. Gunther thought there was a dead person here and called us."

Terrific. Ish didn't need to know I was the one who'd made the call. Why not hang a sign around my neck? *Major Trouble-maker.*

Ish leaned so close, I smelled barbecue sauce on his breath. "I just met this woman, and she gets the cops coming after me?"

"My mistake," I said. "I didn't mean to cause you problems."

"I guess you came here for some other reason." He turned to Stevie. "You wanted something for the class and couldn't wait for our next session?"

She gazed at the floor, shaking her head.

The police listened.

Ish faced me. "Did you want something here?"

"Yes." I hitched up my chin. "I wanted to ask about Pierce Trottier."

Detective Renwick appeared more interested. So did Stevie, staring at me.

"What about him?" Ish asked.

"He was your accountant." I was proud to convey that information in front of police.

"And?"

"And . . . he died."

Ish squinted at me. His cheek twitched. "So do you plan to find out who each of his clients were and go visit them?"

Good point, now that I thought about it.

"Are you a private investigator?" Ish asked me.

"No, but Mr. Trottier was also in your stop-smoking class."

"So was your cousin. So do you think quitting smoking killed the man?" He aimed his pointed stare at Stevie.

Redness flamed up her cheeks.

Darn, I hated to see this man make her so embarrassed.

Detective Renwick stepped up to me. "Did you find some other connection between Mr. Muller and the victim?"

"No. But maybe y'all should be checking into all of Pierce Trottier's clients. Maybe his stop-smoking group, too."

"Thanks for your suggestions. It's possible we already thought of that."

"Y'all are so clever," I said and followed him to the door.

"Other detectives and myself didn't make up the procedures, ma'am. They're already written for us to follow."

"*I,*" I told him.

The detective stopped walking. "What?"

"It's *I.* You can't use *myself* as a subject. Sorry, I hate to correct you, but I have this bad habit—among others. I own a copyediting agency and have offices throughout the country. I have to stop myself from correcting people's grammar. I don't mean to do it but often can't stop myself in time."

He stared at me. "What are you talking about?"

"You said, 'The other detectives and myself didn't make up the procedures.' It should be 'The other detectives and I.'"

Renwick eyed me for the longest time. I feared he wanted to slap handcuffs on my wrists. He sucked in a breath. "Is that true?"

"Sure. When you have two words as the subject, and one is a pronoun you aren't sure of, take the other word out. You'll find it's much easier then. You wouldn't say 'Myself didn't make up the procedures.'"

"That would sound real stupid."

I nodded. "Also, *myself* is a reflexive pronoun. Only use it to refer to *I* that you've already used, for example *I* hurt *myself.*

He shook his head. "I wish I'd paid more attention in some classes. We need to write so many reports."

"I didn't make great grades in all of my classes, either. I think we're all given different talents and interests. I couldn't do your job."

"I don't give a damn about your talents or jobs!" Ish stood behind us at the door.

Well, ex-*cuse* me. I didn't mean to bring up the correct grammar thing. Habit. It was one I wanted to break.

"Sorry we troubled you," Detective Renwick told him. "I may want to ask you more questions later." He looked at me. "*May* is correct there, right?"

I did a thumbs-up.

"If you come back," Ish told Renwick, "don't bring all of your troops so my neighbors think I'm a criminal." He slammed his door behind us.

I walked to the driveway with Renwick. "I didn't mean to cause y'all any trouble. That guy is weird though, don't you think? I mean, having a blow-up doll and hanging it from your ceiling."

"If we sent people out every time anyone did something weird, nobody would be around to handle the real emergencies."

"Good point."

He went to his car and drove off. Stevie was already in hers. I climbed in. We took our time buckling up. She started the motor.

"That went well," I said, and her angry face snapped toward me. "I'm kidding, Stevie. Darn, what happened to your sense of humor?"

"It vanished the minute my cousin made a fool of me!"

"What, here? But you thought we should come over here, too."

"Because you made a big deal out of some far-fetched connection between Ish and a dead man." Her voice pitched high.

"Far-fetched connection? The strange guy who lives here could have easily killed that man!"

Stevie threw up her hands. "Easily? How do you know that? How do you know how that man died?" She stretched her face toward me. "It's exactly like when we were kids—you make up the best stories."

"I make up stories?"

"Yes! Like when you went crying to our mothers, saying I pulled your hair."

"That again? Well, you did. And it hurt, so I cried."

"I'm talking about the time we were at Grandma Jean's house, and you ran in whining and told 'em I did it, but I didn't!"

"Oh, that time."

"You decided you'd get even for the time I really did it." She slapped the steering wheel. "Our moms were reading poems they wrote to their mother, but your fake tattling made them stop. I even saw you pinching your palm once you lied."

Oops, she did know my habit. I raised my right hand, admitting guilt. "That was bad timing, but I didn't know it."

"Of course you didn't know it would be the last time they'd get to read their poetry or talk to their mother!"

"Stevie, I didn't know." She needed to back off with the dramatics. I felt bad enough remembering that day.

"Your mom got so upset she took you away from Grandma Jean's house, and mine took me away, too. And later that night, Grandma Jean died."

She was trying to dump too much guilt on me. I didn't want to hear any more or continue the shouting match. I pressed my hands to my ears, letting her know I'd heard enough. I surely didn't want tears to gather in my eyes, but she probably didn't see them.

It was so dark, sitting in the Jeep in the driveway. I envisioned

Grandma Jean the last time I saw her. Normally a calm, sweet person with soft white hair curled close to her scalp, she'd gotten so angry with Stevie and raised her voice, telling her not to pick on me.

And Stevie hadn't that day. We'd had some stupid argument in the yard, and I'd determined it was time to get even. I forced tears while I ran inside Grandma Jean's house and pointed at Stevie, who marched in behind, protesting that she hadn't touched me.

Grandma, she didn't do it. Stevie didn't lay a hand on me that day. I made up that story. I admitted my guilt to Grandma Jean while I sat in the now quiet car. I'd wanted to do it at her wake. But I'd eyed her in the casket and hadn't been able to muster the courage. I'd only cried. I was especially sorry after Mom told me what they'd been doing, she and her sister reciting special poems to their mother. It was the first time Grandma Jean really took notice and understood both of her daughters loved to write poetry. My mom had read a couple of her poems to me but never did after that day.

Stevie was probably also reminiscing and wishing our elders were still near. And that I hadn't ruined their last special time together. I imagined warm tears were coating her eyes, just like they were doing to mine. I looked at her but couldn't see well.

Except for the monstrous face pressed close outside Stevie's window.

"Look out!" I yelled, pointing.

Stevie jerked her head away from the glass. I hit the lock button for all the doors.

The face, I determined, belonged to Ish. He still looked furious.

Stevie slid her window down an inch.

"Are you two planning to camp out here to watch what goes on?" Ish snarled.

Not a bad idea. But I didn't mention that thought.

"No," Stevie said. "We're only talking."

Ish pointed down the road. "Take your discussion elsewhere, or I'll call the cops to come get you for trespassing."

"All right, enough," I said, unable to hold my tongue. "We were discussing our childhoods. We weren't even talking about you. And your . . . toy-girl." I waved my hand toward the top of his gorgeous triangular window.

"Ceal-ie!" my cousin warned, whipping her head toward me.

Ish stuck his face near the opening of her window and glared at me. "I don't care to know a thing about your childhood, which must have been terrible to make you grow up to be the person you are."

I leaned toward him, opening my mouth to retort.

"We're going!" Stevie said and threw the car into reverse. I bounced toward my side. We shot forward so quickly, I grabbed the dashboard. She zipped down the dark winding road. I closed my eyes and prayed.

I smelled fire and looked.

An unlit cigarette stuck out of her lips. She held a lighter, moving it closer to the deadly cigarette.

"No!" I grabbed the lighter, hit the button to lower my window, and tossed the lighter.

"What are you doing?" she screamed, cigarette dangling from her mouth.

I grabbed that and pitched it.

She slammed on the brakes. We stopped.

A horn blasted, and a truck swooped around us from behind. Its inside lights were on, probably so we could see its teenage male driver shooting Stevie his middle finger.

I shot one back but didn't think he saw it. Stevie slapped my hand down. I looked around. Thank goodness no other cars were near when my cousin decided she'd brake without checking both ways.

She heaved a breath, then started the car forward. Neither of us spoke.

Way sooner than it had taken for us to reach Ish's house, we were back at Stevie's. She rushed into the house. I trailed her inside. A door slammed.

I didn't see her. The door to the candle room was the only one shut. She was doing her thing.

Fine. I'd do mine.

My stomach grumbled, wanting dinner. Stevie surely wasn't fixing a meal in that room. I rapped on its door. "I'm going out to eat. Do you want to come?"

I pressed my ear against the door.

"Ahroom. Ahroom." Softly, those sounds echoed from inside.

"Stevie, you can ahroom all you want. I'm going to have dinner at Cajun Delights. Do you want to come?"

I knew she heard me. I tapped my foot, giving her time to wrap up her prayers or chants.

Still nothing.

"I'm leaving. Stevie, I'm getting my purse and going. I can take you with me."

I went to my bedroom, glanced in the mirror, and reapplied lipstick. I fluffed my hair. My shirt and slacks looked okay. I could dress them up a bit by wearing heels. I kicked off my Keds and went for the red spikes tucked into side pockets in my suitcase, still atop the unused side of my bed. If I had to stay much longer, maybe I'd take it down and put a few things in drawers. But I didn't expect to stay long enough. My hanging clothes in the closet seemed enough of a down-home feel for me here.

I opened my suitcase.

My first thought was that the young cop who'd fingered my chamois sweater in the closet had picked through everything inside my luggage. All of my panties were open on top of my other clothes.

Fear gripped me. My back stiffened.

I hadn't opened my panties and strewn them over other things. I'd left them folded in a small neat stack.

I stepped away from the suitcase—and felt the wind.

Jerking around, I spied the sheer curtains flapping.

"Stevie!" I yelled, running out of the room.

She met me in the hall. "What's wrong?"

"Somebody came in my bedroom. Maybe they're in there right now."

CHAPTER 12

Stevie clutched her throat. "Oh no. You saw him?" she cried as we dashed toward the living room.

I shook my head. "Just the open window. And my messy panties."

She slowed. "Your window's wide open?"

"No." I realized I'd seen how much of it was open. "Only about two inches."

Stevie stopped. "You think somebody really skinny came through your window?"

"I don't know. He or she could have come through and rummaged in my suitcase and then slipped back outside. Or opened it wider to come in, and then . . ."

I visualized what she must be thinking. A person, probably a man, shoved that window open wide enough to climb through. And then pulled it back down—just part way. Why? To keep a nice breeze wafting through the room?

Why not either leave it wide open or close it all the way so nobody knows he's come in?

"Cealie, nobody came through that window."

"How do you know?"

Stevie inhaled and exhaled a couple of times.

"You're short of breath," I said.

"It's no problem." She took another visible deep breath. "What about your underwear?"

I glanced toward my room, imagining some large guy stomping out towards us. "I think we ought to get out and call the police."

She grabbed my chin and turned my face up toward her. "Tell me about your panties."

"They're messy."

"Excuse me?"

I withdrew my head from her grip. "I had my underwear in neat stacks in my suitcase but found my panties messed up."

"Your underwear is still in your suitcase?"

"Yes, like a lot of my other things. And still on the bed, and I believe somebody went through it and might still be in that room. We should get out of here."

"Du-uh."

"What?"

"Don't you dare tell me you think someone came in while we were gone so they could mess up your suitcase."

"I don't have any idea what anybody around here would want. Do you?"

"No, and I'm not going to spend another second entertaining the thought of a person being here tonight."

"But—" My fear started to dissipate.

She leaned near my face. "You think someone was watching to know when we'd leave. And then while we were at Ish's house, they came in here?"

"Possible." Not too probable.

"Okay, Cuz, we're going in there right now. We're going to see if anything's missing, or if a killer's waiting in your closet."

That thought zapped my throat dry. "My closet?"

"I'm kidding. When did you turn into a big baby? Never mind, I'll bring you some protection." She sauntered down the hall, muttering so I could hear. "I can imagine calling the cops again tonight. Right-o, Cealie, *you're* going to leave this town soon, but not me. Nope, I have to stay around and have everyone call me a fool."

She said I'd become a big baby? When did that happen—recently in Chicago, when I needed to square off with a killer? Or after I arrived here—and tripped over a body? Okay, I was *not* a crybaby. But being around her, I almost felt like one.

Darn, I was a grown woman. Mature—except when I was around my cousin.

She returned carrying a baseball bat. "Let's go check your room. I'll go first."

She might have been trying to make me feel like I'd cried wolf. But if she really thought that, she wouldn't use both hands to grip the bat in front of her face. She went into the doorway and stopped. Surveyed the room, as I did.

No one visible. No wide open window. Only the edges where curtains met, moving slightly, enough for us to see the window open an inch or two.

Stevie ran across the room, surprising me. She reached the window, yanked back a curtain panel, and bent down.

"Ah," she said and let the curtain drop. She lowered her baseball bat. "The screen is still on the window. Nobody came through there."

Okay, she was probably right. Still, I crept toward the bed, dropped to my knees and yanked up the bed skirt. Only one fuzz ball underneath. I pulled the closet doors open. Nobody and no feet of someone standing behind Stevie's stored winter boots. I shut the closet.

"Satisfied?" she asked.

I went to the window and checked closer. A shiver of fear swept through me. "This screen isn't locked." I grabbed the lock at the base of the screen and tugged. It wouldn't reach the eye hook.

"I had the windows cleaned not long ago. The screens don't all hook."

"That's not safe."

"I didn't get around to having them fixed yet."

"You'd better do that soon."

"I will. You probably opened the window to get some fresh air and don't remember doing it," she said. "You're getting older. Sometimes you might forget things."

"Excuse me, I don't forget. I didn't open that window."

"Right, Cealie." She headed out the room.

"Really. I didn't."

She spun and faced me. "You win. You always win. You didn't do it, okay?"

"I always win?"

"Cealie, I'm going to eat. You can go to your guy's restaurant if you want. I'm staying here. I have leftovers."

"He's not my guy. And I don't feel like going out anymore."

"Fine, I'll heat something for you."

"Fine."

She stamped off, the bat swinging loosely in one hand.

I stayed in my room. I shut and locked the window. I took my underwear out of my suitcase and refolded it, making slender stacks. Then I opened the top drawer of the chest of drawers to put my things inside.

The drawer was half full of magazines. *Playful Girl, Check Out These Dudes* and other glossies showing almost-nude men.

"It's hot. Come and eat if you want to," Stevie yelled.

I slammed the drawer. Took breaths, waiting for my heartbeats to slow. Tentatively opened the second drawer.

Same as the first. I slammed it. Heard footsteps and turned.

Stevie stood in the doorway. "Are you coming?"

I nodded. "Uh-hunh."

"You folded your clothes?"

I noticed I still held them. Rushed to my suitcase and threw it open. "I needed to get them all tidy again."

"Did you want to put your things somewhere else? You don't have to keep that suitcase on your bed."

"No, I'm good. The bed's good." I set my new stacks back inside the suitcase.

"You could stay long enough to unpack your things," she said with a hint of annoyance. She walked in front of me toward the kitchen.

"I think you ought to see a doctor," I said. "You got short of breath."

"I hear you huffing back there. So why don't *you* see a doctor?"

What I needed was to not see so many almost-nude men. "I might."

"Me, too."

I didn't mention the magazines because skimming through them felt like I'd been prying into her private business. Also, she might take them away, and I might want to skim through them—only to see how perverted she had become.

We ate pizza without conversation. I finished eating and helped wash the dishes without thinking about what I was doing until I was drying the last fork. I noticed the clean kitchen. Went over and gave Minnie a gentle pat on one of her small pink bumps. Her stem was straight, and all the puffs on her head appeared plump and healthy.

"I'm going to bed," Stevie said. "Good night, Minnie!" she yelled to my plant with a smirk.

"Me, too. Good night," I said to her and my friend, Minnie.

In my bedroom I rechecked beneath the bed and in the closet. I looked at the window, making sure I'd shut and locked it. Apprehension kept me awake. And the new severe pain in my shins. I massaged them. Somebody needed to discover what killed Pierce Trottier.

And even after they did, would the ache ever go away?

I mourned for the man. My own problem was so slight compared to what happened to him. *I'm okay,* I told myself. *Don't worry about it.*

My shins throbbed. I could barely stand the pain.

I grabbed a cookbook from my suitcase and read a few pages. The last recipe I read, Big Bill's Chili, would have the person who prepared this dish shopping for thirteen ingredients and spending half the afternoon chopping them and stirring in the pot.

Exhausted from the thought, I snored.

Sunshine brightened my sheer curtains. It seemed a spotlight outside aimed at my window the second I opened my eyes. The day definitely had not just gotten started.

I stretched, drew the top sheet tighter to my neck, and slept again.

I woke later, satisfied that I could sleep as late as my body chose to now. My body was ready to get up. I padded to the window. Still locked. I gathered my clothes and looked for Stevie, then remembered it was Monday. She was at school. Another lovely thing about being in business with great people running my offices was I often forgot what day of the week it was.

I didn't forget I'd want to check into more of the people who knew Pierce Trottier. Ish remained high on my list of suspects as a killer, but I'd check others.

I couldn't find the newspaper. I got the phone book, looked up funeral parlors in the area, and called. Pierce Trottier still wasn't scheduled at any of them.

Deciding it was better that Stevie was in school all day and wouldn't know I'd snoop into lives of others in her stop-smoking group, I showered and dressed in a silk shirt. I added comfortable cotton slacks and flats and then stared in the mirror. Uggh.

The face looked rested with no red eyes. But that hair.

Totally red. Totally puffed. My brown eyes disappeared. So did my nose and lips.

I applied liquid makeup to cover pillow creases on my cheek and coated my lashes with mascara. Coral lipstick helped brighten my face. Still, red hair surrounded my head like a bonnet. I ran my fingers through my curls to loosen them, then patted my hair down. A little better. But I needed help.

Stevie left me some freshly brewed coffee. "How nice," I said to Minnie in the kitchen that smelled scrumptious. "And she baked pastry."

I ate a muffin. Flaky, with a trace of blueberries and cream. I had it with coffee, first looking for the paper plates I'd bought. I didn't find them. I washed my few dishes and tossed my napkin. In the trash I discovered an empty container. Stevie hadn't made the pastries from scratch before going off to work. She'd bought a can and baked them. Ah, she was more my kind of woman.

"Miss Pudgy here," I told Minnie as I waddled out of the kitchen. It felt that way, and if I didn't leave Stevie's house soon, that's exactly how I would walk.

The ache struck my legs. They started to buckle. Pain radiated from my knees to my ankles. I needed to help solve Pierce Trottier's death.

I wanted to check on the priest. Yesterday he was probably busy with masses. Today was he busy with those gorgeous women?

I didn't know what church he was assigned to, but did know someone who might have that knowledge. I drove out to Beauty First, discouraged when I recalled that most hair salons seemed to close on Mondays.

To my delight, a car was out front. A sign said *Open*. I went inside, met by the pleasant scent of potpourri. The TV blared on the wall. Nobody visible.

"Hey, Audrey. Are you here?" I yelled.

She bustled through the beaded curtain. "Cealie. You're back."

"I thought you might've missed me."

"I did. So what can I do for you? Doesn't everyone love your hair?"

Possibly. They all stare at it. "People notice. I have one slight problem. Could you tone it down a little? And maybe not have it stick out so much?"

Her forehead creased, like she might be hurt about everyone not loving her creation. "Sit up here."

I climbed in her chair. Tension in my shoulders told me maybe I shouldn't. But I really hoped to get information.

She whipped a plastic drape open and wrapped it around my neck. Audrey peered down at my hair, parting sections and murmuring. She mixed lotions in a container.

"One thing I've noticed in the last few months," I said to her, "is that my eyelashes don't show up as much as they used to, even when I put on mascara. My eyes aren't large, so without the mascara showing, they almost disappear. Especially when my hair is so large."

She quit mixing her brew, mouth tight. "Large hair?"

I patted it down on top. "I have worn it this puffy." Of course that was decades ago, when puffy was in. "Or instead of smaller hair, do you have any idea how to make my eyes look bigger?" I snickered, trying to make it sound like we were good friends, playing around.

She stared at my reflection. "Get younger."

"Excuse me."

"Your eyes look smaller because you don't have as many eyelashes as you had when you were young. When you get older, they break."

"Oh, crap. You mean that's gone, too?"

"Yep." She squeezed my head into a tight cap. Using a knitting needle, she tugged sprigs of red hair through tiny holes. Each time the needle reached down, I cringed.

I was exhausted from pain once she put the needle down. She painted a solution with stench onto patches of my hair poking out from the cap. "Now we wait a few minutes," she said, "while the color sits."

"Do you have an aspirin?"

"No. Why?"

"Never mind." I resigned myself. The pain in my head would soon go away. I'd come here for information. "The other day I met a priest, Father Paul Edward. I wondered where his church is."

"He's pastor of Our Lady of Hope. He's really nice."

"And crippled," I said, thinking maybe she'd say nope, he doesn't have a physical problem. And then I'd know he was faking his dipping foot and need for a cane.

"Of course the man's a cripple. Did you see him walk?"

"I did."

"Okay then." Her expression said you-must-be-really-stupid. It was an expression I often encountered and was learning not to mind.

"Is his church around here?"

"About ten miles west. It's the most beautiful building you ever saw."

"Does he ever keep any ladies around? You know, like hookers?" Ouch. I hadn't meant to say that last part. But unwanted words too often slipped out of my mouth.

"Hookers? Father?" She shook her body like she experienced a giant shiver. "Girl, where do you get your ideas?"

"It's a long story," I said. He'd had all those women, four at one time.

Audrey slunk away through her curtain beads.

My thoughts couldn't jell since the TV blared. Somebody in that soap opera was getting married but discovered her fiancé's dad was also hers. And then a gunshot fired. A man yelled, asking why the killer did it. What killed Pierce Trottier? Why?

"Could you lower that TV volume?" I called.

Audrey came and pressed the remote. "Why are you rubbing your legs? Are they cold?"

I shook my head and let go of my legs. No use trying to explain. I hadn't been aware that I was rubbing them, but they burned like fire. Phantom pain? I hoped so and hoped it would leave me soon.

I wanted out of here. "I'm done enough. Rinse me please."

"It's up to you. But you won't have much color change."

She tugged the swim cap off, intensifying my headache. Audrey washed and towel dried my hair. She grabbed the blow dryer.

"Not that," I said.

"What's the problem?"

You blast my hair with that and make me look like I'm wearing a red exercise ball. "I need to go. I'll let it air."

"Okay. Did you want me to wax your mustache?"

"What!"

"Older women often get a few dark hairs above their lips."

I hopped off her chair, paid her, and drove off, wet hair soothing my achy scalp. I needed to find the priest and his hooker friends. I hoped I wouldn't grow a beard by the time I got there.

CHAPTER 13

Our Lady of Hope was easy to find. I followed my hairdresser's directions and drove west. After a while, I hooked a left on Pine Drive. A few tiny wooden houses were scattered along the barren scene on the bumpy drive straight up. The road made a sharp turn to the left. It ended near a cluster of trees in a parking lot next to a church. One car beside it.

The church looked so natural it could have been another great log cabin, except for the large wooden cross on top. It was bigger than any cabins I'd seen but wasn't huge. Windows on two visible sides took up most of the walls.

I pulled closer to the church and saw movement inside.

One person. No, two, three of them walking. I parked and got out. Then decided to be sneaky so I might see if Father Paul Edward was doing something in there that he shouldn't. Of course I did lots of things I shouldn't do, but my concern here was learning about a man who died and whether this man or his cohorts could have killed him. There was a time when I believed priests and teachers and adults of certain other professions would never harm a person. Then I discovered the naiveté of that thinking. People were capable of good. And the unthinkable.

I sneaked against a solid section of wall. Stepping to the first long window, I bent low and peeked inside.

A familiar-looking attractive woman stood near the glass. Smiling, she bent and waved at me.

I considered waddling away, staying as short as I was while she watched. And then I'd slip into my car and drive off. But that thought came because I was embarrassed.

I wanted information from this place, and I was old enough to stop being concerned about what others thought about me. That lesson was difficult to learn, but I was on my way toward mastery.

I straightened and walked to the church doors. One sucked open, and the spry cousins met me. Today's slinky dresses were royal blue—bright and tight. Bling-bling dangled at their ears and into their cleavages.

"I saw you out there. I guess you were peeking in 'cause you thought it was locked and wanted to see this pretty place," said the one who'd waved at me.

"Right." I pinched my palm, especially not meaning to fib while I entered a church.

"I'm Lois, and that's my cousin Sue," she said, and Sue and I gave each other big smiles. "We met you at that restaurant. Isn't the food there great?"

"At Cajun Delights? Yes, it's terrific." *So is the owner.*

"We just stopped by," Sue said, "but we were leaving. So nice to see you again."

I watched them teeter out on spiky shoes, wanting to ask why they stopped by, but couldn't think of a nice way to ask it.

The door shut. I was alone. I looked over the church. A car started and left.

Striking hardwoods had been used to create this building, with nooks and crannies along the walls. I walked around the wooden floor, enjoying the saints or whoever stood in those recesses. Each one appeared to be in his or her home, at ease in that place.

The Virgin held a place of honor on a shelf. I smiled at her. A strange feeling came over me that she might be glad to see me. I wasn't any religion, only from never getting attached to one of them. I did believe in the Almighty. Here was his mother.

Warmth spread inside me.

I wrenched my eyes away from her to look over everything. The altar in front seemed a special place, with beautiful carvings and candles and a crucifix. I lowered my head a moment and prayed. I prayed for discovering what was right with my life and my family. I prayed for the man who'd died at Stevie's house and the people who loved him.

I took in the view from the wall of windows. *Spectacular.* Countless trees stretched beyond the glass. They ran down the hill and jutted into surrounding bluffs. Their varying shapes and shades of green kept my eye spanning them. I almost felt I was outside, immersed in the forest, touching their frilled and fine textures, smelling their new-leaf scent, until a voice made me jump.

"Can I help you?" the voice said, and I knew it wasn't Jesus or his mom. The sound of a door opening registered, and then a *thunk* like a stick hitting wood. The priest.

Father Paul Edward shuffled into the church cavity using his walking cane. "Did you want to come to confession?" he asked.

I could give you some real doozies, I thought, but decided not to mention them.

"Oh, is that what the other people who were here came for?" I asked.

He started a nod, then must have realized he was giving away some hush-hush churchy stuff. "Confidentiality," he said with a slight wink.

A priest winked at me? He'd had those other women, four of them at Gil's restaurant and two of those four now. Maybe he gathered women like some priests gathered little boys.

I gave myself a mental head slap. Many people, not only

those of his profession, went after children, but priests made the news.

"No, thanks. I never do anything bad," I said, pinching my skin. God might make this building crash down on me for telling such a fib. "I'd like to talk to you without the confessional."

"Sure, let's sit." He leaned his pronged cane outside a pew and slid in.

I'd hoped he would come outside but decided not to suggest that since he might need to sit. I mentally confessed I'd had those thoughts about knocking his cane out from under him.

Purged of guilt, I slipped into the pew and sat near the priest. He did a closemouthed smile. I gave one back to him. "Father, I'm Cealie Gunther. We met at your stop-smoking session. I was with my cousin Stevie Midnight."

"We also saw each other at Cajun Delights and the drugstore."

I nodded. "How well do you know the people in your quitters' group?"

He leaned forward. "If you want to know whether I've heard confessions from all of them, the answer is no."

"I wouldn't ask that." *Unless I thought you'd tell me.* "But how about the women?"

He glanced toward the front door, where two attractive women had gone out moments ago.

"I don't mean do you know them, like really *know* them," I said. I actually wanted to discuss Ish with blow-up dolls but thought I'd get him off guard by talking about the women first. This conversation didn't seem to head where I'd hoped.

He chuckled and rolled his round shoulders back. "There's Fawn. I believe she's doing quite well with the program. And Jenna. I'm not sure about her. And your cousin is having a rough time but making a go of it, right?"

"Probably. And how about the men?"

He considered me a long moment. "You aren't just doing a

survey, are you? For your cousin's sake?"

"No. One of the men from your group died in her yard. I fell on Pierce Trottier. Accidentally, of course. And I can't get it out of my mind. I didn't know the man, but I'm trying to learn what I can about him."

"Pierce seemed a good man. He wanted to break his smoking habit."

"And he did." I said it, then gave myself a mental head slap. "Sorry."

He grinned slightly. "What else can I tell you?"

"How about the other men in your group?"

"There's Kern. He dresses well."

"I noticed."

"And our leader, Ish." Father grinned and shook his head.

"Is he funny?" I couldn't imagine that being true.

"I think so."

I decided to throw out my explosive information. "Did you know that Ish has an inflatable doll? A life-size one."

Father smiled wide. His foot pumped faster.

"You find that humorous, Father? I find it quirky. The man is strange. He has a blow-up doll. It was hanging in his window."

Father chuckled. His foot kept still.

"I'm sorry, but I can't imagine what would be funny about a grown man having something like that," I said.

Da-dunt, da-dunt, da-dunt, played in my purse. I answered my phone.

"Cealie, we have a big problem." The manager of my San Francisco office sounded frantic.

"Betty, relax," I said. "Whatever it is, we can fix."

"It's our Sterling Bryst account." Sterling Bryst was one of our largest customers, selling numerous personal products. "Instead of their sunscreen ad saying *Great Protection from Sun,* our copy said *Great Protection from Fun.*"

"Protection from fun?" I said with a laugh.

"And it's too late to change. It's on the air."

"Damn."

I saw the priest glancing at me.

"Cealie, I am so sorry," Betty said. "Liz edited the work, and I looked over it. But my grandson had a high fever and I was so worried. I wasn't paying enough attention."

"How's your grandson now?" I asked.

"He's better. I'm so sorry I let you down."

"That's okay. Don't worry." I worried for the both of us and shoved up to my feet, my mind whirling. How could I fix this? What would happen if I didn't?

I might lose my largest account. I could get sued and lose my entire business. And all of the people who worked for me would lose their incomes.

"I need to go," I told the priest as I left his pew. I got out of his church, which might have been a good place to come up with answers, but not with him in it. Not with him thinking it was funny for Ish to have a doll dangling from his ceiling.

I drove away, letting Betty Allen give me all of the details she wanted to, then I reassured her that it would be fine. None of this would be a problem.

And then I envisioned the man I'd seen on the cross in church and his mother. I prayed to them that I was right.

Chapter 14

I returned to Stevie's house where I would have quiet. I needed to come up with solutions for the situation with my business and then make important phone calls.

I went in the front door, locked it, and took my laptop out of my carry-on bag. I brought the laptop to the kitchen table.

"Bad news," I told Minnie. I set her down next to my laptop. For some reason, I felt reassured having something alive beside me.

I powered up my laptop. The Sterling Bryst account was also tied to the Woodlands account. I knew owners of both companies planned to merge soon. They would create one of the largest conglomerates in the personal hygiene and grooming industry. If I lost the Sterling Bryst deal, I could shut down my company before they did it for me.

I scrolled on my cell phone and reached Betty Allen. "Betty, are you sure? You've seen the ad?"

"I'm afraid so. I did go over the copy. I checked, you know? I read the words and thought they were correct." She didn't speak for a beat. "Cealie, you are so considerate. You try to make things right. But I screwed up. That's all there is to it."

"You didn't create the ad."

"No, but I should have checked closer. You know that. I'm the manager here, and proofreading copy is my responsibility."

I couldn't argue the point.

"You'd have to let me go, but I'll keep you from having to do that and save myself some humiliation. I quit." She sighed. "I love this job—and you. But I don't work for you or the company any longer."

"Betty, I don't want to lose you."

"I'm sure you'd want to make everything all right. But it's not. And it's mainly my fault."

What could I say? She was my good friend. She'd managed that office ever since my husband and I started the business. Our first office was there in San Francisco. I wanted her to stay—but couldn't let her. I'd warned all of my office managers about what they needed to do. They did not have to actually write copy, unless they wanted to create something for a special client or take on something they enjoyed. But they did have to closely proofread everything—everything that other employees in the office created. They were responsible for customer satisfaction. Without it, they could lose their jobs.

"But you know the satisfaction clause," I said. "The customer must inspect his copy thoroughly before he accepts it and signs off for the job. Did they do this?"

"Yes."

We were silent. Both of us knew we could insist that legally, Sterling Bryst was at fault for not inspecting the job we did before they accepted it. But we also knew probably eighty-five percent of our clients did the same thing. Whichever of their employees signed our invoice probably scanned our work. But most of those people were accustomed to working with money. They knew finances, but probably not grammar as well as we did. They expected that *we* knew what we were doing in that department. They trusted us to know.

And now that trust was gone.

Betty sighed. "I'm going to tell Liz she's in charge now, until you decide something else. Maybe hire a new person to run this office. Cealie, I'm sorry I let you down."

"You didn't."

"I need to go," Betty said and hung up.

I stared at my cactus. "This will turn out fine." I hoped that belief would sink in to me. Taking out a legal pad, I copied from my laptop the contact info for some of our largest accounts.

I called the first one and reached the CEO within minutes.

"Hey, Cealie!"

"Hi, Frank." I used his first name, as he'd told me to do. "How're things going in Orlando?"

"Real good. Great weather. The Marlins should have a great season."

"I hope so. Frank, I'm really calling to see how you're doing and to see if you have any problems with my company."

"The work your office does for me works out great. We keep getting more business. Our customers must like your ads."

"Good. Please let me know if you have any complaints, okay? I can hop a plane and be down there."

"You're the best, Cealie. I wish all the companies we work with were like yours."

"I appreciate your vote of confidence." We hung up. I phoned more people to check on their satisfaction. If the talk about our agency was basically good, perhaps if others heard about our major mistake, it wouldn't go over too badly. Maybe people who worked for me wouldn't all lose their jobs. I was going to have to contact Sterling Bryst's CEO. First, I needed to speak with a few others, make sure they were satisfied.

The *plat-plat* of footsteps registered as I was entering another number. Someone was walking from the den, not from the garage door where Stevie would come in.

I jumped up, throat dry, scanning the countertop for anything I might use as a weapon. I'd rather run out the back door but the gate might be locked. And it dragged, making it hard to open. I yanked up the coffee carafe, hoping it was still hot.

It was cool, plastic. I needed something heavier.

I threw open the cabinet doors under the sink where Stevie kept dishwashing detergent. "Yes," I whispered, seeing aerosol cans.

I grabbed window spray and bug spray. I considered the oven cleaner but only a second. I couldn't do that to a person's eyes.

Armed with my sprays, I determined I'd use one or both. "Get out of here!" I yelled in my huskiest tone. Deciding window cleanser wouldn't do any harm, I dropped it and grabbed a heavy pot. "Go away! I'm warning you!" I tried mimicking a man's voice, slamming the pot down on the stove, hoping the noise might scare off the intruder.

A hand swung forward as the person stepped into the room.

I shrieked and slammed the pot down.

"Golly, Cealie, what's going on?" April quit walking right inside the kitchen. Cherish cowered beside her mom. "Why are you holding that pot up like that? Are you swatting mosquitoes or something?" April grinned.

I swung my gaze to the child. She ducked behind her mother. I lowered my arm with the pot.

"I thought a man was coming in." I set the bug spray on the countertop and slammed the pot down on the stove. Oops, the stove didn't look too good. It was an electric cook top, black to match her refrigerator and dishwasher. And now one burner was cracked. The central part of the stove looked dented.

"You broke it." Cherish stood near her mom, glaring at me and the stove.

"Not on purpose," I said.

Cherish and April hung gazes of guilt on me a moment longer.

"How'd you get in here?" I asked.

April showed me her key ring. "Cherish said somebody came home, so I figured it was you and Stevie."

"She's teaching today. Didn't you know that?"

"Yes, but she could have come home early." April blew a pink bubble. It withdrew. "Or maybe with you here, she'd take some time off to visit."

"She can do that? Schools let teachers take vacation days whenever they want?"

"No. But since you're at her house, I thought she might call in sick to take you around to some places."

"Does Stevie lie?"

"I don't know. I just thought she might."

Cherish moved to the table and picked up Minnie. "What's this?"

My instinct was to grab my plant out of her hands so she wouldn't break it. "That's my plant, Minnie. She's like my friend. Isn't she cute?"

Cherish pursed her lips.

"Don't touch that thing. It'll stick you," April told her.

Offended, I said, "My plant doesn't stick people. Go ahead, try it. But don't press too hard."

The girl touched the thick green stem. "That don't hurt. It feels good," she told her mom, then pressed all the fingers of one hand against my plant.

I took Minnie from her. "But most cactus plants really pick," I said, "so you won't want to touch them." I set Minnie on the countertop near the back wall.

Cherish gave me harsh eyes. Her eyes shifted toward the glittering objects hanging over the sink, catching sunlight.

"Pretty, aren't they?" I asked, hoping to distract her from my plant. "And all of those pretty rocks." I stared at the stones Stevie had arranged on a small table. "Do you ever play with them?"

"She don't let me."

Pop. Pop-pop. April stopped the rapid-fire popping of her bubble gum. I didn't ask her to stay and visit. I couldn't stand that gum. The way she chewed it made me think she needed to use up nervous energy.

"Just tell Stevie we came by," she said, for which I was grateful. She and her child started toward the front door.

I walked with them. "Did you need something?"

"Cherish wanted to show her the new outfit she got."

"Where is it?" I asked, seeing their hands empty.

Mother and child turned toward me. April said, "She's wearing it."

Cherish stuck out her lower lip and hung her head. Her outfit, a periwinkle blue shirt and skirt, were not new. *Panther Girls* was spelled out with rhinestones. The *t* was missing, so the first word said *Pan her*. There was a pull in her knit skirt.

"Yes, I see now," I said, trying to repair the child's spirit I had maimed. I stooped next to her. "This is such a pretty shirt and skirt."

She spun away and went out the door.

April gave me sad eyes. I gave a sorry expression back to her. She walked out.

I locked the front door, my chest feeling like it held much less oxygen than before. My mouth often didn't wait for my brain to kick into gear before shooting off, but this time I'd hurt a child. I would have to find some way to make amends.

Maybe I could buy her some cute outfits, I thought, spirits brightening. Then I realized that would only remind her I knew what she wore was secondhand. The new toy she'd come to show "Aunt" Stevie hadn't been new and this new outfit wasn't, either. And why did the child always want to show off her things to my cousin? Didn't she have any real relatives?

Probably none around this area, I determined, also wondering if they had friends. I hadn't noticed any people coming to their house. Of course I hadn't been looking. They could have many friends I wasn't aware of. And I didn't need to concern myself with their business. My own was causing enough problems.

I returned to the kitchen. I made more phone calls, checking out customers to assure their satisfaction.

Unhappy tones came from Benton Hadley, one of the owners of the new hotel chain called Just Like Home. "I don't especially care for the ad your office came up with. We want to start a new advertising campaign soon, and now I'm not sure your company is the one we'll want to do business with."

"I apologize. Please give us a chance to create something you'll love," I said. "I can get back to you soon with that."

He agreed to a brief wait. I thanked him and punched in the number for my office in Austin. Brianna Thompson, my latest hire with tiny thighs, ran that office.

"Brianna, did you know Just Like Home doesn't care for their latest ad?"

"Someone from their office told me it was nice. He didn't say they didn't like it."

"Send a copy to my e-addy now, okay? I'll take a look."

"I'll send it right over, Mrs. Gun—Cealie."

She shot me the attachment, which I opened on my laptop.

My first impression: a neat look to the page, good colors—blues and greens that blended well and soothed, as a person would want a stay at a Just Like Home hotel to achieve. A touch of brown added an earthy tone, also a nice feeling, and the slenderest splotches of red added interest. I liked the colors. The ad showed the first of the company's hotels nestled on a hillside with attractive nearby trees. Good eye appeal.

I checked out the wording. *From your house to ours. A stay with us is just like being at home.*

It wasn't too many words, and they were spread into precise spots on the page. We wanted our ads to catch the eye at a glance, to attract it like a piece of art. This was our art, our singular, individual artistic creation. The piece I was inspecting looked good. Enough empty spaces to look peaceful, like the part of a canvas not painted. To me, it looked nice. But the ad had to satisfy our client.

Motion through the open blinds on the back door snagged my attention. Someone was in the backyard.

A pinch of fright skittered down my back. No one was trying to break into the house. But back there was where a person died.

I grabbed my cell phone and yanked up the bug spray. If a threatening person was out back, I'd run out the front of the house, calling police as I ran. But in case anyone came at me before I could get away, I could zap his face and make a dash.

Creeping to the door, I peeked through the blinds.

Two men. I'd seen them before. They wore sheriff's department uniforms. They were taking down their yellow tape.

I stepped out to the porch. "Good morning," I said.

" 'Morning. We're only removing this," the older one said. The young one pulled the last section of yellow tape away from the fence and went off through the gate.

"What has your office learned about Pierce Trottier's death?" I asked.

"We should have something to give you soon."

"His death probably wasn't from natural causes, right?"

"Probably not. But we're making sure."

"Let us know as soon as you have something definite, okay?"

"Yes, ma'am, we will. Do you have a lot of bugs?"

"Huh?" I noticed I held the bug spray. I squirted it around in the air. "You sure need to work hard to keep them away."

"We're finished here. You might want to lock this gate after we go out. And it drags. It's probably a good idea to get it fixed." He walked out and tugged the gate to make it close.

I went into the yard, carefully walking outside the area where the dead man had lain. To lock the gate, I needed to lift it to get the locking mechanism even with the part on the fence that locked it. I tried lifting the gate. Much too heavy. I shoved against the locking mechanism but couldn't get the gate high enough.

This gate needed to be locked. I felt uncomfortable with it the way it was. Anyone could get in Stevie's yard. The police. A man coming here to die. A killer?

I shivered and scooted away from the spot where Pierce Trottier died. Before going on the porch, I stared at it. Anyone who stood back here could see inside Stevie's kitchen.

I walked around her backyard. The grass was long, the bushes and trees many. The side of the house near my bedroom held neither. But something made the sound outside there a couple of nights ago. I inspected the grass near my window. Tiny yellow flowers grew there. Nothing else of interest. The wooden fence for the backyard started a couple of feet behind my window. A scrap of paper lay near it.

I grabbed the paper. Bubblegum wrap. Blueberry flavor.

I stared at April's house. A common wooden fence separated her yard from Stevie's. April chewed bubble gum. The way she and her child zipped back and forth from there to here, she could have easily dropped the wrapper. The paper could have landed here today. But the bubble she'd blown was pink. Blueberry flavor probably meant the gum from this wrapper was blue.

The gum wrapper reminded me of something that goes in the mouth. It was almost one p.m. Time for lunch. I went inside and tossed the gum wrapper in the trash.

From the table, my laptop stared at me. Ugh. I wanted to go off and find food. But I'd told Benton Hadley I would get back to him soon. Soon would be now.

I jotted my ideas, sent them off to my manager Brianna, and

got her on the phone. "Check your E-mail now, and if you agree, get the concept off to Benton Hadley, please." With work done, I grabbed my purse and took off.

I wanted to talk to more people from The Quitters Group but wanted food first. I needed to avoid Gil, who might be at his restaurant, so I couldn't eat there. He was tempting. It seemed as I grew older, I became worse at handling temptation.

Driving east I spied a couple of restaurants. Both tiny with not many cars. Lots of cars meant good food. I gave in to my urges, turned around, and drove to Cajun Delights.

As I approached, I thought I'd gotten my directions wrong and was reaching a different restaurant. This one looked like all of Gil's places—tall gray cypress in front and slinging lower toward the rear. Tin roof. Hot-pepper-red words *Cajun Delights* on a muted green background. But no cars in the large parking lot.

Passing by, I glanced back. A silver truck was near the fence in back.

Something was amiss. It was Monday, they should be open, and many people should be eating.

I returned to Gil's restaurant. Probably the day manager would be there. I'd ask her if anything happened.

I trotted to the front door. Locked. I rapped beside the door's stained-glass insert, knocking as hard as I could.

An image became visible through the glass. A person approached, a person larger than Babs Jacobs.

The lock clicked, and the door opened.

I steadied my legs.

Gil's smile widened. "What a nice visitor."

CHAPTER 15

I started to walk in but noticed all the lights were off. I was standing close to Gil, a deadly place if I wanted to avoid an intimate encounter. Private parts of my body came to life.

I swallowed. Looked at Gil. Backed outside.

He kept the door open. "Aren't you coming in?" he asked, tone husky.

Mine would get husky, too, the longer I stayed near him.

"Uh, I wanted to eat. But you're closed."

Gil glanced at his empty restaurant like he was considering what I said.

Jealousy ran a little streak down my backbone. Suppose he wasn't alone? He might have a woman in his office or any place else in this large, dark building.

"You want food. This is the place. Come on in." He opened the door wider.

"But no cooks. Look, no people," I said. Maybe he was just arriving and hadn't noticed. But Gil did notice things. Many things.

He kept holding the door wide open. I had to walk in. He glanced down at me. "Had your hair fixed differently, didn't you?"

I patted the top of my hairdo. "Do you like it?"

"I like anything you decide to do, Cealie."

My, what a sweet man. I hoped he didn't notice my mustache. He led the way toward the restaurant's rear. Faint lights were on, mostly small wall lanterns. "You didn't have a silver truck," I said.

"The other one leaked oil. I didn't want to turn on all the lights," he said, "because we're closed today. I didn't want to attract customers."

"You're really closed on a Monday?"

"I guess you didn't see the sign. One of our large fryers caught fire last night."

"You had a fire?" I envisioned Gil trapped in a roaring fire. An instinct struck to protect him.

A mother instinct?

No-o-o, my increasingly horny instincts told me.

I stepped away. This man didn't need protecting right now. He loomed a foot taller than me, his shoulders extra wide through his knit shirt. His eyes extra dark. His lips extra sensual.

"It was only a small fire," those lips said, "and they put it out right away. Someone will fix the problem later this afternoon. But we're closed until then, since we have so many customers during the days of our grand opening. Many of them want their seafood fried."

"Mmm, crispy and hot," I said, then noticed him staring at my lips. The invisible magnet tugged. I took a deep breath. "So you need to get it fixed, and I need to go somewhere and eat. I'm starving."

"I have something for you."

"I wanted seafood."

"I know." He looked me in the eye. "There's gumbo in small packs in the freezer. I'll heat some for you."

How could I resist?

He led me to the kitchen, a vast space with stainless steel appliances and the tempting aroma of fried seafood, tainted by the slightest burnt odor. Gil turned on lights in one section of the kitchen. Everything looked new and sparkly. There were vats for frying and burners and ovens and refrigerators and a microwave. Gil went into the walk-in freezer and came back with a small package. He placed its contents in a bowl and heated it in the microwave. "I'll see what else I can find for you."

While he went off, I sniffed the air. I looked around, disappointed not to see any empty sacks. On second thought, maybe the sacks didn't come into the kitchen.

"You're checking for boiled crayfish, aren't you?" Gil asked, coming near.

I nodded and smiled for real. Beyond him, I spied stacks of the large plastic trays used for serving boiled seafood.

"This restaurant is getting crabs now, fairly large ones. But I'm afraid we don't have any crayfish yet. I checked."

"You do know me." I smelled the well-seasoned mixture of seafood gumbo in the bowl he set in front of me on the long stainless steel counter. As in his other restaurants, this was where cooks would set orders for waiters to pick up.

Gil pulled a stool close to my food. "Enjoy. I've already had lunch." He walked off and returned with a tall glass of milk. He set it beside my bowl, then got me a chunk of French bread and a dish of potato salad.

Yum. The gumbo was brown and thick from the roux. It held a little rice and lots of shrimp and crabmeat. I ate three crab claws, sliding the flaky meat off with my teeth.

"That food really turns you on." Gil stood near with a smile. "Finish that, and I'll get you some more."

I grinned at him. Dug into my bowl. Savored the textures and tastes. I bit a piece of bread. Some bites of potato salad, especially good with a pinch of onion. I spooned a small oyster out of my gumbo.

"The Cajun aphrodisiac," Gil said, his grin wicked.

"It's a good thing you're only part Cajun," I said, and then ate more of this food for the gods. "And it's a good thing you can't have this."

"Not with shrimp in it, but I could eat lots of oysters." He was allergic to shrimp but not oysters.

Gil moved closer while the food in my bowls emptied. I noticed him. Noticed the darkness beyond our space.

"That was terrific," I said.

"Ready for dessert?" He stood near, no dishes in his hands.

He placed those warm hands on me. Gil wrapped his arms around me. "I missed you." He kissed my lips. Pulled his lips away. "I really miss you when you're not around." He kissed me longer. Drew his mouth away. "You're so important to me, Cealie."

"It hasn't been that long," I said, immediately annoyed with my lame response. This man was terribly important to me.

But I didn't want him to be.

He shifted even closer. Gil pressed his firm chest against mine. His steel-gray eyes held my gaze. My traitorous body reacted to his.

This man wanted me. And I wanted him.

No, I don't. I slid off the stool on the opposite side from him. I wanted my freedom. I needed more strength to keep away from him. I called up my mantra—*I am woman! I can do anything! Alone.*

If I gave in to Gil's urges and mine now, I'd be back where I was some time in the past. I'd want to be with him all the time. Depending on him.

That last part would be the problem. My self-worth couldn't depend on having a man near me again.

I gazed at Gil. He watched me from the opposite side of the backless bar stool. He was tempting, definitely.

My body told me, *Get him. Jump his bones. Do it now!*

And he would love that. So would I.

But then . . .

I shifted my eyes. I needed to call up an image of Gil wearing a crown and sitting on a throne, knowing exactly what he wanted and having all of it set before him.

And then me, the broken half of a couple. Once Freddy died, I no longer knew what I wanted from life except to be with him, and that choice was gone.

So then, who was I?

That's exactly what I had finally begun to find out. Rediscovering Cealie needed to come first. I wanted romance with Gil. But that would mean I had to give away the freedom to be a complete person, the newfound sense of being an individual who didn't *need* anyone to feel whole.

His sexual draw pulled my body.

I placed my hand on the bar stool. I wanted to shove it to the floor and grab the man. Then he and I might go down to the floor, too. No, not in this kitchen. We'd kiss and fondle all the way to his office, which must hold a comfy sofa.

No, no, Cealie. You are woman, remember?

He could have smiled, which would have made me angry and broken the moment. Gil might have smiled because he knew the dilemma jamming my mind. He knew me, and knew I wanted sex with him.

He was also a man, one with desire in his eyes and in his heavy breaths. He didn't break the moment, dammit.

I stepped around the bar stool. Moving close to him, I swallowed. Watched his eyes appear to darken while I stepped nearer.

Da-dunt, da-dunt, da-dunt.

"Does that make you want to dance?" I asked Gil, moving away from him and grabbing my phone.

Harsh eyes told all before he spoke. "You don't have to get that."

"Yes, I do." I needed it for my salvation, to keep me from giving in to what my body wanted, but my mind knew better. It was increasingly harder for mind over body to function when it came to Gil.

I stepped farther from him and cheerily answered my phone.

"Where are you?" Stevie sounded worried.

"At a restaurant. I had lunch."

"You're just eating now?"

I eyed Gil, eyeing me. "Yes. Why? Are you home?"

"We're having recess. I wanted to find out what you were doing."

"Just—eating." I broke eye contact with the man making me lust.

"And I wanted to find out what you want for dinner. Would you prefer for me to cook, or for us to go and eat at that Cajun restaurant?"

"No!" I watched Gil and took steps farther away from him, heading for the hallway where we'd entered. "That restaurant isn't open today," I said to explain my sharp reply to my cousin. I couldn't tell her the food wasn't the only tempting thing here. On second thought, I could tell her, but then she might expect to see a romance blossom, and that wasn't going to happen. I waved good-bye to Gil and mouthed, "Thank you."

No satisfaction touched his expression. He didn't wave. Didn't nod. Gil stood in place in the half-lit kitchen, watching me walk out.

"We could go somewhere else, or I could cook," Stevie said.

"Don't worry about cooking." I made my way through the dim restaurant. "I can pick up something from a supermarket that we could throw in the microwave. I won't need much to eat."

"We'll see. But don't pick up any food. I need to go outside now and walk around. This is when I want a smoke the most."

"Exercise is much better. See you later." I reached the front door, discovered it locked, and grinned. I hadn't noticed Gil locking us inside. I glanced back and listened for him.

No sound of his approach. He was probably still in the kitchen, unhappily cleaning my mess and putting away my used dishes.

I could at least do that myself, I considered, but only for a moment. And then I turned the lock on the door.

I rushed out and away from Gil's restaurant.

The moment I drove off from Cajun Delights, my shins hurt.

This wasn't funny. Had they been hurting all along, but being near Gil made me not notice? Or was the pain starting now, maybe from the position of my legs?

I shifted and gave both legs different angles.

The pain remained. About the width of a dead man's thighs.

I wiggled my legs, trying to get rid of that feeling and lose the image. The feel of a dead person beneath them and the sight of him stayed. I had to learn more.

I connected with Information on my phone while I drove and had them get me the sheriff's office. I got Detective Renwick on the line.

"People from your office came to my cousin's house and took down that yellow tape," I said. "I'm sure removing it means you have more information about Pierce Trottier's death."

"I do."

"Please tell me."

"When we're sure about our findings, I'll contact you and your cousin."

"Couldn't you share a little now? I won't tell. Promise."

"It shouldn't be long. I'll get back to you." He hung up.

I needed to get my own information. A combination gas station and pancake house came into view. I hooked into its parking lot and bought a newspaper out front. Inside, I sat at a booth with coffee and turned to the obituaries.

More listings than I would have expected. Almost a whole

page worth. Possibly this paper ran obits for longer than one day. I skimmed faces and felt sad for each of them but especially for their families.

Yes! *Pierce Trottier.*

His obit was brief with no picture. I knew what he looked like dead but would have liked to see him with his eyes open. Alive. Flecks of cut grass had been stuck to his shoes, I recalled now, wondering about that since Stevie's grass was extra long.

He was fifty-three, a native of Tallulah, Mississippi. Survived by a son and a daughter and a cousin, Jenna Griggs. Jenna was his cousin? And curiously, his children weren't named. Even more curious, his short obituary said no services were held. It did mention that he was studying to become a minister. It didn't say a thing about his fiancée that Audrey Ray told me about.

I had little connection to the people in The Quitters Group but knew I would speak with all of them.

A phone book was attached to the public phone. I looked for *Jenna Griggs.* She wasn't listed. Maybe Stevie had numbers for all of her group members. I still didn't know how Stevie had not seen Pierce Trottier in their small group. Didn't know if I believed her.

From The Quitters Group, I had spoken to most of the people away from their meetings. I'd gone to see Father Paul Edward and Ish Muller. Ugh, I hated to think of that scene. Besides those men, there was one other man. And then Stevie and two other women. Fawn, the straw sucker, had come over. Maybe I'd talk to her again, maybe not.

In the phone book, I looked for the man I hadn't spoken with, recalling his name was like an ice cream treat and started with *P.* I ran my finger down *P*'s. *Parfait.* I'd never eaten or seen a real one, but pictures of them always looked tempting.

The phone book showed no person with that name. It listed a business, Parfait's Parlor.

I returned inside the pancake shop and asked for directions. A man told me which way to go but had never been to the business.

I drove off, hoping it wasn't an old-fashioned parlor filled with antiques. I hoped it was an ice-cream parlor. I really hoped its owner would be the man I was looking for.

CHAPTER 16

"Yeah," I said, seeing Parfait's Parlor served ice cream. Even if the guy from Stevie's quitters' group wasn't connected with it, I would enjoy being here. Not that I wasn't already stuffed. But the pictures outside the building were super tempting.

Parfait's appeared a perfect ice-cream parlor. Extra clean outside. The pink, red, and white paint was bright. All of its windows were shiny. Pictures on the windows displayed long-stemmed glasses, wide on top and slender at the bottom. The glasses held tilted layers of multicolored ice cream and crushed fruit and syrup. Whipped cream piled on top. Adding to the temptation, tall plants growing on both sides of the parlor were trimmed to resemble parfait glasses.

My stomach made happy jumps. I parked near four other cars and went in.

Red leather bar stools enhanced a counter. Small round tables created intimate eating spaces. A family of three appeared happy, gobbling their parfaits. So did the other eaters, mainly couples. A young guy and girl wearing shirts and caps with pink, red, and white stripes took the orders. No sign of the Parfait man I'd met at the stop-smoking group. Possibly he wasn't connected to this place.

I really shouldn't eat more, I told myself, but then convinced myself I should. I'd had gumbo for lunch. Gumbo seemed filling when you ate, but it contained lots of water. I'd probably get hungry again soon. My mind showed me the potato salad and French bread I'd gobbled along with that gumbo, but I blanked out that picture. I wanted a parfait.

"I've never eaten one of those," I told the family at a table. "What kind is good?"

"Chocolate!" the young boy said.

"Chocolate!" the smaller girl repeated.

Both had layers of chocolate syrup with their vanilla ice cream. Chocolate surrounded the girl's mouth.

"I like crushed pineapple best," the woman with them said, using her long spoon to dig pineapple out of her glass. "Blueberry is great, too."

So many choices. I wanted them all.

"I'll try strawberry and banana," I told the girl taking orders.

"Yes, ma'am, and would you like chocolate with that?" She must have noticed my indecision. "I'll put in a little bit, okay?"

"Sure, why not?"

I sat at a table away from other people in case the Parfait man from The Quitters Group was here, and I'd get to talk to him. If he wasn't here, I'd have beautiful scenery through the window. Thriving trees and rolling hills made me think of Our Lady of Hope Church. Why would Father Paul Edward laugh at someone who hung an inflatable woman from his rafters?

"I hope you like it," the girl who'd taken my order said. She placed a heavenly concoction in front of me. A large cherry topped the swirled whipped cream.

"I'll blame you if my clothes don't fit anymore, okay?" I asked her, and she nodded. "Oh, sweetie, is the owner here? And is he a Parfait?"

"Yeah, he's here. And his name is Parfait. Isn't that cute?"

"Adorable. Do you think I could talk to him?"

"I'll check."

I dug into my parfait. Yum. Sweet layers of red and yellow and white and brown soon lowered in my tall glass.

I was stuffed, but almost half of my parfait remained.

A man walked out from behind the work area. The first thing I noticed was his neat appearance. His extra-wide shoulders looked nice in his knit shirt, and his slacks fit well with no wrinkles. His shoes were highly polished. As he neared my table, I noticed his baby-smooth complexion. He probably didn't eat the rich treats here.

"I'm Kern Parfait. You wanted to see me?"

"Yes, hi. I'm Cealie Gunther. We met at your quitters' group," I said, and he looked curious. "I'm Stevie Midnight's cousin, in town for a visit."

"Ah, yes."

"Would you join me a little while?" I waved to an empty chair.

"I'm kind of busy." But he took a chair across from me.

"This is terrific." I took another bite of parfait.

"Thank you." He leaned forward, apparently wanting to return to whatever he was doing.

"You could have called this place Parfait's Parfaits," I said. "That would have been cute. But then you'd have had to put an apostrophe in front of the *s* on the first *Parfait* but not the second one."

He blinked a couple of times. I couldn't tell whether he got it. I decided to hurry and get to what I wanted.

"That was so sad about the man from your group dying," I said.

He nodded, his gaze leveled at me. "It was."

"I never met him," I said and then thought maybe that wasn't true. I found him under my legs. Of course that didn't really count as a meeting.

Parfait watched me, waiting for my purpose. Which was . . . ?

"Do you have any idea what happened to Pierce Trottier?" I asked. "Or why anybody would want to kill him?"

He leaned closer. "What's your connection to Pierce? Are you a detective? Journalist?"

A nosy woman. "He died in my cousin's yard. I found him."

This seemed to spark his interest. "Really?" He leaned back. "What did you want to know?"

"What can you tell me about the man? I find myself needing to know about him."

"He wanted to quit smoking."

"And did he?"

A corner of Parfait's lips twitched like he wanted to grin. "Before he died? I don't know. He didn't come to the class after we were supposed to quit. I think that's the day you showed up."

"I arrived on your group's quit day. Maybe somebody from the group got so angry after they quit that he or she wanted to kill someone and saw Pierce. Then he became the victim of stop-smoking rage."

Parfait stared at my face. He did not find any humor in this.

Neither did I. "Please," I said. "I need all the information I can get about him."

"He and your cousin never came to class on the same nights."

"How do you know that? How could you remember who attended each meeting?"

"We've been meeting once a week. I always set up the chairs. I open the exact number we'll need. We've always had one extra. Twice, Pierce was absent. Twice, it was your cousin."

I sighed. "Stevie told me she never met him."

"And you didn't believe her?"

"You believe all of your relatives?"

He grimaced. "My uncle's been locked up for twenty-five years for a murder he told us he didn't commit."

"Sorry. What else can you tell me about Mr. Trottier?"

"Else?" His expression blanked. "I didn't really know him."

"Did other people from your group know him well?"

"I have no idea. We weren't a social gathering." He glanced at the front entrance, where the woman and kids went out. A group of teens headed inside. "I need to go," he said.

"Thank you for talking to me."

"I don't know much to tell you." He accepted my hand. His grip was firm, as I'd expected. Parfait went off behind the counter. The teens reached it and gave their orders to the young people working there.

I checked the concoction in my dish. The ice cream had melted. My slim lines of colors blended together. I took a bite. Liquid banana split. My stomach had time to know it was extra full. I'd avoided fatty foods like banana splits ever since I'd gotten older and put on weight. For some reason, my height did not continue to expand like my width. I stepped away from the table and stumbled as pain shot across my shins.

I grabbed a tabletop to stop my fall.

Teens looked concerned about me. I shrugged, smiled, and walked out.

The ache will go away. Cealie, you're okay.

I was normally a positive person. I was positive now that I needed to discover what happened to the man who lay dead under my legs.

Another possibility besides phantom pain came. Maybe when I fell over him, I chipped a bone. That would explain why my shins hurt and I'd almost fallen. I smiled. A bone would heal, and then the ache would go away.

But two bones? Both shins?

I drove, trying not to think of my legs. I considered the quitters' meetings. What Kern Parfait told me ruled him out as a killer. The night Trottier died, I attended their meeting. Two extra chairs were open in their semicircle when my cousin and I went in. She sat in one chair and I took the other, the one Kern

Parfait had expected their other member to sit in.

Of course that would have been a first. The first time every member attended at the same time.

There was one other person in The Quitters Group I hadn't spoken to outside of their meeting. Jenna Griggs. I knew she hadn't quit smoking on stop-smoking day and she'd walked out of the meeting. I'd spoken to her briefly at Gil's restaurant, and she wasn't too pleasant.

Also, she was Pierce Trottier's cousin. And the phone book didn't list her number or address.

Of course Trottier had many more contacts than those in his stop-smoking group, but I didn't know them. I needed to keep myself busy, feeling like I was accomplishing something meaningful during the time I felt forced to stay here.

A school bus crossed the intersection in front of me. Stevie might be home from school. I returned to her house to wait. She might know where Jenna lived.

Parking in front, I walked up the steps, gripping the rail to stop my fall. My shins burned.

This was too much. I needed to do something about my legs.

Taking my time to get inside, I limped around the house. I grabbed the phone book and dropped to a kitchen chair. I needed a doctor.

I checked the yellow pages for physicians. On my laptop I pulled up a map of Gatlinburg, the nearest fairly large city, so I could get directions to an office once I made an appointment. I called a few doctors' offices, telling them my name and I'd prefer to come in today if possible, and no, I wasn't already a patient.

One secretary after another told me their patient list was full today and tomorrow. Most said if I had a problem that couldn't wait, I should get to a hospital's emergency room.

Emergency? An emergency room was where you went when

you couldn't breathe or experienced a major ache in your chest. Or your child got real croupy during the night. Would I go in one and say, "I feel a man pressed against my legs. Do you see any sign of him?"

Enough silly thoughts. I needed to know if he'd left any damage that might be permanent. A broken bone would not be permanent.

I was running out of doctors in the area when I lucked out.

"Doctor Wallo just had a cancellation for this afternoon. Can you be here in twenty minutes?"

"Absolutely." I glanced at Minnie. "Dr. Wallo will see me today." I punched in addresses on my computer for Stevie's house and the doctor's office, considering his name. "Pigs wallow in mud. So how do you think he's going to look, eh?" I said to Minnie. An indenture between two of the tufts on her pink head appeared new, almost like a grin.

Directions from here to the doctor's office popped on my screen.

Noise from the garage startled me. Stevie came in from there, huffing. She lugged her purse and a bulky book bag. "You didn't hear me hitting on the door for you to open it?" she snarled.

"No, I didn't." Maybe my hearing worsened while I was busy growing a mustache. I helped her slide all the things off her arms to the countertop.

"I used my elbow," Stevie said, hair falling on her face. She glanced at the table. "What did you do all day? Play Solitaire?"

"I don't like your attitude. I didn't play a thing."

Her gaze hung on my open computer. "Looks like you did."

I reeled in my anger. It wouldn't do any good. I replaced it with positive imagery. Acapulco's tropical beaches I would soon lie on. Stretching on a towel on warm sand. A breeze filtering the air fluttering over me. I'd listen to waves lapping while I luxuriated in a novel. Sea birds would sing and swoop for meals.

Mine would get delivered to me. It would come with a tall glass, a little umbrella on top. Why not add a hunky guy in a swimsuit leaning over me with a smile as he handed the drink to me?

Stevie released a bloodcurdling scream. "What happened to my stove?"

"Oh that." I moved closer. The stove's top was crimped with potholes. "It looks worse now than when it happened. I'm sorry. I'll get you a new one."

"*You* did this?"

"Accidentally." I gave a quick explanation. "I'll buy you another stove." But I'd wait till I was ready to leave town. That way she wouldn't cook so much while I remained, and we wouldn't have all those fattening meals and pots to wash. We could eat something light and quick and toss our paper plates.

Stevie stared aghast at her appliance. She grabbed a bottle of water from the fridge, took a deep breath, then swigged water. "I called the police before I left school."

"What did they tell you?"

She sucked in an audible breath. "Nothing."

"Stevie, are you okay? You seem short of breath."

"I'm fine." She was pale. "But you took away one of the three pillars of my life."

"What? Your stove held you up?" *How foolish was that?*

"Feng Shui, cousin, or aren't you familiar with the ancient Chinese art of improving your life through your environment? I've arranged my home to enrich my life with Feng Shui principles."

"And that's why you have all those stones and crystals and the altar?"

Her cheeks colored. "Some of those are for totally different things. I'm not really proficient at any of them."

"What do you do in that room with the altar?"

"I'm trying to learn what happened to Pierce Trottier." She gazed at the floor. "I haven't discovered a thing."

She looked so embarrassed, I patted her on the back. "Don't worry, you'll get it. You'll figure things out."

Stevie stared at me. She stared at her dented stove. "In Feng Shui there are three life pillars—the front door, the master bed, and the stove. You destroyed one of mine."

"I'll take care of it. Soon. I promise. And you'll want this mirror on the new one?" I pointed to the mirror standing behind the burners.

"Yes. It faces the kitchen and doubles prosperity."

I held back my grin. Indicating the map's directions on my laptop, I asked, "How long will it take me to get to that area? I have an appointment in about ten minutes. I'm seeing a doctor about my legs. They still hurt from the fall in your yard."

"So sue me." She said it without sarcasm and checked my screen. "Are you going to Dr. Wallo's office?"

"Yes, like wallow in problems or mud." I couldn't stop my grin.

"He's my doctor. He's great." She checked her watch. "Pooh, I'll have to drive so you can get there in time."

She yanked her shoulder bag off the counter, knocking Minnie's pot over with it.

"Watch that. You hit Minnie." I straightened her pot. A pinch of dirt had fallen out. I returned it to her pot.

"How silly," Stevie said. "Talking like a cactus was a person. Come on, let's go."

" 'Bye, I hope you're okay," I told Minnie.

Stevie grimaced. She grabbed her school bag. "I'll bring this so I can get some work done while I wait."

Waiting wasn't what I wanted her to do at a doctor's office. She needed to be checked.

I trotted to her Jeep. "The Mexican Hat Dance" played. I

pulled out my phone. "Hello."

"Hello."

The rumble of Gil's voice stopped me. I leaned on the garage wall, letting sensual tension fill me. I was woman. I liked being with a man who turned me on.

"Hi," I told Gil. "Good to hear from you." Especially as my mind started to replay scenes of me and him close together.

"I'd like to talk to you, Cealie. You were supposed to be in Mexico by now, and I'm glad you aren't. But you didn't tell me why you came to Tennessee instead."

"Nope, sure didn't." And I felt like a fool and didn't want to tell him I'd arrived here and then realized my cousin had convinced me to come because of whatever she imagined from her stupid candles or cards or stones. Or maybe her stove.

The sensual moment passed. I considered those precious stones Stevie kept in her kitchen. She thought Minnie was stupid? Suppose I took one of her stones? Would she miss it?

I grinned—until the Jeep's horn blasted.

"What was that?" Gil asked.

"Sorry. My cousin thinks she's funny."

"Cealie, could I come over and see both of you? I'm free now. I'd bring food. Oh, the restaurant reopened."

"Thanks, but I'm full. And we're leaving."

"Then I won't keep you."

"Okay, 'bye," I said and dashed for the Jeep Stevie had revving.

CHAPTER 17

I hopped in the Jeep, and we raced toward town. The doctor's office was near a touristy area downtown, where traffic crawled. Stevie growled, took loud breaths, and eventually found a place to park.

We went inside. She chatted with the secretary, and I filled in a new-patient form. The place was clean, its rustic décor in keeping with the rest of the area. No other patients waited.

"You can come in now," the secretary told me. "Stevie, do you want to come back here, too? I'm sure Dr. Wallo would enjoy seeing you."

"I'd planned to do some paperwork," she said.

"Come with me," I urged, not telling my motive. "We probably won't be long, and you don't have time to get started with all those papers."

"I wouldn't mind seeing him."

We went to the rear. A nurse met us, told Stevie hi, and asked me to step on a scale.

"I don't think I have to." I backed from it. "I'm only here about pain in my legs. Nobody has to know my weight to treat that."

The nurse's lips thinned. She remained near the scale.

I set down my purse and took off my shoes. If I wore a watch, I would have removed that, too. I stepped on the scale and stared at the paisley-printed wallpaper. Maybe *they* needed to know my current weight. I did not.

"Pretty good for a woman your age," the nurse said and wrote on her folder.

"Really?" I stepped down, loving the part about a good weight. Not so thrilled about *for a woman your age*.

"Yeah, Cealie's always been in great shape," Stevie told her.

Me? My cousin was saying this about me? The nurse measured my height, and I knew I was standing much taller than my five feet two.

The nurse led us into a room. "You can remove your clothes and slip on this paper gown," she told me. "Then sit up here." She pointed to the paper-covered bed.

"I won't need all my clothes off. I'm only here to see about my shins."

"That's up to you. The doctor will be with you shortly."

I sat on a chair next to Stevie. She frowned at me like I had done something wrong. I imagined she was still mad at me for ruining her "life pillar."

The nurse went out. Quiet minutes passed. The urge came to ask Stevie what her doctor *wallowed* in, but I kept my thoughts in tow.

Until the nurse returned, followed by Dr. Wallo.

Yummy hit my brain and almost came out my mouth.

Distinguished. Oozing sex appeal, the man stood about six four. His eyes were the softest blue I'd ever seen. His black hair was threaded with gray, pure white at the temples.

"This is my cousin," Stevie said after she and the doctor greeted each other. Old friends. Patient and doctor—who had seen all of her body? Why hadn't I hopped up there on that paper sheet and stripped all my clothes off, as the nurse told me? Maybe I could do it now.

I smiled at Dr. Wallo, my smile fading as I considered the cellulite and drooping body parts he'd see if I took off my clothes. It was bad enough that nothing would hide the wrinkles on my face or neck. They weren't all that bad, but at the moment I wanted to look especially good. Ugh, and was I growing a mustache?

Dr. Wallo scanned the papers I'd completed. "Mrs. Gunther, I'm Dr. Wallo. I see that your shins are giving you trouble?"

"Not much," I blurted. Then Stevie shot me mean eyes. "Yes," I amended, "they have been bothering me. Sometimes I have a bit of pain across here." I was wearing slacks, so I pulled both pant legs up to my knees. I was also wearing knee highs. Cute.

I rolled them down to my ankles. What a pretty sight for him—a stocking roll above my shoes now and indentations under my knees. Any attractiveness my legs might have had was destroyed.

"When did this pain start?" he asked, checking my legs.

"When I tripped over something."

"What did you trip over?"

I'd hoped I wouldn't have to tell him.

"It was a person," Stevie said. "A man died in my yard. Cealie fell over him," she said with vehemence, as though I'd chosen to do it.

He looked at me. "Is she kidding?"

I shook my head. "The police are investigating what happened. But ever since I fell, I've felt pain across here." I rubbed my shins. "Well, almost all the time."

He knelt in front of me. Inspected and pressed on my legs. "Does this hurt?"

I shook my head. He touched more places. I didn't want him to know how his hand on my legs was affecting me. I jammed my lips into a grin, shook my head that it didn't hurt, and enjoyed the feel. There was a time when a man's hands on my skin was a common occurrence, but since I'd reached a certain age, that time had passed. And my husband died, and I no longer let Gil keep his hands on me . . . probably.

This hunky man pressed on my calves and my knees and then above them.

My smile widened.

"Cealie!" My cousin's tone said I'd done something wrong.

Maybe she wouldn't appreciate a man's hands roaming her skin. I loved it.

"I don't think anything's broken," he said. "You might have some bruising inside. It could take a few weeks to totally heal. I could prescribe something for pain if you think it's bad enough."

"Oh no. I don't take medicine unless I absolutely need it." And your hand rubbing my legs was great medicine.

I gave myself a mental head slap. *Bad girl, Cealie.*

"Good, but in case it persists or gets worse, let me know and we'll x-ray," he said.

Stevie stood up to leave. I didn't.

"Doc," I said, "I'm worried about Stevie." As I expected, Stevie's head whipped toward me. Her jaw fell open. "She's been really tense, and she's getting short of breath."

"I am not!" she snapped, her shoulders drawn up near her neck, her eyes wide at me. Her breathing appeared scant.

Dr. Wallo watched her, looking concerned. He lifted his stethoscope, pointing to her chest. "May I, Stevie?"

She glared at me, huffed, and nodded.

The doctor listened to her chest. He asked questions, and listened to her back. "Aren't you a smoker?"

"Not anymore."

"Good for you."

"It's only been for a few days," I interjected, and my cousin narrowed her eyes at me. "I'm really proud of her for quitting and hope she never sticks one of those deadly things in her mouth again. But I thought you should know, Doc."

"Maybe there are things about *you* I think he should know,"

Stevie said, "but I don't go around blabbing all of *your* business."

The doctor grinned, seeming to enjoy our exchange. He spoke to Stevie, "We could do an EKG."

"No way. Not because she thinks I have a problem."

The doctor nodded. "Maybe your increased tension and difference in breathing both come from giving up smoking. It's great that you quit, but maybe you could use a little help that might take the edge off and help you to stay quit."

She shook her head. "I don't want any pills. I've tried them. They didn't help."

"Sometimes it takes more than one try, just like trying to quit smoking," he said.

"And this time I'm here with you," I told her.

With a loud exhale, Stevie opened her hand. "All right, I'll try them again."

I didn't look at her. If we made eye contact, I might have grinned. Then she probably would have told him to keep the blasted things.

"Another thing that would help," he said, "is exercise. Even walking a few times a week would help with stress and weight control."

She didn't comment. As we all made our good-bye exchanges, the doctor's stomach growled.

"Sorry," he said. "I was too busy for lunch. I need dinner."

"Me, too," Stevie said. "I thought we'd go back to that Cajun restaurant this evening."

My hearing antennae came to life.

"I figured I'd go there now. You were my last patient," Dr. Wallo told me.

"I'm starving," Stevie said. "Going there now sounds great to me."

"Maybe we'll see you and your wife at Cajun Delights," I said.

His face lengthened. "She and I aren't together anymore."

I shook my head. "I'm sorry."

I took a final look at the eye-candy doctor, and we left. "If you're going to that restaurant, please bring me home first. I'm not hungry," I told Stevie. I also didn't want to see Gil if he was there. He was too tempting. She didn't need to know that.

"*I'm* tense?" she said, ignoring my statement. "Since when did you think *I'm* tense?" Her pitch screeched extra high.

"Ever since—"

"And you think I'm short of breath? Maybe you should listen to yourself."

I didn't need this discussion. She was making up things to get back at me for telling the doctor about her. Keeping my mouth shut, I focused on the street. I had no idea where she'd bring me.

After a short drive, she turned into a small shopping center. She parked near a drugstore, gave me a pointed glance, and grabbed Dr. Wallo's prescription sheet off the seat. She held it up so I'd see it, as if she were shouting *You did this to me.* She went in the store.

I stayed in the car. With the tension removed, I could think. The problem with my legs was probably psychosomatic. My mind created the ache in my shins, so changing my thoughts should delete the ache.

Fine. I could do that.

I considered Pierce Trottier. I definitely needed to do everything I could to hasten my departure. My cousin and I didn't need to stay together much longer. I considered her hair, rich chocolate brown way back when, and always short and stylish. Long, drab gray and thin now. If I had to stay near her much longer, I'd surely yank it like she used to do mine.

She walked out of the store carrying a medium bag and thrust it on the seat. "I'll come back for my meds later. I bought paper plates." She raised her eyebrows at me.

"Paper plates are nice to have. You do remember that I bought you some."

"I remember everything," she snapped. "And I don't usually have paper plates, but now my stove is broken." She shoved the bag closer to me. "So you can heat yourself something from the fridge in the microwave. I'll be going to that Cajun restaurant."

Oops, I saw her point. I'd made her get the meds for her tension. And I'd ruined her stove, which the silly woman liked to cook on. Darn, I'd also kicked away one of three of her life pillars. Not a good thing.

I crossed my arms. "I'll replace your stove."

She turned her nose up and cranked the motor.

I couldn't ignore the frigid feel in her car. I dreaded getting more of that feeling in her home. As soon as Stevie dropped me off, I'd try to discover how to contact that final person in The Quitters Group. Maybe she was the killer. That would be perfect. Then I could let the police know, and they'd let me leave town. I imagined Acapulco's palm trees swaying. I'd contact the Royal Acapulco, where I was scheduled to be staying right now. I would get a suite and spend an extra week or two luxuriating in tropical breezes.

First, I needed to locate another person. "Would you happen to know where Jenna Griggs lives?" I asked.

"Why do you want to know?"

"Just wondered."

She glared at me a moment longer and then sped on. Maybe she had a folder out at the house with contact info for her stop-smoking group members.

Stevie dumped me in front of her house. She slowed barely long enough for me to slide out before she rolled off.

Fine. I didn't want to be with her anyway. I certainly didn't want to hold a conversation. Blame, blame, blame, that's all she did to me.

I trotted up to the porch, pulled out my key, and aimed it at the door's keyhole, turning the knob a pinch. The door opened.

Stevie might have forgotten to lock this door. She was angry at me before we left her house. But she hadn't come to the front.

I stood on the porch, shrugging off the sprinkle of apprehension that crossed my shoulders, and shoved on the door. I wanted to freshen up and have time alone to clear my thoughts. I stepped through the doorway.

Noise in the house froze me in place.

I swallowed. Listened. Maybe her house was settling.

The noise repeated. Someone walking in a room? Or shutting a closet door?

Da-dunt,, da-dunt, da-dunt, played in my purse.

I jumped back, reached in my purse, and opened my phone to make it stop ringing. I shut the door quietly, scooted to my car, and drove off.

Who was in that house? Should I call the police?

Second thoughts made me decide not to. That noise inside Stevie's house could have been a person walking or rummaging, but people's houses had different sounds. Maybe I'd heard her refrigerator dumping ice. Or her air conditioner's compressor.

Stevie could tell me if her house made sounds I hadn't noticed before. I knew where she was going. I could phone her at Cajun Delights and ask.

Yeah, right. She'd probably hang up on me.

I didn't know what caused the noises but I wouldn't return there alone. It was getting dark. She hadn't left lights on inside when we left her house.

When I had to pause for a red light three blocks away, I remembered to check for the missed phone call. It was my Austin office. I pressed its number.

"Oh, Cealie, they love what you came up with for Just Like Home hotels," Brianna said, voice bubbling with enthusiasm.

"Good."

"It is a large account, you know." She seemed to want enthusiasm from me.

Now wasn't the time. "I know, and I'm glad. I'm just a little busy."

"Oh. Sorry."

"That's okay. Call anytime. I'm really glad they like it."

"Me, too. I'll let you get back to whatever you're doing. Bye now."

" 'Bye." What I needed to do was locate Jenna Griggs. Maybe the phone book I'd looked in at the gas station was old, or Jenna would be listed in a different one. She could be married. I was no expert at detecting but had to try something.

I pressed *0* on my cell phone and asked about a listing for her name.

As I expected, there was no Jenna Griggs.

"But," the operator said, "I do have a listing for J. P. Griggs. Do you want that?"

"Sure. Oh wait. To make certain, what's that address?"

"Two-forty-three Hill's End Road."

"That's it. Thanks," I said and listened to the phone number. I sure hoped that when I arrived, J.P. would be the woman I was after.

CHAPTER 18

I drove up a slim road on a steep hill. It was dark, and I wasn't wearing my bifocals.

I pulled over next to a streetlight at the end of a long driveway. Digging my glasses out of my purse, I put them on and pressed numbers the operator gave me.

The phone rang and rang. I decided I should hang up when a man walked out of the nearby house. The huge man made me think of the Hulk. He wore a navy robe and stalked across the driveway to my car.

I locked all my doors, then opened my window only enough for us to talk through.

He lowered his angry face to the crack in my window. "Did you need something?"

I was still holding the phone to my ear. I jerked my finger to it, letting him know I was only there to call someone.

His expression softened. "Poor thing, you can't talk?"

I lifted my eyebrows. Shrugged.

"That's probably one of those phones you can text messages on, right?"

I waved my free hand around and wiggled my fingers. My other hand holding the phone was about to close it.

"Hello," a woman said, answering after about fifty rings.

I hated to speak since the Hulk was leaning against my car. I motioned him away.

He backed his hands off my door, and I nodded. Without

thinking, I said, "Thanks. Have a nice day."

"What?" he roared.

I drove away. A glance in the rearview mirror let me see him waving his arms in angry motions.

"Hello," the woman repeated on the phone. "Dammit, they call me away from my housework and then hang up."

"Wait," I said.

"Who's this?" she snapped.

"Cealie Gunther—Stevie Midnight's cousin."

She didn't reply. Maybe Stevie's name didn't register.

"Stevie from your quitters' group," I said.

"Oh. You came with her the other day, and we met in that restaurant."

"Right."

This was the tricky part. I'd thought I would plan what to say if I found her, but other problems made me forget to come up with a script. And she was waiting.

"I'm doing some research about people who smoke and try to quit, and I need to ask you some questions." I considered pinching my palm but decided I'd told the truth. My research might help Stevie stay quit. And I did want to know things about this woman.

She pondered while I came up with more. "And I need to come over there so I can take your picture to attach to my research. You are such an attractive woman." *Liar, liar, pants on fire.* I pinched my palm extra hard.

She stayed quiet. Ready to hang up? Blushing and thinking of how pretty she was?

"Who are you doing the research for?" she said.

"Um, Ingram and Bradshaw and Herman." Pinch, pinch, pinch. My palm was going to bleed. Those were a book distributor, former football player, and guy I dated in high school.

"I guess I can spare a minute." She gave me directions.

I drove, barely having enough time to put together a story. I ran into a store along the way for a disposable camera so I could take her picture. I also bought a pen and legal pad to write on since I was supposedly doing research.

I grinned all the way to Jenna Griggs's house.

Parking in front, I took my camera out of its packing and skimmed the directions. I walked up the path to her house that was tiny and old. Bright lights lit her porch. She opened the door the second I touched the doorbell.

"Hi," she said. "I remember you. Come in."

I carried my legal pad and camera high in front of me to make sure she saw them.

She pointed to the sofa. "Sit down. I was changing clothes. I'll only be a minute longer. Do you want something? Water. I could make tea." She held her tan blouse closed, either taking it off or putting it on. She wore snug jeans and tennis shoes. Fresh fuchsia lipstick too far over the edge of her bottom lip.

"No thanks. I'm good."

She rushed off. I surveyed the living room. Small with wooden floors and walls, an antique fireplace, high ceiling, two chairs and stiff sofa. I sniffed the air. Yep, stale smoke. She probably still hadn't quit.

Her decorations were a mirror and lavender vase above the mantle. One other vase held silk sunflowers on an end table. I looked for photographs and spied some on the wall in the next room. I checked them.

A dining-room table topped with lace and lots of papers anchored this room. I stared at framed photos on a wall.

Lots of old people. Maybe her grandma with siblings? Jenna stood between people I guessed were her parents in a fairly recent photo. In the photograph beside it, I saw Stevie.

"Do you like them?" Jenna stepped behind me. For such a large person, she moved with stealth.

"I do." I looked her over. Different shirt, a bright emerald green. She wore snug black jeans and kept the tennis shoes. Her earlobe-length brown hair looked freshly brushed. Eyeliner smudged the skin beneath her right eye. "You look nice."

"Thanks. These are just some clean things I threw on."

"I see my cousin." I looked closer and recognized most of the people.

"Stevie was there the day we all got together and decided to quit our killer habit."

Staring at the framed four-by-six snapshot, I noticed the group gathered in front of the hall where they held meetings. No one appeared happy. They were strangers, thrown together, knowing they'd have to suffer to achieve a worthwhile goal. The women stood together, Fawn and Jenna, with Stevie behind them. Ish wasn't there. He must have taken the picture. Kern and Father Paul Edward stood with two men I didn't know. "Who's this?" I pointed to them.

"That's Gerald Gibson," she said of the bald stout one with a slim mustache. "He came that first day and never attended a meeting again."

"I guess he decided it was too difficult to quit," I said, giving her an out if she didn't quit, either.

"It's difficult but not impossible. Thousands of people quit smoking every year."

"So you quit?"

She gave her head a brief shake that halfway resembled a nod. "Gerald came around once after that. He showed up after the meeting and wanted to know how we made out. He really pissed me off 'cause he stood close to all of us, and he was smoking."

I recalled smoke coming from outside the meeting hall. Behind one of those bushes. I'd thought it was Jenna smoking. Could it have been Gerald?

"And this poor guy." She touched the head of the other man mainly hidden by the others. "He wanted to quit smoking for his health, but something else killed him. That's Pierce."

"Your cousin. I tripped on him." I slapped my hand over my mouth. Too much information sliding out.

Jenna stared at me. "I knew he died in Stevie's yard. You tripped him?"

"No! He was already down."

She narrowed her eyes.

"I didn't. Promise."

"How did you know we were cousins?"

"I read his obituary," I said, and she nodded. "Your name was listed, but not the names of his children. That was strange."

"Sometimes people might not want to be associated with someone." She gave me a haughty look.

"His children didn't want their names with their deceased father?" I asked, unable to grasp such an idea.

She stared at me, eyes hard. "Are you doing a dissertation on Pierce?"

"Oh, no. I just wondered." I flung my gaze back to the picture, wanting to get off the topic of his family so I wouldn't turn her off. "Wait. He's in this picture. So is Stevie. She said she didn't know him." Kern Parfait also told me she and Pierce never attended a meeting together.

"This first night, all of us sat in a straight row instead of making a semicircle with the chairs like we do now. Now we can see who's there. That first night I was so worried about having to give up my cigarettes that I sure didn't pay attention to who else might be there."

"Are you kidding me?"

"You have no idea what a smoker goes through to quit, do you?"

"I guess I'm fortunate that I don't."

188

"You sure are. When you're thinking about giving up something that's such a large part of your life, you certainly aren't concerned about who's around you."

"That might explain it," I said and reached for my aching shins.

"What's the matter?" Jenna sounded concerned.

"My legs." The pain intensified. I rubbed them and then hobbled toward the door. "I need to go."

"Wait. Didn't you want to interview me? Take my picture?"

"Right." I turned, raised the camera, and pressed the button. Nothing. She held her pose while I quickly scanned the directions. I needed to roll that little wheel to the right until it caught. It finally did. I aimed the camera. "Say *parfait.*"

"Parfait." Her lips spread in a nice angle. Maybe I'd start using that word instead of *cheese.*

"One more," I said.

She turned her head in a slightly bent tilt. "Par-fait."

I snapped three more shots. "Nice. I need to go. I'll get back to you with more questions for the interview."

My aching legs made me nearly fall off the bottom step. Something needed to be done about them. Those pain pills Dr. Wallo wanted to prescribe tempted me. Maybe I'd even go to an emergency room.

Driving away, I noticed the pain lessening. I didn't think it was my position that changed the way they felt. Maybe sitting was better, and standing made them ache? At Stevie's house I would be able to stretch out. I'd get my legs up on the sofa or my bed.

I tapped the brakes. I'd heard those noises in her house and her front door had been unlocked when I'd arrived there earlier, and she wasn't home.

No way was I going into Stevie's house by myself.

She was at Gil's restaurant now. With cutie Dr. Wallo.

I didn't know if Gil was there, but at least one good-looking man was.

Cajun Delights, here I come.

CHAPTER 19

I walked into Gil's restaurant, heard familiar laughter, and spied Stevie at a table. Beside her sat brawny Dr. Wallo.

Hmm, he could help me with my leg problem. I could also look at him again. How therapeutic was that?

Waiters carried fried and boiled seafood. Their aromas kicked in. I was starving.

Actually I only craved the food here. I'd eaten tons of fat grams since I woke up and didn't need lots more. Just thinking about all of the entrées I desired made my waistband snug. Many of my favorite slacks had some elastic in the waistline, and I wore them with fitted shirts on top. I should have worn that instead of these slacks with a zipper and button in front.

"Hello," the doctor said with a happy smile as I approached.

Stevie looked annoyed. She took big swallows of her icy drink.

"Nice to see y'all," I said, half pretending to be surprised to find them here. I placed my hands on the back of the empty chair nearest Dr. Wallo.

"Nice to see you, too," he said. "Join us. We've ordered, but you can eat with us."

Heat rushed out toward me from Stevie. It was animosity and not a spell she was casting, but her anger made me yank my hands off the chair.

"That's okay," I told the doctor. "I'll wait. I'm joining someone."

Stevie gave me a pleasant nod. I gave one back while surreptitiously squeezing the hell out of my right palm.

My satisfied expression was fading.

"But we had to wait quite a while for a table," the doctor said. "Look, there's a long line. It seems everyone wants to try this new restaurant. I've heard the food is really good."

I hadn't noticed all the people waiting but did now. They sat on benches and stood. I'd passed lots of folks on the swings outside.

I was not going to go out there to wait now that the food tempted me. I ignored my cousin, pulled out the chair next to the doctor, and sat.

The air between Stevie and me turned frigid.

A waiter approached, and I ordered. Then looked away from my cousin.

Lots of happy folks, smiling and chatting. A trio of musicians played soft jazz. Babs, the manager, stood beyond them, checking her watch. Fawn, the shapely straw-sucker from The Quitters Group, appeared apprehensive, sucking on one now. She sat alone at a table in the right-hand corner of the room, in the place usually reserved for Gil whenever he was at his restaurants. Obviously, he wasn't here now.

Disappointment plopped down in my chest. I tried to shrug it off. I was sitting near an extremely handsome man, and he wasn't young enough to be my son's classmate.

He unwrapped crackers and ate one. He didn't slather it with butter.

Stevie did. She spread a quarter-inch of butter on her crackers and crunched on them, dropping the empty wrapper on top of two she'd already opened.

Fawn again drew my attention. Only a glass of maybe iced tea sat on her table, along with her napkin which still looked rolled, like she hadn't taken the silverware out yet. She saw me.

I smiled and waved as though I'd known her all my life.

She pulled the straw out of her mouth and gave me a tiny wave, like she had no idea who I was. And then her gaze shifted to my side, and she smiled, jabbing her finger toward Stevie.

I touched Stevie's arm.

"What?" she snapped, drawing her arm away.

I pointed to her friend. She and Fawn gave each other sociable waves. Stevie put her hand up to her mouth and made a motion as though she were inhaling on a cigarette.

Fawn shook her head. She held up her straw, inhaled through it, and took it out of her mouth. She pursed her lips and blew. Then pointed at Stevie, eyebrows raised.

Stevie made a big show of shaking her head, letting Fawn know she hadn't smoked. She shoved half a cracker in her mouth. Then held up her fork, probably to show Fawn she was putting food instead of cigarettes into her mouth now.

Fawn nodded. She did a thumbs-up. A waiter served her a bowl of gumbo.

My stomach growled, wanting my own dish of gumbo.

"I'm really proud of you," Dr. Wallo told Stevie. "I saw your friend there inhaling on her straw. She must have quit smoking, too."

I nodded. "Yes, great job, Stevie."

She grimaced at me, confirming I was not off the hook.

"She and that woman are in a stop-smoking group together," I said.

"That's great. Support really helps," he told her.

"And I'm here to support you." I grinned at my cousin.

She grabbed her purse. "I'd better try one of those pills now."

"I'm glad you filled the prescription," I said and turned from her annoyed face to the handsome doctor's. "She'll probably really want a cigarette right after her meal since smokers want to light up the most after meals and sex."

He grinned. "I've heard that. Were you ever a smoker?"

"Uh-uh, tried it once or twice and choked."

"You're lucky. You were probably allergic to the smoke," Stevie told me, "because if you'd gotten hooked, you would see how hard it is to get off of it."

"I know. And I know you tried to quit before. I really hope it works this time."

She opened her pill bottle and shook some pills out. Then squinted at the label, put all except one of them back, and popped the pill in her mouth. She sipped her drink.

"Good girl," Dr. Wallo said. "It's certainly not easy to quit. I know."

"You do?" I said.

"I smoked for fifteen years."

"That's nothing," Stevie told him.

"I guess not." It seemed the doctor didn't want to argue with her, especially since their meals appeared. "Have some of this filet mignon while you're waiting," he told me. "Here, I'll cut you a chunk. And you can have some of these fried yams."

"That's okay, I'll wait," I protested but not too intensely. My hand happened to nudge my little empty dish closer to his plate. He easily sliced the steak, then placed a chunk on my saucer with a few fries. "And a little of your gravy, please," I said, and he spooned some onto my steak.

Yum, such heavenly food at Gil's places. I ate what the doctor gave me and eyed Stevie's large seafood platter. She saw me and drew her plate closer to herself. Surely she could share one of her shrimp or an oyster. A tiny bit of her soft-shell crab would hit the spot in my rumbling belly.

"The Mexican Hat Dance" played. I grabbed my phone. "Sorry," I said to those at my table, normally remembering to turn off the ringer before I went out to eat. I answered the phone.

"Gram, I'm back!" My granddaughter.

"Hey, Kat, how was your trip? Did you fall in love?"

She laughed in her cheerful tone that had been missing for so long. "Not quite. Maybe Dad did, though, while I was gone."

"I'll want to hear all about it."

"Just a minute," Kat said. "Somebody's calling me."

An angry exchange of voices right beyond the restaurant's stage drew my attention. The balding night manager and striking day manager were both apparently trying to convince each other of something.

Customers between them and me quit talking. Smiles faded from the faces of seated people watching them. Babs stalked toward the exit. Jake stepped up on stage. He spoke to the trio, and they stopped playing. Jake reached the mike.

"Welcome. Thanks to all of you for being with us. I'm sorry the food seems a little slow being served tonight, but we apparently didn't expect so many of you to want to dine with us."

Customers applauded. I was one of them.

"Gram, what's going on?" Kat asked me on the phone.

I missed some of what Jake said onstage but then saw a woman rushing up there.

"I think a joke contest is about to start," I told Kat.

"Oooh, you're with Mr. Gil. You're at his restaurant somewhere."

Heat struck my cheeks. I could only surmise it was because most thoughts of Gil included nudity. Maybe not great thoughts to have while talking to Kat. "No, he's not here."

"Yeah, right. Well you're obviously not in Mexico where you said you were going, but wherever you are might be more interesting. A friend of mine is holding and needs to talk to me. I'll check with you later, okay? Oh, Dad sends his love."

"Mine back to him with kisses to both of you. Call again. Love you, sweetie."

I shut my phone. People nearby looked grateful.

"So Boudreaux never did it again," the woman onstage said. Patrons laughed and applauded.

I'd missed a Boudreaux and Thibodaux joke. Normally I heard those only when Gil was around and made certain to have them told for me.

I checked his table.

Nope, he wasn't there. Only Fawn, spooning food into her mouth.

I was famished. And getting horny, thinking about Gil.

"Want some?" Dr. Wallo said. I met his eyes and matched his smile, then noticed him shoving his plate toward me.

I shook my head. Another woman went to the stage, a young mother–type this time. A tall person, she leaned to the mike.

"Boudreaux drove, with Thibodaux beside him. They were in a rush for an important meeting and couldn't find a place to park. Boudreaux said, 'Lord, if you help us find a parking place, I'll give up drinking and go to church every Sunday.' Miraculously, a parking place appeared. Boudreaux said, 'Never mind, we found one.' "

I enjoyed my belly laugh. My waiter came with my food. I considered telling the doctor about my legs. Neither of them ached now. But he didn't need a patient mentioning an ailment while he was eating out.

The jokes and a handsome man at my side and a crab platter approaching me made me happy I'd decided to come here. But why B and T jokes now? I broke a leg off my fried soft-shell crab and ate it, looking again at Fawn's table.

Gil was standing beside it. Happiness danced inside my chest. He bent and spoke to Fawn. Then he saw me.

Gil strode forward, sharing intense eye contact with me. Heat welled up inside my body.

A waiter stopped him. The young man looked apprehensive.

Uncharacteristically, Gil seemed to brush the employee off.

He still eyed me, his expression no longer happy. His gaze shifted to the man seated near me—the good-looking man who now leaned his head close to mine.

"These fried yams are delicious," Dr. Wallo said. "Cealie, how about a few more?"

"Uh-uh." I raised my hand at him, kind of a signal that he should back off. I didn't believe Gil liked this scenario.

"Hello, Cealie." Gil bent and kissed me full on the lips.

Umm. I might be persuaded to forget my food. I was sure he had a nice big office out back, a lock on its door.

No, Cealie. You're woman. You want to do your own thing—no strings attached. He could easily become a permanent attachment.

I withdrew my lips. "It's nice to see you." I worked to still my torso from shaking. This man always shook me up. "And here's my cousin, Stevie."

He clasped her hand. "So nice to see you again."

She wiped her mouth with her napkin, a happy smile brightening her face. "It's wonderful seeing you. I love your restaurant."

"Thank you. It's especially nice to see repeat customers."

"I'll be back a lot. I'm telling other teachers how good your food is, and the joke contests are a wonderful treat."

Okay, what was the deal with Stevie? She was gushing. It seemed she had a crush on Gil. Well that would never work. And here she had this fine-looking, unmarried specimen of a man for a doctor seated at her side.

Gil turned to the doctor, all happiness gone from his face. "I haven't met your friend here."

Ah, Gil was jealous.

Sweet.

"Gil Thurman, Dan Wallo. *Doctor* Dan Wallo," I emphasized.

They shook hands. The doctor smiled. Malice darkened Gil's face.

How neat was that? It had been *so* many years since a guy had fought for me. *Go, Gil, go!* I mentally cheered. Of course I didn't tell the doctor Gil owned this place and others like it.

Gil straightened, his stern gaze swinging toward me. So what should I do—tell him to go away so we could finish eating without any tension between him and the other great-looking guy?

Was I stupid?

"Sit down, Gil. Join us," I said.

Yes! He drew back the empty chair and sat.

Dr. Wallo's plate had remained toward me. I pulled it closer to my plate, ate two of his cold yam fries, and smiled. I looked at Gil.

His lips pressed together, their corners jammed back. His steel-gray eyes stared at me and the doctor.

I needed to eat, and my crab dishes wouldn't stay warm forever. I took a spoonful of the seafood gumbo. Mmm. I nibbled a fried crab claw. Yummy. I ate a crab ball—sinfully delicious. I was going for the stuffed crab when I noted the uncomfortable feel of quiet at our table. I didn't want to talk to either man. But maybe Stevie, chewing her last bites of food, would give me her attention now without being annoyed.

"Guess who I saw at a drugstore," I said to her.

"Santa Claus."

I grinned, pretending she'd said that to me with good intent. "Close. It was Father Paul Edward. He was with some of those sexy women."

She spooned the final shrimp from her bowl into her mouth.

To make sure I got her notice, I spoke louder, "And they were laughing near the rack of condoms and picking up packs of them." *Let's see you ignore that.*

She aimed her empty spoon at me. "He wasn't buying cigarettes, was he?"

"Not that I saw."

"Hmgr." The cigarettes seemed her only interest.

But not Gil. Grinning, he leaned close to me. "Did those condoms make you think of something?" he said near my ear while Stevie listened to something Dr. Wallo told her.

I punched Gil's arm.

"Cealie!" Stevie said, staring at me wide eyed.

"A flake of dandruff on his shirt. I was getting it off." I didn't even have to pinch my palm for that one. Gil did have a flaky head if he thought the mention of condoms would turn me on.

His gaze shifted toward the doctor. Oh, of course. He'd spoken to me like that because he wanted this other hunky guy to know we had something going on between us. Well we did—but not anymore. I'd never again give in to my urges concerning this man.

With him close, parts of my torso screamed *Liar.*

"I'll let all of you finish your dinner. I have business to tend to," Gil said. "Nice meeting you, Dr. Wallo." He and the doc shook hands, their gazes sizing up each other. Gil nodded to me. He exchanged a smile with Stevie and sauntered off.

"Well," I said and speared a popcorn shrimp with my fork.

"Dr. Wallo!" Gil called.

"Oh, my God!" a woman yelled. People around wore shocked expressions.

The doctor shoved back his chair and dashed to Gil's table.

Fawn was slumped over, facedown in her gumbo.

CHAPTER 20

Stevie and I rushed from our chairs toward Fawn. So did others in the restaurant.

"Stay back! Give them room! She needs air," manager Jake Bryant shouted.

People stopped and stared. We left space between us and Fawn. Dr. Wallo and Gil were gently laying her on the floor. I stood on tiptoe to see between people's shoulders. The doctor felt the side of Fawn's neck. He listened near her nostrils. He looked at Gil, his look void of hope, and started mouth-to-mouth on Fawn.

The part of her face that I could see appeared swollen.

Jake stretched his arms toward our group. "We need this room for medics to come through. Move—please."

We pressed to the side of the pathway from the door. People began slipping outside. The kind thing to do was leave.

Stevie and I went outside. We stood in front of Gil's restaurant like most other people. I glanced into the dark at the street, where sirens screamed their approach. Everyone jammed together on and near the restaurant's wooden bridge. Most patrons and workers stayed quiet. Some complained.

"I just got my food," a man said.

"Me, too. I hope they'll give us a rain check."

"What if their food killed her?" a woman said.

"Yeah," some others agreed.

My fighting instinct struck. I yelled, "Their food didn't hurt her! If you think the restaurant owes you something, I'm sure they'll give you a rain check for another meal."

People glanced at each other. "That's not a bad idea," someone said.

"I'll check with them tomorrow," another agreed.

Groups started toward the parking lot. Sirens wailed closer.

"I'm not eating here anymore," a departing man said.

"Neither me," agreed a tall one.

"Their food didn't kill anyone!" I hollered.

The tall guy faced me. "Then what did?"

Scores of people waited for my answer. "We'll find out soon enough," I said, my voice not as loud or as certain. "But you can be sure it wasn't the gumbo."

I had no idea what was wrong with Fawn, except she didn't appear to be breathing. Trembles made my gait unsteady.

No one looked satisfied with my answer. Some shook their heads.

"Let's go," I said and touched Stevie's arm. We watched an ambulance and police cars approach, then walked to our cars.

Vehicles drove away from Cajun Delights. I imagined most people inside them did like me. Prayed.

Stevie and I got into our cars without speaking and drove away. Would this horrible incident affect Gil's restaurant? I hated to think so but had heard those customers griping.

And what if Fawn died? My gosh, she seemed a sweet person. She had a family. She couldn't be dead.

But if she was, she would be the second person in that small stop-smoking group to die. Would whatever happened to her be connected to the man I'd tripped on—whose leg imprints on mine now throbbed?

I'd need to get Dr. Wallo to x-ray my shins.

I followed Stevie toward her house. We were a few blocks from it when another problem sprang to mind.

I tooted my horn, put on my flashers, and nosed to the road's shoulder.

She pulled over and walked back to my PT Cruiser. "You have car problems?"

"No, but your house might. I was going in it this evening, and the door was unlocked."

She leaned close, her stare intense. "Didn't you ever forget to lock the door?"

"And there was noise inside."

"What kind of noise?"

"Maybe a person moving around. Or your house settling. Or ice dropping from the ice maker."

"It's been a really trying, long day. I'm going home." She jammed herself back into her car and sped off.

I followed, hesitantly now that I recalled the noises. Big chicken that I was, I really slowed down to let her get there a bit ahead of me. Stevie wasn't scared.

Soon she was reaching her house. I was almost three blocks behind. She shouldn't go inside alone.

Bad girl, Cealie. Go help her.

I shoved the pedal to the floor.

Flashing blue lights came to life. A police car roared after me.

Curses sprang from my lips. Then an idea came. I tapped my brakes and slowed. Putting on my flashing lights, I continued down the street to Stevie's house.

The police car followed, lights swirling, siren wailing.

Front doors flew open. People popped out of houses to see what was going on.

Exactly what I wanted was happening, except the policeman might give me a speeding ticket. Not a big problem. I would have wanted police to come to Stevie's house, just in case a bad person was inside. Now I was getting a policeman there.

Porch lights came on at her neighbors' houses. Doors opened. Adults stepped out to their porches and stared at me.

The cop's car closed in.

I replaced my flashers with my right blinker and pulled in front of Stevie's house.

Her garage door was shut. If someone had gotten into her house, that person would have heard the siren coming and rushed away. At least that's what I hoped.

The cop car stopped behind me. It shut off its siren. Swirling lights atop it cast an odd blueness.

I shut off my motor and got out. I knew the police would want a driver's hands up where they could be seen, so I raised mine. I glanced at Stevie's house—still no sign of life. No visible lights.

"You again," the deputy said.

"Oh, hi." I recognized him as the first one who'd come here when Pierce died.

"You didn't know we had speed limits?"

"I screwed up," I said with a weak smile. I heard people excitedly speaking and glanced around.

Most of my cousin's neighbors were in their yards, watching us. I looked at April's house. She wasn't outside. Still no light inside Stevie's. I might have to get this deputy to come in.

"Where were you coming from in such a hurry?" he asked, writing on a pad.

"Cajun Delights restaurant."

His face snapped up toward me. "You were there, too?"

I nodded, hands high. "Why?"

He shook his head. "Somebody dies, and you're there. Why doesn't that surprise me?"

I lowered my arms. "Fawn died?"

"And you know her." He shook his head harder.

My eyes stung as I thought of that young woman. Fawn

seemed so full of life. But not anymore.

Stevie's porch lights sprang on. She walked out the door.

"You're all right!" I said.

"You thought something happened to her, too?" The deputy scratched his head.

"I could have guessed this," Stevie told me in disgust. "My neighbors call to say the cops grabbed someone in front of my house."

She returned inside, slamming her door.

The deputy lowered his pad. "I won't ticket you since you just experienced a tragic incident in that restaurant. But you might be called in for questioning regarding that woman who died tonight."

"Why? Do you suspect she was murdered?"

"We'll need to investigate. But stay close. You may be called."

He went to his car, and I walked up to the porch. People still watched from their yards. I waved to them all to let them know I was friendly.

Some of the women waved back. Since the cop car was leaving, I imagine they decided I wasn't going to pull out a gun and shoot them.

I clasped the doorknob.

It wouldn't turn. Stevie had locked me out!

I was going to ring the bell, but she'd purposely done this. While everyone in the neighborhood stared, I made a big deal out of digging the key out of my purse. I held it up, unlocked her door, and went in.

"Do you know how embarrassed you made me?" Stevie screamed as I entered the den. "Everybody's calling, telling me to be careful—there's a cop following someone toward my house. And I peek out—and it's *my cousin* with her hands in the air!"

"Sorry about that." I glanced toward the rear of the house.

"Have you checked everything? Did anyone break in the back door?"

"Grrr." She threw her hands upward and stomped off.

Feeling safer since the deputy had made lots of noise, I clomped to the rear of the house to inspect. Imagining Fawn dead made me shiver. My heart went out to her and the people who loved her. Fear about who or what might be killing people around my cousin made me pretend to be brave.

I flicked on the kitchen lights and spoke with a loud, deep voice. "Good, this looks good. Nobody came in here, right?" I glanced at Minnie cactus. What appeared especially good was that no one had ransacked the room, although I couldn't imagine what anyone might steal from a kitchen. What mainly satisfied me was that the door wasn't busted or open.

What didn't look good in here was the stove.

It looked like someone had used a sledge hammer on it. No wonder Stevie seemed ticked off at me. When she'd parked in the garage and entered this room, she'd seen this again. Tomorrow I'd need to replace it. Right now I needed to inspect the back door. Maybe it was unlocked, a bad person standing right outside.

I opened my cell phone in case I needed it. "Let's see if this door is still locked," I said in my deepest tone. "Nobody better be here because the police are still near."

I reached out and tried the knob. Still locked.

Braver, I checked the ice maker and found the metal arm up. I pushed on it, trying to make ice drop so I could tell what that sounded like. The arm didn't lower. I didn't want to force it and break another of Stevie's appliances. I could easily replace them but didn't believe she'd be happy if I broke all her things.

She slammed the door to her bedroom. Her action assured me she wasn't happy.

I didn't think I should be the one to tell her Fawn was probably dead.

I went to my room. Everything appeared normal. I checked the window and closet. Thank goodness, nothing.

I changed into my nightgown and pulled back the bedspread. Uneasiness clung to my skin. I peeked under my bed.

No person. But on the clean floor near the foot of the bed lay a round pink object. I grabbed it.

Ugh, chewed gum. I went to the trash can to toss it, then stopped. I stared at the gum wad and squeezed. It moved easily between my fingers.

I didn't think old chewed gum remained pliable for long. The floor was so clean, there weren't even any dust bunnies. Had April been in here? If so, it must have been a recent visit. Why would she come in?

Returning to the window, I peeked between the curtains at her house.

Through her sheer curtains, I could see bright lights in one room. I wished I'd checked that earlier, soon after all the other neighbors were outside watching me. If she wasn't home then, it would have made sense that she hadn't called to check on the commotion or been outside, rushing over here to snoop.

Of course a light on now didn't prove anything. She and Cherish might have gone out, although it seemed rather late for that. But what did I know of their habits or what they did with their lives? Only that cute nosy April had bright blue eyes and chewed pink bubble gum and drank lots of diet lime drinks, and Cherish called Stevie her aunt but she wasn't.

I squeezed the gum. It had stiffened during the time I held it. I tossed the gum, determining I only imagined its changed feel.

In the hall bathroom I soaped my hands. I was tempted to knock on Stevie's door and ask about April being in my room lately. Reason told me I'd better not. My cousin seemed to like

April much more than she liked me.

I slipped into my bed and tossed around. Shapely Fawn who sucked straws to keep from smoking died in her gumbo. She was probably in her mid-forties with two children and a husband. What could cause such a young person to die?

In less than a week, two people from Stevie's group mysteriously died. I imagined the group like Agatha Christie's *And Then There Were None.* One person after another was found dead.

My heartbeat thrust up against my throat. I needed to keep Stevie away from everybody else in her quitters' group.

CHAPTER 21

Stevie was gone when I awoke. Apprehension grasped the nape of my neck. I tiptoed, searching her house, envisioning her friend facedown in gumbo and Trottier facedown in tall grass. I recalled the unlocked front door to this house and the noise.

Had someone snatched Stevie?

I almost grabbed a phone and darted outside. But the kitchen treated me to the rich aroma of brewed coffee. Stevie's washed cup, saucer, and spoon were drying in the drain. The newspaper lay neatly folded on the table.

I picked it up. Tuesday. Another school day for her. The wall clock said it was late morning.

I brought coffee to the table to savor with the local newspaper. I spread the paper open. Headlines snapped me to full senses. *Woman dies in local restaurant.*

Near the headlines, a close shot of Cajun Delights restaurant.

The brief article did not mention Fawn's name. It said all of the woman's close relatives had not been notified yet. The cause of her death had not been determined. A physician, Dr. Dan Wallo, had been eating at the restaurant and tried unsuccessfully to revive her.

The reporter quoted restaurant patrons who said they left once a customer died. They were shocked, seeing a woman with her face in her bowl, which held chicken gumbo, restaurant manager Jake Bryant was quoted as saying. Bryant told reporters the gumbo also contained andouille sausage, okra, garlic,

208

and other seasonings. This new restaurant was owned by Gil Thurman, who was not available for comment. An investigation into the woman's death was continuing.

I breathed. Studied the picture. Gil's restaurant, the grand opening poster.

I reread the article. Exhaled. What would this death do to the business he was trying to establish?

Not interested in other sad news, I left my eyeglasses on the table and took a quick shower. In my underwear, I faced the mirror and opened my bottle of liquid makeup. A glob dropped into the lavatory basin.

I'd been taught to be frugal. Besides, there wasn't much left in the bottle. It was supposed to prevent lines, and I needed all the help I could get to pretend this stuff diminished them. Maybe it would even cover my mustache.

I leaned over, positioning my hand between the glob and the drain. I used my free hand as a scoop. And heard heavy footsteps approaching.

A chill jolted up my spine.

This wasn't April. Without a doubt, a man was walking toward this room.

The only nearby thing I might use as a weapon was my makeup bottle or mascara wand.

A tap came on the wall outside this room, followed by the shoes slapping the floor inside here.

I bent and held onto the lavatory, giving myself leverage as I prepared for him.

He rushed toward me, speaking.

"No!" I yelled and drew my right knee up. I slammed my right foot back, using all my force to hurt him where it would count—and recognized his voice. I tried to yank back my foot. Too late.

"Cealie, no!" Gil yelled. He doubled over, grabbing himself

where my foot struck. He grabbed the wall for support.

"Gil, I'm so sorry. I didn't know it was you." I moved closer.

He put his hand up to stop me. "It's okay. I'm—" He shoved himself straighter. Groaned and bent over. "I'll be okay." His voice held pain.

"Why did you walk in here without warning?"

He grabbed himself, then moved his hand away. "I rang the doorbell and then knocked. Nobody answered. I tried the doorknob. The door opened."

"Darn, nobody locked it last night." I tapped my head. I should have locked it. "There was so much commotion." I noted the pain in his face. "Are you really all right? Maybe I should bring you to a doctor."

Gil's hand had remained near the area where I'd hurt him. He jerked his hand to his side and stood ramrod stiff. "No, I'm fine." He smiled slightly. "At the last minute, I saw what you were ready to do, so I pulled back and turned. You didn't score a direct hit."

"Good thing I'm not a good aim."

"I'll make sure you never have target practice."

I realized how I was dressed. "I wouldn't have greeted you in a pink bra and panties."

His smile was real. "Those are nice. And I especially like the black lacy ones." Gil moaned but seemed to try to keep his smile. "I'll have to ravage you another time."

A frightening thought came. "You will be able to ravage again, right?"

He awarded me a half grin. Gil started to bend, pain obvious from the new deep creases outside his eyes. "Cealie, you were there last night. You saw that woman drop her head in her dish."

"I didn't actually see when it happened. We had smiled at Fawn, and she and Stevie pantomimed with each other about smoking straws."

"You two knew her?"

"She was in Stevie's stop-smoking group. I'd met Fawn there, and she came over once since then."

Gil shook his head, looking sad. "What a horrible thing to happen to her."

"She was sitting at your table. Were you friends?"

"I didn't know her. I'd come out of my office but wasn't going to eat until later." He always let customers sit at the table considered his until it was time for his meal. Once people left his table, he sat and ate.

"You spoke to her," I recalled.

"I asked if her gumbo was all right. She said she hadn't tried it yet."

"And a few minutes later, she died." I released a deep sigh. "Do you know what killed her?"

"Not yet." He leaned back against the wall. Gave me a smile filled with anguish. "You know how to hurt a guy."

"Oh, baby, I'm so sorry. Let me put something on you. Some ice or medicine."

"No!" He put up a hand, maybe making sure I didn't try to touch his privates. "I'm good. Really." His nostrils narrowed while he inhaled. Then he pushed himself off the wall. "I'll be going."

He took tiny steps out of the bathroom. Gil let out little *ooh*s along the way.

I cringed, wanting to take away his pain. I shrugged into my robe and followed. "Why did you come over?"

"I felt so bad about having someone die in my restaurant last night. I wanted a friend, a shoulder to lean on."

"Ah, Gil." He'd tugged at my heart. I threw my arms out to hug him.

He cringed and leaned forward, allowing only the top portion of his body to touch mine. "Ow." He stepped away and used baby steps toward the front door.

"You really should see a doctor," I suggested. "I could probably get you in with the one I saw yesterday, Dr. Wallo."

Gil stopped. *"Dan?"* He said the doctor's first name like ice dropping off his tongue.

"Yes. He seems like a nice guy. It's a shame he couldn't save Fawn."

Gil's eyes crimped with sadness. "He tried. He knew she was gone, but still kept trying." Gil nodded, admiration in his face.

"So maybe you should let him check you."

"No way."

He walked out the front door. I went with him to the porch. Suffering etched his expression. He gave me a light kiss. "Maybe you should only attack vulnerable body parts on enemies."

"I'll try to remember."

It was a good thing Stevie had a railing for him to hold onto as he hobbled down the stairs. Otherwise, he might have tumbled.

"Oh. Oh-oh." Gil descended each step like it was a major hurdle, and he was a ninety-year-old man.

And I had done that to him.

"Be careful!" I called. "Let me know if you need anything."

He shook his head. Getting into his car at the curb caused him to release more yelps.

"Wait!" I called. "It doesn't have to be him. There are other doctors you could see. Let me phone one and bring you in."

He gunned his motor and sped off.

I considered what I'd done. I'd caused him major damage. I hoped it was reversible and would soon heal.

Oh my gosh, suppose I'd caused Gil long-term difficulty. Suppose his sexual ability was over?

I leaned against the porch wall, considering how I had maimed him. *No, no, no, Cealie, what have you done now?*

"Hey. Nice to see you," a woman said.

I quit shaking my head.

Two women with white hair stood on the sidewalk. Their jogging suits made me recall that they were the ones we'd seen walking behind Stevie's fence.

"Hi," I told them.

"We saw you out here last night," the one wearing pink said.

"Yes, well . . . it's nice outside." Okay, and yesterday a cop followed me here. And just now you both saw my former lover hobbling away. And I caused his hobble.

They started walking, arms swinging briskly.

"Wait," I said, and they turned. "A man died here a few days ago. Did you see anything?"

"No," the one in pink said. The other one shook her head. They strolled off, faces ahead, arms swinging.

Directly across the street, a young woman walked out of her front door and grabbed the newspaper from her porch. She spied me and gave a big wave.

I waved back. Were all of Stevie's neighbors so friendly?

Back inside, I slipped into slacks and a dressy shirt and flats. I made a pit stop in the bathroom. The liquid makeup glob now staining the lavatory made my heart sink. I'd hurt Gil.

I should stop aiming for vulnerable body parts whenever I felt threatened, I told myself, swiping a little mascara on my lashes. I shook my head. Body parts became valuable things to hurt when no weapon was around and I needed help. I dabbed on tinted lip gloss, grabbed my purse, and went out.

Somebody somewhere had information about the man who'd died. Could his death be connected to Fawn McKenzie's?

Probably the same medical examiner was trying to discover why she and Pierce Trottier died. Nobody could convince me his death stemmed from natural causes.

I was going to investigate one person from the stop-smoking

group again. I had an idea he knew much more than he was saying.

More cars were at Parfait's Parlor than I'd thought I would find during the late morning. I parked, and the sweet smell of chocolate drew me inside.

College-age youths sat in clumps, their voices loud. They ate from tall glasses, the swirls of their parfaits attractive. I wanted one.

I shook my head, reached back with both hands and patted my butt—ammunition for avoiding temptation. I poked my stomach way out, feeling how extremely tight my slack's waistline became since I'd arrived in this town and eaten so many rich foods.

"Mrs. Gunther, do you have a problem?" Kern Parfait stepped up to me.

"No, why?"

He stared at my belly, then leaned toward my butt. "You seemed to have problems with getting some body parts to stay in place."

That was rude. Nearby kids heard and snickered.

I looked at them. Looked at him. Raised my voice. "Don't you ever feel like your ass has gotten too big?"

Kids guffawed.

Parfait's grimace intensified. His hands at his sides clenched into fists. "Did you come over here to check yours?"

"Maybe." I pulled in my stomach as hard as I could. Then poked it out. I pulled in and poked out. "This is really good exercise. You might try it."

I stopped my stomach workout and shoved my butt way back, then tucked it in. I repeated the motion, while young people howled with laughter.

Parfait grabbed my arm. Not gently. His teeth clenched. "Unless you order something and sit, you're loitering."

"Come sit with us," a guy in a red T-shirt yelled. He shoved over in his already-crowded booth.

"Yeah," other teens said. Young people in the place cheered.

I smiled and slid into the space close to the boy. I winked at all the others in the booth.

Kern Parfait seethed. "What can I get you?" he asked me. "I'll have someone hurry it to you."

"We need another round of all this." I pointed to the group's half-filled glasses.

"Oh, yeah," the biggest guy said.

"I'll take water." I glanced at all of the tables holding young people. "And let's have refills for everyone."

Cheers and whoops resounded.

I stood, moving my face close to Kern Parfait's. "Again you're dressed spotlessly," I said. "And there's not a speck of grass or dust on your shiny shoes. Why was there grass in the cuff of your slacks the day Pierce Trottier died?"

His teeth clenched while he whispered, "Don't ever come here again."

"The grass was cut outside my cousin's fence that day." I pulled two hundred-dollar bills from my purse and shoved them at him, speaking louder than he did. "I'll enter this joint any time I want."

"Yeah, you're right!" kids hollered. They were stomping their feet and pounding on tables while I strolled out.

Getting inside my car, I sat quietly. I didn't know that I'd accomplished anything in there except making its owner angry. Oh, of course I did help feed the masses.

I grinned. Those growing young adults needed nourishment, although double doses of ice cream and syrup and surgery fruit might not be the first requirement on the food chart.

My stomach growled, reminding me I hadn't eaten a thing

yet today. I always ate breakfast, but not today because of Gil's visit to Stevie's house. And now the sweet scent of ice cream remained with me. I needed food.

I also needed to see Gil and find out how he was doing.

Chapter 22

The parking lot at Cajun Delights held only nine vehicles. Nine. And it was almost noon.

I parked there and checked my car's clock. Twelve-thirty.

Maybe they were closed. I strode to the front door, pulled it open, and went inside.

The vast room filled with black-and-white squares on tablecloths looked like it waited for massive checker games. No music played. The restaurant was almost silent. No seafood scents.

A waiter stepped up to my side.

"You're open?" I asked.

"Yes, ma'am, we opened a couple of weeks ago. Would you like a table near a window? And will you be eating by yourself?" His voice was void of cheer.

We moved farther into the restaurant. Four men in work clothes ate together. I saw Gil, the only other person eating. He sat at his table, gaze down. He looked solemn.

"I'll eat with him," I told my waiter.

"Oh, yes, ma'am."

Gil only glanced up when I stepped near. He didn't smile—probably a first for him when he saw me. "Hello," he said, tone lifeless.

"Hello."

The waiter drew a chair back for me, the chair Fawn sat in when she died last night.

I took a breath and sat in it. "I don't need a menu," I told the waiter. "I'd like seafood gumbo, please, with iced tea."

He went off. I edged my chair closer to the table. Envisioned the white gumbo bowl at this place, Fawn's face inside it.

I shoved the chair back and stood. "Four chairs at this table," I told Gil. "I pick the one closer to you." I took the chair beside his, leaned over, and kissed his cheek.

"I wonder if anyone will ever want to sit there again." Gil gloomily stared at the chair Fawn had died in.

"Oh, sure," I said with little conviction. "People will hardly even know about it."

His gaze speared my eyes. He looked at Fawn's chair that I'd left. He looked at me.

Enough said.

I drank some tea the waiter set in front of me. Its coldness going down accentuated how tight my throat had become.

Gil stared across the room, gaze vacant. His gaze had always held his vision for an even better life than he already had. And whenever he gazed at me, his gaze held love. Lust. A mingling of both.

But not today.

I touched his arm. "You could get rid of that chair. Put a new one there."

"I'll attach a sign—I'm brand new, not the chair a woman died on."

"I see your point."

"This is rush hour. Or should be." He scanned his nearly empty building. "A birthday party was scheduled at noon. It was cancelled. So were three group reservations." He scraped his fork alongside a flounder stuffed with crabmeat languishing in his plate.

"Last night I saw a waiter stop you when you were on your way to our table. And I heard raised voices exchanged between your managers."

Gil shook his head. "Both managers seem competent, but there's a problem. He often runs late. She voices her unhappiness in front of customers."

"Customers did seem to notice."

His expression darkened. "Those are situations I'll need to deal with. I've spoken with both of them about those habits they need to break, or I'll have to hire new people."

"Hiring competent people to run your business can be tough, especially when you don't even live in their state."

"You know how that is," he said.

I nodded. We quietly sat, hanging our heads. The waiter brought my gumbo.

"I need to wash my hands," I told Gil. "They're sticky." The stickiness came from syrup on the table where I'd sat at Parfait's. I didn't need to tell him I'd gone there to nose around.

He didn't seem to notice as I walked away.

I soaped my hands in the restroom. A toilet flushed. Good. Maybe new customers had come in, and one made a pit stop here.

A stall door opened. It was only Babs, the manager. She nodded at me and washed her hands.

I dried my fingers. "You don't like to drive at night," I said.

"Excuse me."

"I've seen you getting annoyed with the night manager. I'm Cealie, a friend of Gil's. We met at the supermarket near the grapes," I added to reassure her I wasn't a person off the street trying out psychic mumbo jumbo.

"Yes. You're right. I can't see well driving when it's dark."

"I knew it. I'm the same way. Ever since I turned forty, I've had problems seeing to drive at night."

She gave me a small smile, dried her hands, and walked toward the exit.

"I really think you should give him a chance," I said, and she turned to listen. "Jake. He might frustrate you now and have faults, especially not being on time. But you could help him with that. He just seems like a good person."

"Yes. Well . . ." She nodded briefly and went out.

I happily sighed. I loved to play matchmaker.

Gil didn't think it was a good idea since he believed people meant for each other would find each other on their own. He probably wouldn't like to know I'd tried fixing up people he'd hired, especially since he was having problems with them.

But he'd be pleased if they started dating and became happy with each other instead of miserable. Then this restaurant would become more cheerful when they were together.

I smiled as I walked out to meet Gil. Passing the bar, I heard muted voices from the wall TV and glanced there.

A national news station showed my face. I stood among others outside Cajun Delights, the restaurant where they were telling the world a woman died with her face in a bowl of gumbo.

My legs wobbled. News stations were showing this everywhere. What might this coverage do to all of Gil's restaurants?

I rushed to the table, hoping he hadn't seen or heard that news. Maybe the cause of Fawn's death, a natural cause, would be discovered shortly, and all of this horror would be over.

Gil sat, his expression still sad. I forced a smile and sat with him. I picked at my gumbo, which was cooler than I liked, but didn't want to complain or send it to get reheated. Gil didn't need any more complaints. I dreaded having him learn about making the national news.

"You aren't eating?" I asked.

He didn't hold any silverware or drink. His stuffed flounder, normally a choice entrée, was surely cold. "I need to go to the bathroom," he said.

"The men's one isn't working?"

"It works fine."

"Then why don't you go?"

He grimaced. Took a deep breath. Bent forward.

"Oh, my gosh, you must be really hurt."

Gil gave me a forced smile. Creases formed between his eyes. He let out a moan.

Tears warmed my eyes. "Can I do anything?"

His smile widened. Still didn't get happy. "After the customers leave, I'll try getting there."

Ooh, how badly he must hurt.

There were customers at only two places—the four men and me. The men were paying for their meals. I gobbled my lukewarm gumbo so I could leave, too.

Gil's face looked drawn and expressed pain when I tossed down my napkin.

"Can I help you?" I asked.

He seemed to be gritting his teeth. Shook his head. "I'll be fine."

"Good luck. Call me." I pecked a kiss on his cheek and went off.

Driving away, I imagined Gil shoving himself up with much effort, then hobbling and moaning to reach the bathroom.

My chest ached for what I had done to him. The more I envisioned Gil hobbling, the angrier I became. I'd only struck him out of fear—the fear that came from two people near me dying.

I needed to learn what caused at least one of those deaths. I needed more answers. At least one person—or group—that I didn't trust should be available now.

People often made up excuses as crutches for their negative behavior. Some of them went to confession at churches. Maybe I could kick away one man's crutch and draw out a confession on my own. I whipped my car around the corner and headed for Our Lady of Hope.

CHAPTER 23

Sunlight glittered against the church's steep windows, momentarily blinding me as I drove near the church. No cars around. No people visible. No sound except my shoes patting on dirt while I got out and walked to the church.

I tried both doors. Locked.

Trotting to the side wall, I peeked in a long window.

The confessional door was closed. No motion. Not one person.

The house beyond the driveway looked extra small. Wooden frame, natural finish, a tiny porch. I walked across the dirt road, stepped onto the porch, and rang the doorbell to what I imagined was the priest's house.

No response.

I rang and rang it again, more frustrated by the moment. I needed to question someone, needed some answers. Needed to get rid of the feeling that I'd caused Gil anguish. Stevie wasn't happy with me, either.

The bell might not work, I decided, and slammed my fist against the door. Instead of finding solutions, I was bruising my knuckles.

I breathed in deeply and turned to go.

"Yes?" a woman said, holding the door open.

"You're one of the twins."

She nodded. "Lark." Lark looked exhausted. Mascara smudged under her droopy eyes. Other makeup was bright red on her lips and cheeks. She wore a flimsy pink robe.

This didn't look good. If this was the priest's house, she probably wasn't his housekeeper or the cook taking a brief nap before she washed the lunch dishes.

"I'd like to come in."

"Father's not here. It's just me."

"You'll do fine."

Unhappily, she let me inside.

Blue. Bright, in-your-face ice blue, the same color as the shirt Pierce Trottier wore when he died. That's what the little house held.

We walked directly into the petite living room with blue walls. Lark dropped to a cushioned blue chair and indicated I should sit on the blue sofa. I sat and scanned wall pictures—outdoor scenes in navy frames. The coffee table painted ice blue. Through a door I saw an old-time stove in what seemed to be a matchbox kitchen, reminding me I needed to buy Stevie one. The other door was shut.

"So Father lives here?" I asked.

"Yes. And sometimes he lets us stay."

"Ah." It was worse than I thought. He let how many stay? Both twins? All four women?

I didn't want to envision that scene. I stared at the bright blue coffee table, my stomach churning from being engulfed with the solitary color, the color of the dead man's shirt. "He favors blue, doesn't he?"

Lark leaned forward, her face sincere. "He's a good man, no matter what you think."

I forced a half smile. "I'm sure he is."

"I mean it. Father is a wonderful man."

I kept nodding. I knew how it felt when a woman was convinced that a man was wonderful.

"We're hookers," Lark blurted.

"No!" I said in a shocked tone.

I wanted to gush about how I couldn't believe it but could not make myself utter one lying word.

"Me and Clark. I don't know about Sue and Lois. I think so, but they won't admit it."

"Who would've guessed?"

"I worked last night and was taking a nap." She rubbed at the mascara smudges under her eyes. "Father's been trying to get us to stop our profession. He really is a good person."

"Lark, did he know Pierce Trottier?"

"The man that died? I heard Father mention him once. Don't remember what he said." She reached out and squeezed my fingers. "Father Paul Edward always behaves like a gentleman."

"Then why are you here and dressed like that?"

She stared at her robe. "I should've changed. But he left right after I got here. He lets us stay when we don't have a place." Seeing the accusation in my face, she said, "We don't sleep with him. He sleeps in his bed whenever we need to come here to rest, and we get the sofa or bring a sleeping bag and stay in this room."

"That's hard to believe."

"He only has one bedroom. He offered his room and said he'd sleep in here. But the only way we'll come is if he stays in his bed, and we crash in another spot."

I leaned closer. Her stale liquor breath made me draw back. "I saw all of you getting condoms a few days ago. You were laughing and picking out condoms with a priest—who happens to also be a man."

She shoved back against her chair. "He's been trying to get us to quit hooking."

I skimmed her tired face and pink robe. "It doesn't look like he succeeded."

She turned her eyes away. Kept quiet a moment. Then faced

me. "No, me and the other girls have kept our profession that's paid our rent for a while."

"There are other professions. Other jobs."

"I know. Father tells us about some of them. He was trying to help us that day. He insisted that if we wouldn't change our ways yet, we needed to use condoms. He made sure we knew where to find them."

"You never used condoms?"

"Sure, I keep a stash. But we went along with him that day. We were laughing about all the different kinds and sizes they come in."

I tried to smile. Didn't succeed. Especially when the ice-blue chair she was sitting on blended with the blue of the coffee table, and I stared at the sofa I sat on. Putrid blue. My stomach protested.

"What about Ish?" I needed to ask. "Did he ever mention that name?"

"Ish Muller? Sure, he and Father are good friends."

"They are?" Blue walls and furniture swallowed me. "I need to go."

Lark stood, her look sincere. "He really is a fine person."

I rushed out the door. I dashed to the end of the porch and bent over. Dry heaves made my eyes cry. I fought to shove away the image of Trottier's blue shirt engulfing me.

I straightened, taking big gulps of air. Assured that I wouldn't throw up, I slid into my car. I was in no condition to question anyone else. I drove to Stevie's house, hoping she wouldn't be home yet.

Stevie stood in the kitchen. I would have preferred quiet, without the need to talk.

"You look awful," she said when I stumbled in.

"You look gorgeous," I told her, noticing her drab tan dress.

226

"Are you sick?"

"No." I leaned on the broken stove, then pulled my hand off it. "What kind of stove do you want?"

She squinted at me.

"Okay, I broke it. I'll get you another one. What kind do you want? Does it matter?"

"*It* is the mouth of the home. Does it matter!" She threw her hands out. Stomped off. Slammed a door.

The mouth of a home. What the hell?

I peered down the hall. The candle-room door was shut. Had she gone in there to meditate? Or call on bad spirits to attack me while I slept?

Cealie, Cealie, I thought, shaking my head. *You don't believe in psychic foolishness, yet you keep coming up with thoughts that it might work.*

Exhausted, I dragged myself to my bedroom. I shut and locked the door, threw myself across the made bed, and slept.

Knocking came from my door.

"Cealie," my cousin said, "if you're sleeping, it's time to get up."

I burrowed my head deeper into the pillow.

She rapped on my door. "Cealie, get up. If you're sick, I'll bring you to a doctor, but get up. You won't be able to sleep tonight."

I was sure I looked as exhausted as Lark had when she'd opened the door to the priest's house. I opened mine.

"Ugh," Stevie said. "You look bad."

I fought the retort pushing across my tongue only because I had to rush to the bathroom. Gil crossed my mind as I wondered how he'd made it to the bathroom at his restaurant. I would call him. But maybe, like me, he needed a long nap this afternoon. I'd check with him later.

"Food's ready," Stevie called soon afterward, hearing me open the bathroom door.

I entered the kitchen, and enticing aromas greeted me. "What'll we have?"

"Pizza. And special dessert, blueberry pie."

More blue?

"I'm not hungry." I rushed out of the kitchen before I had to look at the pie.

Moments later Stevie came to my room. I sat in a stuffed chair, taking deep breaths and then closing my eyes and sending my thoughts off.

"Were you sleeping again?" she asked.

"No, trying to meditate."

"Great. Was it working?"

"I don't know. I was imagining myself on a beach."

She nodded. "Good start. Now feel the ocean breezes across your skin. Listen to the waves rolling in. Immerse yourself in this scene."

"I did."

"So what's the problem?"

"After all that, I pictured myself on a beach towel in a bathing suit. And my gosh, do you know how much weight I need to lose?"

"What?"

"I've been sitting here, trying to hold in my stomach. I've imagined the huge weights I'd need to use to tone my arms. And my legs are so pathetic. Cellulite's striking my behind."

She actually looked amazed. "You could see all of that in your mind's eye? Maybe *you're* the one in the family with extra-psychic abilities."

"No way. I just know my body's gone to pot." I stood up.

"You look great, Cealie."

I peered at my stomach which had disgustingly gotten too big to hold in without great effort. And I looked at Stevie's face.

Her smile looked genuine. Sincere.

I was flattered. "I need to shed some pounds," I said demurely. "And I've got to tone my arms and legs. Probably do some exercises that are supposed to tighten the skin on the neck."

She turned away, no longer interested. I hadn't even mentioned my mustache.

Stevie, I noted in her overlarge long dress, could probably stand to do all those exercises and much more to regain any semblance of her previous body size.

But who was I to analyze another person's changed shape and weight?

"As long as I have to stay here, maybe I can exercise," I said, following her out my room. "You go to a gym, right?" I groaned inwardly, not believing I'd asked that. We were supposed to work out earlier this week, but problems had stopped us.

"Okay, Cuz, I get the message. I'm too fat. I'll start doing something about it."

"No, you're not fat. I'm fat. Look, this is fat." I poked out my stomach. Made my jaw slacken.

"You're right. You need to lose weight."

I stared at her as she walked away from me. What did she mean? Had I become *that* overweight?

"I've got a meeting," she said, heading for the kitchen. "You can come if you want."

"Not with those stop-smoking people? You said you wouldn't go around them anymore."

"I know, but I need them."

"One of them might try to kill you."

She inhaled. Exhaled. "So would a cigarette. And I sure want a lot of them."

"Are you taking those pills Dr. Wallo gave you?"

She nodded, face tense.

"Good, but don't go to the meeting. You and I will exercise and meditate together, and you'll get rid of that urge. You'll see." I smiled wide.

"We'll start tonight, two a.m. But right now, I'm going to that meeting."

"You can't." I clutched her arm.

She swung it away from me. Stevie went through the doorway to her garage. I rushed behind. Jumped in her car and buckled my seatbelt. Watched the dark mountainside without seeing anything while she drove. She did say two a.m., didn't she?

"Why did you groan?" she asked.

I shook my head. Didn't need to give up on our exercise plan so soon.

CHAPTER 24

Only a handful of cars were parked near the building where Stevie's group met. She left her car with theirs. My hair blew in a warm breeze while she and I walked on the faintly lit sidewalk between shrubs toward the meeting hall. I recalled a smoke smell. The glowing tip of a cigarette.

"I'll come in there in a minute," I told Stevie.

She made a face and went inside, possibly thinking I needed to pass gas.

I elbowed through the thick shrubs that someone had hidden between when we met here, the same day Pierce Trottier died.

Behind tall shrubs, I stood in almost total darkness. A faint bit of light reached back here from a pole light near the sidewalk. I kept totally still. No smoke smell lingered from anyone who might have just been outside. Could a person here have seen who was up there on the sidewalk?

I couldn't. I shifted around, poking my head from one tiny space to another one. I discovered a spot where I could see, and probably no one out there could see me.

A bug flitted near my face. I swatted it, finding I didn't want to make too much noise or too large a motion. Maybe someone else from The Quitters Group would arrive, someone who could be a killer.

I held my breath. Didn't want to make leaves rustle.

Sound came of a car moving near. I ducked. Stooped.

Someone had smoked back here that night. Maybe put out a cigarette?

I studied the small area I could see and ran my hand across the ground, shoving my fingers as far as I could reach. I felt something soft—a smashed cigarette butt. I slipped it into my purse and felt around for another one.

A car door slammed. Clicking heels approached on the sidewalk.

Before the woman could come near and see me jumping out from behind bushes, I shoved out of my hiding space. I'd just reached the sidewalk when she walked near. The wind blew up her brassy red hair. Here, under the lamppost, I spied her black roots.

"Hey, uh . . ." she said, trying to place me.

"Cealie Gunther. I came to visit you." I put out my hand to shake hers. "Hi, Jenna."

Her frown at my palm made me notice the dirt on it. "Sorry," I said, and wiped my hands on my slacks. We walked inside the building.

"How's your story coming along?" she asked.

"Great."

I'd faked writing a story about her and taken her picture. She was the one who hadn't quit that first day. She'd walked out of the meeting and hidden behind those shrubs to smoke. Did I have a butt she'd smashed out?

We didn't have time for more conversation before reaching the room with the others. I did feel braver having her walk in there with me. I doubted that many in that room loved me.

Stevie sat in the same chair as before. Ish stood in front of her. As I entered, he turned away. Kern Parfait sat, his shoes shiny, not one blade of grass on them or his cuffs. He squeezed his face into a prune-like expression, keeping his stare aimed at me. Father Paul Edward wasn't there. I took an empty chair beside Stevie.

Something wasn't right with this group. One of them, especially, hadn't given me answers that made me satisfied.

A poster on a tripod was entitled "Ten Steps to Staying Quit." Ish passed out papers to everyone except me. Stevie's paper had the same heading as the poster.

"Tonight we learn how to *stay* quit," Ish told the group. "You've all been through the really hard part of quitting smoking. Now you'll find out what methods you might use to keep from ever smoking again."

"I've done number one on the page," Stevie said. "I take deep breaths and hold them. Then count backwards."

"Is that really relaxing?" Jenna asked, and Stevie nodded.

Ish eyed me. "What are you doing?" he asked, annoyed.

"Inhaling. Holding my breath and exhaling."

"But you never smoked, right?"

"Only twice at the graveyard, but I choked." I grinned at him.

He faced the others. "This number two is an excellent thing to do, especially now that it's late springtime. Exercise. Any form will do. Running, jogging, swimming. If you get tense, you can walk outside and take a brisk stroll around a block or two."

I pretended to hold something to my mouth between my fingers. I took a deep breath and then puffed my cheeks and blew.

Ish stared. "Would you stop pretending you're smoking?"

"I'm not. I'm sucking on a straw. Remind you of anyone?"

A gasp came from Stevie. A sharp inhale from Kern.

"I'm not trying to be rude or defame anyone's memory," I said. "I just think somebody needs to be remembered here."

"That's a good point," Jenna said. "Let's all say a silent prayer for our friend, Fawn."

I lowered my head. Didn't close my eyes. I wanted to see

what others were doing.

Stevie crossed herself. The men didn't even lower their heads.

"Now," Ish said, "let's move on to point three."

How discouraging. How little concern for the dead woman I'd thought might have become their friend.

I needed to find out more.

I made my hand form a tight circle and brought it to my lips. I inhaled hard, sucking in my stomach. Then moved my hand aside, puffed my cheeks, and blew.

Ish's cheeks reddened. "Could you be less distracting while sucking your pretend straw?"

With my hand making a circle, I brought it to my lips. Shoved my chest way out while I inhaled. I blew exceptionally hard into my hand.

"Cealie!" my cousin said, but I ignored her.

Ish stomped to right in front of me. "So what in the hell was that?"

"I'll give you a hint. It's not a balloon." I waited a second while veins protruded in his neck. "I'm wondering what it's like to blow up a really big doll. One that I could hang from something. Like a rafter."

Kern let out a sound of disgust. He pushed back in his chair.

Jenna looked at me curiously.

Ish's vision appeared to go inside himself. He seemed to make a decision. Looked at me.

"I don't know that it's any of your business, but maybe I can get you to shut up. Father Paul Edward and I are good friends. We have been for a number of years."

"Really?" I said. "Did you go to school together?"

"Yes, the seminary. But I decided it wasn't for me."

I couldn't envision this man as a priest.

"We used to play pranks on each other," Ish said. "Paul was coming over for a barbecue, but somebody needed him at the last minute, so he couldn't come."

I pictured four people who supposedly often needed the priest. Pretty people.

"So you got a doll instead of him?" I asked, even more confused.

"He'd been telling me I was too lonesome. That a man shouldn't stay by himself."

"So that was your girlfriend we saw?" I said with disgust and pushed to my feet.

"No. That was *me*." He swung away and walked beyond the poster. "I'm a miserable, lonely man, but no, I don't stoop to dating a woman you'd buy in a plastic bag. It was supposed to be me." He poked his chest with his finger. "I couldn't find a male doll, although I'm sure they exist. And I wasn't trying to kill it. I'd dressed it like a man and wasn't trying to hang it. I was only trying to make it stay upright."

I put my hand up to stop him. He looked too sad, too miserable standing there, confessing to me and this group. "That's okay," I said. "You don't need to go on."

"Yes, I do." He aimed his finger at my face. "You're the one who blamed me. Now I want you to know. I want all of you to know what a pathetic creature I am."

"Oh, crap!" Kern shoved up to his feet. "I didn't come here to listen to this."

"I never put a cigarette to my lips, but I might after dealing with you," Ish told me.

I wanted to rush out. Or drop and crawl away for causing this man such anguish. He owed me nothing. No explanation. "That's all right," I said. "Please stop."

He continued, "I was making the doll that represented me stay up straight. I'd tried tying the rope under its arms, but the head kept falling." He threw his arms out with a huff of disgust. "And I didn't put lipstick on it to make it a woman. I was trying to make the person smile, me, to show I was happy."

I cringed. My stomach clenched in a knot. I didn't want him so miserable.

"So that's it," he said. "I fooled you, didn't I?"

I nodded, disgusted with myself. Oh, he'd certainly fooled me. "I'm really sorry."

His cheeks remained pink. "Please sit down," he told Kern. "You can stay. I'm not a pervert, no matter what some people here might think."

I sat in my chair. Felt Stevie's stare on my face.

After a long moment, Kern sat.

Ish cleared his throat. He took up his meeting, continuing with the third step in remaining a nonsmoker.

So many negative thoughts about what I'd done thumped around in my head, I couldn't hear his words. I'd heard enough of them anyway.

"You are some judge of character!" Stevie griped the minute the meeting ended and we stomped out of the building.

"But I thought—"

"Hush!"

"But—"

"No!" She flattened her palm across my lips.

We reached her car before anyone else from the group came outside.

Neither of us spoke all the way to her house. Stevie threw herself out of her car, hurtled inside, and slammed the door.

I tried lifting my chin, giving myself good self-talk. I hadn't purposely made the man feel bad. And the only reason I made the police show up at his house the other night was I thought he'd killed a man, or someone had killed him.

See, Cealie? You're not a horrible person. I stood in the garage, trying to make myself believe that thought. I forced a smile.

Gave up when it drooped.

Walking inside, I recalled that I needed to check on Gil.

"The Mexican Hat Dance" played. I dug in my purse, felt something soft, and smelled a foul odor. I pulled out the object. The nasty cigarette butt. It made my purse stink. The song kept playing. I grabbed my phone and saw the call came from Gil.

"How are you?" I asked, stopping in the kitchen.

"My, uh, leg feels a little better."

"Great." That's what I needed. Something cheerful. Gil was improving.

I noted the butt I held. Plum lipstick around it. I set the butt on the countertop.

"You haven't seen the news tonight," Gil said.

That wasn't a question. "No."

"Cajun Delights is closed."

I plopped on a chair, distraught. "Oh, Gil, you closed your new restaurant?"

"Every one of my Cajun Delights restaurants has been shut down until further notice."

CHAPTER 25

"Who shut down your restaurants?" I asked Gil.

"I closed them. Not even one person came here to eat tonight."

"That's not fair. Fawn died in your restaurant, but it was probably from natural causes. And why all of your restaurants? They couldn't have all been affected."

"Business in all of them slowed to almost a halt since the national media sensationalized the death. We announced that we decided to shut down until investigations here are complete."

"But that could take a while. And so many employees depend on you for their income."

"I'll keep paying them."

I knew Gil did well financially. But what he was talking about could probably break him in no time.

"Can I help you with anything?" I asked. "I have money. And a shoulder to lean on."

"Getting too close to your shoulder can be painful."

A dual meaning. I kicked hard. And I'd left him before, so he couldn't leave me. Our partings hurt both of us. "I'm sorry," I said.

"At least you weren't wearing pointed toes. But I'm better. I have to go."

"Let me know if I can help."

"Right." He clicked off.

I considered a minute and realized I'd hurt his manhood

again. It wasn't enough that I'd kicked his family jewels. Now I'd offered the man money.

I needed to use better judgment before I acted or spoke.

Stevie's candle-room door was still shut. I pressed my ear against it.

Eerie utterances. Possibly in her voice, but much deeper.

I didn't want to figure out what to do now. I shut down all thoughts and took a shower. Crawled into my bed and slept.

In the morning I woke with negative thoughts. Gil, bankrupt. Ish, explaining his blow-up doll to others because of me. Gil, in pain because of me. Stevie, maybe still in that room with candles. Angry at me.

I slid out of bed to make sure she hadn't fallen asleep in there.

My legs hurt, then gave way. I fell to my knees. "What the hell?" I blurted.

I held onto the bed and pulled myself up. My shins ached. And now also both knees.

I limped down the hall. Stopped at the room with the shut door and tried the knob. Locked. "Stevie," I said, knocking. I sniffed the door. No burnt candle odor. She must have gone to school.

The scent of cinnamon rolls vacuumed me into the kitchen. I was glad to note that my legs started to feel better.

A saucer held two rolls. I ate one before touching the door of the stove. It was cold. The rolls were on the counter beside a toaster oven. I felt inside that oven. It was hot.

Ravenously hungry, I ate both sweet rolls and touched Minnie's soil.

"Still damp enough," I said to her. Minnie looked healthy, from the poufs on her bumpy pink head to her triangular thick stem.

I mentally patted my back. I'd done something right. At one time Minnie kept slumping. Her poufs spread. Then I'd learned I shouldn't water her so much. Cranberry juice was also a no-no. And now she was looking much better.

"If this were my kitchen," I said, standing beside her to drink orange-pineapple juice, "I wouldn't replace the stove. There would be no need to." I grinned, noting the fridge, microwave, and toaster oven. What more did a homemaker need?

I washed and put away my glass and saucer, deciding today I would buy Stevie more toss-away cups and plates. I'd also get her a stove since she seemed to like them.

I checked the phone book for places that sold appliances. I was near the back door and heard a man holler. I went to the porch.

"Come here!" he yelled, making me take a quick step back. And then he whistled. A dog barked. It sounded not far outside Stevie's gate. "Come here, Rezo," the man yelled.

From the porch I saw him near the road. Large man in a tan sweat suit. Black cap.

Pumping their arms as they walked behind him were the two women with white hair. None of them glanced at me.

I went through the house to the front, got in my car and drove off, worried. Two members of the group that Stevie belonged to had died.

The only ones left were Kern, the priest, Ish, Jenna, and Stevie.

Fawn McKenzie's death confirmed a connection to the death of Pierce Trottier, at least in my mind.

I'd spoken a bit with all of the male members of The Quitters Group. I'd had to rush away from Jenna's house when I told her that fib about wanting her picture and a story. The notebook I'd bought and disposable camera were still in my car. I drove to her house.

Parking in front, I rang her doorbell. Jenna didn't respond.

A vacant lot with overgrown grass was to the left. The frame house to the right of hers was dull yellow, a new white truck parked in front. I went there.

A woman with a round face opened her door an inch and kept the safety chain on. "Yes?"

I plastered on my nice-grandma smile. "Sweetie, I've been working on a story about your neighbor, Jenna Griggs, and I need to take a couple more pictures of her." I held up my camera and notebook. I'd told the truth. I was making up a story about Jenna right now.

The woman's face softened. "What did you need with me?"

"I'm trying to find her, and she doesn't seem to be home."

"Did you try Westell Brothers?"

"Where's that?"

"On Bowman Road. Jenna's probably working right now."

"Thanks." I was turning away but noted her disappointed stare at my camera. "Before I go, it would sure add to the story if I could snap a picture of Jenna's neighbor. What did you say your name is?"

"Gwen Allen."

I held up my camera while she unlocked her safety chain. Gwen stuck her face in the open doorway and smiled. I snapped her picture. "Another one?" I said, and she changed pose. "Got ya. Thanks." I took another picture and headed off her porch.

"What magazine did you say that will be in?"

I kept going, pretending not to hear.

"What magazine?" She walked right behind me.

"Good Girls."

"Is that new? It's not porn, is it?"

"No, ma'am, and you'll be in the first issue that hits the stands." I pinched my palm.

Her smile widened. I slid into my car. "What's the article

about?" She poked her face near my window.

I cranked the motor and drove off. Thinking up too many lies created by my first lie was more untruths than I could handle. Maybe she'd think I hadn't heard her final question.

I needed to decipher what was truth and what wasn't in two people's deaths. Maybe a person who killed once did what I did with lies: became proficient with practice. I didn't want to lie. I especially didn't want anyone to kill, particularly not the people around me. I needed to find Jenna Griggs.

Jenna was the first person I saw inside Westell Brothers. "Hello, how *are* you?" she said with a huge smile, gliding toward me like a salesperson hoping for a smashing sale. She put her hand out and made eye contact. Recognition registered.

"I'm great," I said.

"You're doing that story about people who quit smoking."

I nodded but didn't believe she had quit. And I didn't need to get her against me by mentioning that guess. I glanced into the store to see what products she'd sell here. "You have appliances."

"With the best prices in town. Guaranteed."

"I want a stove."

"Right this way. Gas or electric? Built in or freestanding?"

I paid so little attention to stoves I wasn't certain what type Stevie had. I did usually pay attention to color. "Black."

"Here are black ones." She swept her arm toward a large array.

I rubbed my hand over their shiny tops, deciding not to tell her all I normally did with my own stove was dust it. She wanted a sale. I wanted information. We could fulfill each other's desires.

"Pierce Trottier's death was a horrible thing," I said, fingering knobs on a stove.

A rush of air left her nostrils. "Can you imagine?" she asked.

"Imagine what?"

"If it was *your* cousin."

Fear for Stevie gripped my chest. "Why do you say that?"

"Can you imagine what it would be like if yours died? Pierce was my first cousin."

"Yes, I read that in his obituary." And now might not be the time to ask about his two children again.

Jenna nodded. Her gaze slid toward the rear of Westell Brothers, making me realize I'd spoken too loudly. She might get concerned about her job.

I opened the stove's oven and looked in, pretending to care. Jenna's boss might be looking. My action showed I was interested in stoves.

"What killed him?" I asked.

"Pierce?" Her eyes looked fearful. I needed to convince her that she could trust me.

"Yes." I gripped her hand. "Jenna, I'm so sorry about your relative. I'm sure you know he died in my cousin's yard. I fell on him. *Fell* on him. And still feel him against my legs. I care. I need to know what happened."

Her face softened. "We weren't really that close."

"I understand. Stevie's my cousin. We aren't really close, either." Our relationship was on and off, but that didn't matter at the moment.

She glanced worriedly toward the store's rear.

"Look in here." I pointed inside the oven. "Make believe you're happily selling me an appliance." I grinned at the oven.

She bent to it, plastering on a smile. "He might have died from nicotine overdose."

I let go of the oven door. It slammed shut. "Nicotine overdose?"

"He had a heart condition. That's why he needed to quit smoking."

"I thought he quit the night before, the night Stevie and most of the others did."

The store's front door opened. A couple entered and glanced at us. They moved toward the rear. A male salesman aimed for them.

"I need to get back to work," Jenna said.

"You're working now. I'll buy something. Smile." I plastered on my own grin.

She smiled, too. "So this is the kind of stove you need? Freestanding?"

I tried to picture the one in Stevie's kitchen. "Yes, it is."

"Okay, good."

I envisioned something else I had seen. And the smell. "It looked like Pierce had gum between his teeth when he died. And he smelled of vomit."

She looked wounded.

"I'm sorry. I'm just remembering."

"It's okay. Yes, they said he had chewed nicotine gum and vomited."

"Why?"

She took a breath. "He was probably poisoned."

"From nicotine gum? People chew it all the time and don't die."

"It wasn't only that." Jenna glanced away. She didn't want to speak of this.

A woman in a tan pantsuit came near. She eyed Jenna and then me. Jenna's boss.

"Hi. Nice stoves," I told her. "Jenna is about to sell me a really nice one."

She nodded and ambled away.

"I'll have to get busy," Jenna said.

"I really want a stove."

"This one?"

I checked out the stove's burners, trying to recall Stevie's. There were flat burners on both sides, except for the parts I'd dented. Yes, it was electric.

"Let me check the other black electric ones you have," I said like I knew something about these appliances. She pointed to three others. I glanced at them, comparing prices. I moved toward the last one that cost hundreds more than the others. Shiny black top and oven door. A couple more thingies on top, one of them maybe a grill. "This one's probably better," I said.

"Definitely."

"Good. I'll take it."

She looked relieved and wrote up the order. "They'll deliver tomorrow. Someone has to be there."

"I will." I paid, again grateful money was no longer an issue in my life. Right now solving a murder was. Or possibly two of them.

"Can I call you at home later?" I asked.

She diverted her eyes. Kept them down. "You can try to reach me."

I thanked Jenna and left Westell Brothers determining she would screen her calls. Mine would not be answered.

I'd met one person who knew Pierce Trottier's fiancée and might know and be free with gossip about him by now. Glancing into my rearview mirror, I wondered how my strawberry waves would look nipped a wee bit. My next stop—Audrey Ray's salon.

Chapter 26

The car parked at Beauty First made me feel better about my choice of hairdresser. Today I wasn't Audrey Ray's only customer.

I parked, left my car. Stopped walking as another woman came out.

Her hair was red like mine was now, only hers was flaming. Sunlight highlighted its bright yellow tones.

"Hi," she said, tossing her mane and touching her hair like she wanted to make certain I noticed it. Only a blind person wouldn't.

I told myself I shouldn't go in this place. I took a breath going inside, remembering I was only coming for information and a nip, not more color. The strong sting of perm solution hit my nostrils.

"Cealie, hello." Audrey Ray quit sweeping brown hair into a dustpan. "Is something wrong with your hair?"

"Not at all. I thought you might give it a trim."

"Already?"

"It grows real fast, and I like sitting in beauty salon chairs."

My right palm almost bled.

"I understand that. Come on to the washbasin."

She washed my hair and had me sit in front of those horrid brilliant lights. The black plastic drape around my neck made my loose skin stand out, blending well with my spotlighted face wrinkles. She enhanced the picture by pinning up little patches of my wet hair.

"A trim, right?" she asked. Blue glitter shone from her thick mascara. "Does everybody love your new color?"

"They think it's unique."

"Great." She started nipping.

"You told me about someone," I said. "Pierce Trottier's fiancée."

"Yes, Kelly's so pretty. A great customer."

"She must have been devastated when he died."

"Yep." Audrey stared at my reflection. "She was so pissed, she would've killed him herself if he wasn't already dead."

"What?"

"He had sex with somebody else before he died."

"You're kidding me. Who?"

"Nobody knows. And I shouldn't talk about it." She yanked bobby pins out of my hair and resumed cutting.

"Audrey, he died in my cousin's yard. I didn't see him when I shoved her stuck gate open, and I tripped on his body." Jitters ran through me, picturing him, feeling the man against my skin. "I *need* to know what happened."

Her reflection held on mine. She broke eye contact in the mirror and cut my hair. "Kelly said he had fingernail scratches all over his back, especially around three nicotine patches that were stuck on him."

"Three? I think I saw one. The bottom of his shirt was pulled up. I thought it was a bandage."

"They think the woman he had his *afternoon delight* with probably slapped them on him. He might not have noticed since it seemed she got wild with him. He probably couldn't reach where they were, much less put them on straight. They were close together behind his heart."

"And he had a heart condition."

She nodded, letting another patch of my hair down. "He

didn't smoke a whole lot, but his doctor had told him he needed to totally quit. Kelly said he chewed nicotine gum."

"He didn't get her to put those patches on his back?"

"They both knew better than that. The gum's instructions said not to use any other nicotine product at the same time. The guy teaching his stop-smoking class told people in the group that, too."

"It's hard to believe using the gum and patches could kill a person. I'm sure other people have done that and survived."

She leaned toward my image. "But none of them had extra nicotine added to the patches."

I leaned closer toward *her* image, eyes wide. "Extra nicotine?"

"They did some tests. Pierce and the patches all contained too much nicotine." Audrey Ray kept snipping. "And his partner might have suggested he smoke a few, just that once, after their sex. Mega doses of poisonous nicotine."

"Wow, so nicotine really killed him." I noticed what she was doing. "You're cutting a lot. I only wanted a slight trim." I glanced at hair on the floor.

She grabbed my chin and lifted it. "Stay straight. You don't want me to mess this up, do you?"

I shook my head. Then realized what I'd done.

"Oh, pooh. Well, I can probably fix that." Audrey Ray stared at the back of my head. I was scared to ask.

"How could patches have extra nicotine?" I asked, getting my mind off whatever she was doing back there with her scissors.

"Somebody could have injected some."

I jerked toward her image. "You're kidding."

She shook her head. Then stared at the rear of my hair and looked grim.

"I should go," I said, fearing what she'd done.

"Let me straighten this out first."

I focused on not saying a word to distract her. I kept my gaze away from the mirror, considering what she told me.

"All shaped up." She plucked the remaining bobby pins out of my hair, ran blue gook between her fingers and through my waves, and picked up a blow dryer.

I touched her hand to ask something before she made noise. "You say his fiancée is terrific. But maybe she found out he had an affair and went into a rage and killed him."

"Kelly teaches fifth graders. She never left school that day. The cops checked."

"It was after school hours when I arrived at my cousin's house and found him."

"Kelly tutors until six. Her students and some parents swore she stayed with them. She's not the kind of girl to do that anyway."

Audrey Ray blasted my head with hot air. Her dryer kicked up my hair's volume.

"That's kind of high," I said, pressing it down on top.

"What?" She didn't shut off her noisemaker but used her fingers to draw my waves up even higher.

I looked like I wore a scarlet crown when I walked out. I waited till I sat in my car to flatten the top and press against the sides. I had refused politely when she'd offered a hand mirror for me to check the back.

"It's a kind of combined Retro and Afro," she'd said of that part of my hair, and I didn't want to see what that meant.

I did want to see how Gil was doing. I punched his number on my cell phone.

He didn't answer. No request for a message came on.

I didn't know if he was staying in Gatlinburg or around Pigeon Forge but had an idea he might be at his restaurant.

I went there.

CLOSED UNTIL FURTHER NOTICE. That large sign out

front of Cajun Delights made my spirits plunge. A ball of tears stuck in my throat.

One truck was there, a dark green one.

I went to the entrance and pulled on the doors. Both locked. I peeked through the stained-glass.

All dark inside.

I walked to the rear of the restaurant. A gray cypress fence matched the building. I opened the gate and walked through the small enclosed yard, went up the two steps and pulled on the door.

It opened.

"Gil," I yelled. "Gil, it's me. Don't shoot," I said with a laugh. He never carried a weapon.

The employees' lounge I entered was dark. So was the rear hall. I ran my hand along the walls and door frames as I moved. I knew where Gil's office should be, but everything was so black I wasn't sure I was heading in the right direction.

"Gil, it's me," I called, reaching a wall, determining I should turn left. And then cold dread washed through me.

A woman had just suspiciously died in this place.

Suppose a killer was in here now instead of Gil? The truck he used wasn't green, was it? No, the one he'd had here before was silver.

A door creaked open. It sounded down the hall to the left.

I stood spellbound, deciding what I'd do if a thug came out, especially one carrying a gun.

Shrugging my shoulder bag to get its weight, I already knew it was feather light. I kept it, like my life now, free of most things that weighed me down. I mentally scrolled through it—wallet, keys, tissue, lipstick. Nothing that would hurt a person.

Lights were on in the room beyond the door that was slowly opening, letting me glimpse my surroundings.

This hall was kept neat and clear like in the rest of Gil's

restaurants, making me angry. If it held junk like large pots or possibly knives, I'd have a weapon. Running back through a straight hallway wouldn't provide me much protection if a person aimed a gun in here.

A few chairs were stacked near the wall. I grabbed the one on top and with my other hand, dug keys out of my purse. Keys jabbed into a person's eyes would really slow him down but I doubted I could do such a thing. Unless I felt severely threatened.

The door yanked all the way open.

I shrieked and pulled on the chair.

The stack tumbled between me and the person coming out of the room. I jumped back, but held my arm straight, aiming my keys up toward the person's face.

"Cealie, no!" Gil ducked, seeing my keys up, although they didn't get close to him.

The chairs did. Some struck his hip.

"Oh, no," I yelped, trying to block all the chairs from getting him. They clattered to the floor.

Gil jumped aside before the whole stack slammed his body.

"You didn't answer when I called you," I said, wincing. I straightened the bottom chair. Pulled the next one on top of it.

"That's okay. Let's leave those alone for now." He stood on the opposite side of the fallen stack. "Come into my office, Cealie."

I squeezed alongside the downed chairs, reached him, and puckered. He gave me a quick kiss on the lips.

Gil took baby steps, groaned, and bent like an old man needing a cane.

"I'm sorry. Did I do that to you?" I put my hands out to hold him in case he fell.

He limped to the chair near his desk. Dropped to it. Moaned. "I'm good."

"I didn't mean to do that. I thought you were a bad guy."

"I can be—whenever you let me." He smiled his wicked, sexy smile and reached for my butt. That movement made him yelp.

I gripped his hand and placed it on his desk. "Did I just do all of that to you?"

He grinned wryly. "I was trying to shuffle out to the hall to complain that you'd really injured me the other day. But that injury is doing much better." He rubbed his hip.

"But not the new one," I said.

He shook his head. "Not that one." He massaged his opposite thigh. "You could do this for me and make it all better."

"Right, and then if you tried sexy moves, you'd yell for sure."

"I'd yell with pleasure." He smiled. Pain crept into his face. "Next time you feel threatened, maybe go a little easier on body parts."

"What would you have me do to protect myself?"

"Throw yourself at me. You might knock me down, but then you'd already be on top. Good position." He gave me his wicked smile, and I was tempted to do what he suggested.

No! Stop that, Cealie.

The man was hurt. And I did not want to have relations with Gil again. Ever. I needed to live my own life, gaining my own certainty like he had his.

"You're tempted, aren't you?" he said with his grin.

"No." I rounded the desk to get opposite him before my resolve broke down. "Tell me what you learned about Fawn McKenzie."

His demeanor turned solemn. "A shrimp killed her."

"Excuse me."

"You know how severely allergic I am to shrimp. So was she. Fawn was sitting at my table. The deadly seafood was probably meant for me."

CHAPTER 27

I dropped onto a chair to decipher what Gil told me.

"Gil, I was eating with you in Vicksburg the day your face swelled like a puffer fish," I said. "I held your hand in the ambulance and prayed like I'd never prayed before."

He sat at his desk and nodded. "That's probably what saved me."

"But that was at another restaurant. It's when you learned you were so allergic." I couldn't get a handle on what he said happened. The doctor had told him if he ever ate shrimp again, reactions could occur much quicker. Gil could be dead before an ambulance arrived. "How could the shrimp be meant for you? It could have killed you."

His gaze scanned his clean desktop as though searching for answers. He looked at me. "Fawn was highly allergic to most seafood. She ordered chicken gumbo. A few chopped shrimp were in it."

My jaw dropped open. I forced it shut. "How did that happen? Aren't the portions frozen? When was that gumbo cooked? Who had access to it? Why would it be aimed at you?" Too many questions came to mind for me to express. Too many fearful thoughts. "She was really murdered?"

"I'm afraid so, Cealie. And I feel responsible." He looked miserable.

I jumped up from my chair and gripped his hands. "You had nothing to do with what happened."

253

The skin between his eyes creased deeply. Sure, he believed he was responsible. "The police are questioning everyone who might have gone into the kitchen."

"That's a lot of waiters and waitresses, besides all of the cooks."

"And others who could have gone in. Nobody else is supposed to enter the kitchen, but sometimes customers slip in for a couple of minutes to check out the equipment and see how things work."

"Or drop in an ingredient that might kill someone."

His gaze shifted to my left. He swung his eyes toward me. "When the waiter turned in Fawn's order, he told the cook he needed one bowl of chicken gumbo for my table."

I knew what that order meant. Because of Gil's severe allergy, the kitchen staff and waiters had been told about it with a warning to be careful not to bring any shrimp to his table. This was the case in each of his restaurants. The only exceptions had been when I was with him, and he'd ordered seafood for me. When we were together, he knew he wouldn't accidentally get my shrimp.

Fawn had been sitting alone at his table.

I squeezed his hands. "Maybe the shrimp was put in there a while ago, before the chicken gumbo was frozen."

"The police are checking into it. There was fresh shrimp around for other dishes. I'll get the reports when they're finished."

"In the meantime, you've closed all of your restaurants. But you might still be in danger."

He appeared to force a wry grin. "Somebody could take me in and protect me," he said with a laugh.

"Tempting. But it's crowded at Stevie's house. She has candles and altars and stones." I kissed his cheek. "Keep in touch. And watch what you eat."

I went out the way I'd come in, quietly picking up the fallen chairs. If Gil heard me, he'd try to rush out to help. I didn't think he'd be able to rush anywhere too soon. My fault.

My main problem now was I needed to help find a killer before this man who was most important to me became a victim.

Lots of people I'd met in this town had come to Gil's place to try out the food. Some seemed capable of murder. One or more might have killed Pierce Trottier. Did they also know Fawn? I didn't want to believe anyone would try to kill Gil.

Big brave man that he was, he certainly wouldn't ask for my help.

But one person had secretly slipped a small deadly item that might have quickly killed him into food delivered to his table.

I needed to protect my man!

I drove to Stevie's house, where I'd quietly sit and consider fearful people and events, maybe getting ideas of what I might do.

Her garage was open, the car inside. Disappointed, I went in through the front.

Her utterances were loud. The minute I walked in I heard them—somewhat like chants and then like sounds I'd never heard coming from a human.

The door to her room with the candles was open. The lit candles flickered. My cousin lay face down. She wore that gauzy white gown. Her guttural sounds mingled with high-pitched ones. And then stopped. Lifting her head, she turned toward me.

Her gaze met mine. Stevie's eyes appeared extra strange, opaquely blending with her fair skin, yet deep and piercing. They looked angry. Sent a jolt of fear through me.

She rose from the floor. Keeping her stare at me, she swept

over to the door and shut it in my face. It clicked as she locked it.

My legs froze in place. I didn't know who my cousin was in that trancelike state. When her gaze turned to me moments before, she hadn't seemed to know who she was, either. My shins ached.

I rushed to my bedroom. Locked my door. Ran my gaze over my room. Nothing out of place. I checked the closet.

No bad guys inside.

I peeked behind the curtains. The window was locked. No new items under my bed. I opened my unlocked suitcase that still sat on my bed. The few items inside looked the way I'd left them.

I thought of Gil and how I'd hurt him. And how I wanted to help him with that problem at the restaurant, too. I wanted to take care of him. To protect him and not let anymore harm come to him.

I sat on the bed and massaged my legs. The ache circled from my shins to my calf muscles. I groaned. Maybe these pains that came and went were all in my head instead of my legs.

Needing to write, I found that the lamp tables near the bed didn't have drawers. I opened the bottom dresser drawer I hadn't checked before, hoping to find paper.

More nude men. These magazines looked worse than the first ones I'd seen in the other drawers.

My face heated. Guilt? Excitement?

I shut the drawer and envisioned Gil's face and body. Hmm, maybe not as firm and chiseled as some of them. But just right for meshing with my mine.

"Stop it, Cealie!" I jerked my eyes open and stomped my foot. I needed Gil's image out of my head.

I remembered the legal pad I'd bought to pretend to interview Jenna Griggs. Stevie surely had paper, but I wouldn't knock on the door to that locked room and ask. I went out to my car, grabbed the notebook off the seat, and went back inside.

Stevie met me in the living room. "You didn't cook supper, did you?"

I shook my head, amazed. She seemed transformed, as though she hadn't been furious with me moments ago.

Or maybe she didn't remember?

"You don't cook too often, do you?" she asked.

"Not if I can help it." I grinned.

She grinned back at me. "I like to cook."

"I know. And when I had family at home, I didn't mind doing it, either. But now it seems such a bother to shop for ingredients for a meal, then spend hours in the kitchen cooking, sitting fifteen minutes to eat, and then cleaning up."

"I'll order pizza. Is pepperoni okay?"

"Yes, but I'll only eat one slice." Pizza contained so many fat grams that this short body usually tried to avoid it. If possible, I preferred not to look like a stump.

Who was this Stevie? I wondered, watching her appear pleased as she located the phone number and ordered.

"I really like your doctor," I said once she hung up. "He's a good man for you to see."

"Dr. Wallo? Yes, having a gay doctor is cool."

I bolted upright. "He is not gay!"

"Everybody knows that's why his wife left him. But they're still friends."

I stifled a grin at this new knowledge, which I might withhold from Gil.

I grabbed my purse to pay for our food. Opened it wide to find my wallet. Got slammed with the stench of dirty ashtray. "Phew," I said and dumped everything on the table. Wallet, lipstick, tissue, keys, tobacco. "Ugh, tobacco." I turned my empty purse over on the trash can and shook it. Only a couple of strands fell out. I rubbed a couple more out of my nice tan straw purse, then smelled inside it. Still horrible.

"What's your problem?" Stevie asked.

"I put a cigarette butt in here and then took it out. My purse still stinks."

"Why would you put a butt in there?"

"I just wanted to."

She watched me a beat. No use telling her I'd gone behind the bushes near her meeting place and found it. Probably because at this moment, that idea seemed stupid.

"It smells that bad after having only one butt in it?" She stuck her nose inside my purse. Handed it to me. "That's not bad."

Without putting my nose close, I was overwhelmed by the odor. "It smells like a barroom."

"You just like to complain."

"I do not. This purse stinks. I'll have to air it out." I sniffed my wallet and tissue. "This all stinks, too." I tossed the tissues into the trash.

"You used to whine and say I pulled your hair."

"You know you did it."

"And you bawled because I took your little jewelry box."

"*You* took it? That was my favorite thing in the world."

"Yeah, when you were six. You even had some jewelry to put in it."

"Just a pink plastic bracelet and a ring. We bent the metal to make the ring fit. It was fake silver."

"I know, but at least you had jewelry. And a special box to put it in."

"I can't believe you took my jewelry box with the dancing ballerina. That box was special. So were the things inside, especially the bracelet that matched my pink barrette."

"Get over it." She turned away.

I grabbed her arm. "What did you do with my things?"

"Traded them with Lucy Black for a Hula Hoop."

"That mean girl, Lucy? And you only got one Hula Hoop for all of my things?"

"Oh, grow up, will you? Forget about that stuff." Stevie yanked her arm away and stomped off.

My jewelry box and jewelry? Grandma Jean gave me the box and the ring. She lived with us only two years when I was a kid and then she died. But she'd pull me to her lap while I was growing, and she would rock and sing to me. That jewelry and box were my only remembrances from her. And Stevie gave them away for a *Hula Hoop?*

My shoulders tensed. I wanted to punch her. I wanted to bawl.

I stood, taking slow breaths to calm myself. Even though that jewelry box and bracelet and ring were most important to me back then, I would only put them away in a closet now, keeping memories.

I loved memories.

But couldn't do a thing about them being gone. I forced thoughts of Stevie's theft away from my mind. I took more cleansing breaths. Picked up my wallet but whiffed its odor. Still too nasty to put in my purse.

On the back porch, I spread my wallet on a rocking chair.

Motion out back snagged my attention.

A truck was pulling off the road to its shoulder behind Stevie's fence. The driver was Audrey Ray.

I waved at her and rushed through the yard and tugged the gate open.

With motor running, she lowered her window. "Hey, Cealie."

"Hi, I saw you stopping. Were you coming over?"

"Actually I was passing by and decided to try to locate where Kelly's fiancé died."

"It was right back there. Do you want to come in?"

"No, I'm tired. Just getting off work."

You had enough business to make you tired? I almost asked, but my brain kicked in.

"Do you live around here?" I asked instead.

"Not really. Well, I'll see you, Cealie."

She drove away. A door slammed.

Stevie stood on her back porch. I was surprised at how well I could see her from the road. Then realized I could see people out here on the road from the porch. Why not the other way around?

"So you were the one who put that butt on my counter," she said, hands on hips, as I walked toward her.

"I found it behind some bushes near the building where your stop-smoking group meets. I want to keep it."

"I threw it away. I'm trying to quit smoking and going through hell making myself believe I don't want one—and you set one of the damned things in the middle of my kitchen to tempt me!"

I reached the porch and looked up at her. "You wouldn't want to smoke a butt. It was nasty. Somebody's dirty butt with plum-colored lipstick on it."

"Who in the hell cares about lipstick? There was a filter and almost half of a cigarette attached to it."

"Don't tell me you would think about lighting something like that and putting it to your lips."

She leaned toward me, nostrils flaring. "Did you ever see an alcoholic trying to quit drinking—and somebody set half a bottle in front of her?"

"No."

"Me neither. But I'm sure it would feel the same way. Thanks for nothing. And what the hell were you doing behind the bushes where we meet? Damn, you're weird!" She swooped back inside.

The screen door slammed.

She took my jewelry box. My beautiful wooden, one and only jewelry box I'd gotten in childhood. And she would have smoked the cigarette somebody else put in her mouth and then mashed on the ground. How nasty was that?

I smelled pizza from out on the porch and walked inside.

Stevie sat at the table, eating the first piece missing from a box. She kept her gaze away from me. From the pantry I grabbed paper plates, took one out, and sat. I grabbed a slice from the box that someone must have just delivered. Anger etched Stevie's face, certainly matched by mine.

I finished one piece. Grabbed another one. Got a bottle of water from the fridge. Sat again and ate the middle part. Sipped my water. She yanked a third chunk from the box. So did I. If I didn't quit eating like this, I'd have to grab my behind to haul it behind me while I waddled.

That thought came and went. I didn't care now. Whatever my cousin did, I could do better. That idea stuck in my brain. Even knowing how ridiculous it was, I clung to the thought.

We each ate five slices. I left the outer rims of my last ones.

Stevie was grabbing her sixth slice. I rushed to the bathroom and heaved. No food came up. Only a determination that I was behaving like a child.

Well, so was she!

And her child was much bigger than mine. That's why she was able to eat so much!

CHAPTER 28

Cealie, get over it, I told myself, tromping down the hall.

In my room I checked out what clean clothes I had left and found few. I chose to go through life lightly now, unfettered by too many things. *Things* needed to be stored and cleaned and sorted and often tied a woman down. I had possessed many things, especially as my business gained success and increased profit. But after years of running around, buying and having to find a place for things, I determined I didn't need most of them. Didn't actually like lots of them. I'd only thought, at the time, that I wanted and could finally afford them.

Now I no longer chased after all the things I'd thought I needed to possess.

Thus I found few items of clothing hanging in the closet. My clean underwear was also scarce.

I returned to the kitchen, where Stevie was tossing the pizza box. "I need to clean some of my clothes," I said.

"There's the washer and dryer." Chill in her tone, she nodded toward the porch.

I gathered my items and took them to the small utility room that opened off the porch, noting that dusk had dropped away to the dark. I tossed my clothes in the washer with washing powder, turned the knob, and walked toward my room.

Down the hall Stevie glanced at me, swept into her altar room, slammed the door, and locked it.

I went to my bedroom, slammed *my* door, and locked it. Immediately felt like a moody child.

Being near my cousin was causing this grumpiness. I needed to take control of my senses and behave like an adult again, even when confronted by her. I needed to learn something definite about the deaths and get the heck away from this town.

Reeling in childish emotions, I grabbed my legal pad and made a list of people I knew who were connected to Pierce Trottier. The police were certainly doing this, and way beyond the investigating I could do. They were also taking care of questioning people connected to the restaurant. I didn't know anything about Fawn McKenzie, except she was attractive, petite, and sucked straws the last days of her life. Also, she belonged to a group with my cousin and a man who'd died. This was the only place I knew to try to connect whoever might have killed both of them.

I listed members of The Quitters Group, leaving lots of blank lines between names.

I stared at the empty spaces, not knowing what else to write.

My mind blanked. It wouldn't wrap around those people's faces and what I'd learned of them. I would have to try again in the morning. I was tired, but my restless mind wasn't sleepy. I dressed for bed and considered reading material. I opened a dresser drawer, grabbed magazines, and took them to bed.

The first one I flipped through was shocking. My cousin actually bought this stuff? I skimmed the second one and shook my head. Horrible. I opened the third one.

Da-dunt, da-dunt, da-dunt.

I shoved up from the covers and grabbed my phone.

"You sound breathless. Were you running?" Gil asked.

"No." I noticed my words were high-pitched. And pictured Gil as I'd seen him often, naked, and knew without doubt I wanted him.

"I thought you might want to know what's going on with me."

"Of course I do." I got ready to hear that his body was all healed. Then we could do wonderful things with it.

"Tomorrow I'm reopening my restaurants."

"Great! All of them?"

"Yes. I don't know if customers will come again, but my hires need to work. I hadn't considered how many people I employ. Business would hurt more the longer we'd keep the restaurants closed."

"I think you've made a wise decision."

"Thanks for your vote of confidence."

I smiled and sat on the bed. "How are your body parts that I mangled?"

"Getting better. Soon I might be able to walk without help." His voice held cheer so that he wouldn't make me feel bad. "What were you doing?" he asked.

I glanced at the pile of half-naked men posing. "Getting ready for bed."

"Need any help?"

"No, thanks, I can do it all by myself."

"I know you can, Cealie. Sometimes I wish you weren't quite so independent."

"And what would you have me be? Totally dependent on a man?"

"No, not totally. Just calm down."

"I've been there, you know, and it doesn't work." After we met I'd told him how I'd depended on my husband, Freddy, to be the other half of a person with me. And then he died and left me alone, needy, not knowing where to take the next step or who I was any longer.

"I'll see you later," Gil said.

I was still huffy when we hung up. I wasn't angry with him. I fumed at the image of myself as I was back then, back when Freddy was dying and then after he went. I became like a bird with one broken wing, with no idea how I'd ever fly again.

Time, friends, and prayers all helped me stand. And now I was rediscovering Cealie and learning more about what I wanted from my life.

I am woman. I can do anything—alone!

My motto flashed through my brain but not too energetically. I gripped my phone. Stared at it. Envisioned Gil.

He hadn't hurt me. If anything, he'd renewed my self-image as a desirable woman. Gil enlivened the dormant side of me. How important was he for doing that?

I needed to let go of the images of any man. Gil. And those men on my bed.

I shoved the magazines back into a drawer and remembered my clothes were still in the washer. I strode outside and turned on the light. In the small utility room off the porch, I dug my clothes out of the washer and tossed my panties in the dryer. Alarm skittered along my skin. A strong sensation told me someone was watching. I smelled smoke.

I looked at the room's doorway, heart pounding.

Nobody visible. Had I imagined a person out there?

I shoved the rest of my clothes in the dryer, punched it on, and rushed out of the room so no one could lock me inside.

On the porch I scanned the yard. Lots of bushes a person could hide behind. The gate was shut. Headlights of one car moved past on the road. I spied a tendril of smoke out beyond the fence. Or was that steam off the road? The feeling remained that someone was out there, watching. I rushed in the house, locked the door, and turned off the porch lights.

Stevie was nowhere in sight. Her bedroom door was open. Her altar-room door shut. A sudden guttural chant sounded inside there.

I rushed to my room. Locked my door, switched on a lamp, and turned off the overhead light. Then I paced, jittery, even more fearful when I walked near the widow. The curtains were shut. I checked the window and found it still locked.

You're making yourself scared. I needed to get to bed and read so I'd quit thinking. I grabbed a new novel from my suitcase and crawled under the covers.

I'd thought the book was a mystery from its cover but hadn't read the blurbs. The suspense thriller scared me from paragraph one. This wasn't what I wanted.

My heart pounded. I heard noise. My arms jerked. I looked at the window, saw nothing different, and determined the sound hadn't come from outside. It was in the house, probably Stevie going to her bedroom.

I threw the scary book against the wall. I didn't need more things frightening me. I was jumpy enough.

Digging in my suitcase, I grabbed my old standby sleep aide.

I slid back under the covers and opened my newest cookbook, *The Best Recipes of the Year.* Baked Chicken Soufflé, which must be made the night before cooking. Coq Au Vin I and II, also great made ahead. The longer they sat, the better they were. Why? Couldn't cooks get it right the first time? Moravian Sugar Cake. Its recipe included mashed potatoes. Potatoes in a cake? I felt myself drifting off even as I heard my light snores.

Stevie was gone in the morning. The scent of coffee called me to the kitchen.

I peeped out the back door. The sun was high. A few trucks drove past. The large bald man with the Lab walked by. He didn't glance at Stevie's yard.

I rushed to the dryer and pulled out my things. Rushed back inside and locked the door. Then felt ridiculous. Did I actually believe a person went out there last night to watch me on

Stevie's porch—and was still out there, watching?

"Guess what?" I said to Minnie cactus. "I was silly enough to believe some guy stood out there all night, waiting to see me in my nightgown." I twirled around so my gown skimmed my hips and enjoyed my laugh. Minnie would probably laugh, too.

I checked her out. The pink poufs that reminded me of sponge curlers looked healthy. So did her thick stem. I touched her soil. Dry. "You're looking good," I said.

Grabbing coffee, I opened the newspaper. Stared at the headlines.

LOCAL RESTAURANT TO REOPEN.

Beneath the words was a picture. Stevie. Me. Many people in the yard of Gil's restaurant watching medics rush in with a gurney that would take Fawn away.

The article reminded anyone who might have forgotten that a patron died while eating there. She died of an allergic reaction to shrimp in her chicken gumbo, the reporter announced. Restaurant owner Gil Thurman could not be reached, but manager Jake Bryant said no one knew yet why any shrimp would be in chicken gumbo. The deceased patron, Fawn McKenzie, had known of her severe allergy to seafood.

Restaurateur Gil Thurman had shut down all of his restaurants, the article told, until detectives could learn more about his customer's death. *Little information has been released by the police at this time, but Mr. Thurman has decided to reopen all of his Cajun Delights restaurants. They will open today, even the local one where many customers saw Fawn McKenzie drop dead.*

A few quotes were included. One customer felt weird to see a person fall on her plate like that. Another had wanted to help but hadn't known how. A woman would never walk inside that place again. She'd always picture a woman dead in a bowl.

An article in Section B would tell readers about allergies and what to do if they experienced severe allergic reactions to anything.

I knew where I had to eat lunch. I swallowed hard, hoping for Gil's sake that I wouldn't be the only person at his restaurant.

CHAPTER 29

I worried about the possible consequences of Gil's decision to reopen now. Concern for him made a lump jam my throat.

Suppose he opened all of his restaurants today, and no customers showed up? Of course he was helping his employees by giving them jobs, but what if people shunned all of his places. Then what would happen to all of the people he employed?

What would happen to Gil?

How could I help?

I could show up at his restaurant. I could contact everyone I knew in other cities where he owned restaurants and urge them to eat at Cajun Delights to show their support.

I picked up my phone, skimmed names, and pressed *Roger.*

After a few rings, my son in Chicago said, "Hey, Mom."

"Hi, sweetie. How're you and my grandchild?"

"Kat's great. Me, too. And yes, I'm still dating her teacher friend."

"Good boy." I'd had a hand in getting them together. And silly Gil thought I shouldn't be a matchmaker.

Male voices and clinks of metal tools sounded. Roger was at his auto repair shop. I couldn't keep him on the phone.

"I need your help." I gave a brief rundown of what happened at Gil's place. He'd already heard about it on the national news. He also knew Gil's recently opened Cajun Delights there in Chicago had closed. But hadn't known it would reopen today. "It will, and I'm afraid people will avoid going because of what happened here. Would you and Kat eat there today? And ask people you know to eat there, too? Including Chicken Boy?" Chicken Boy was a teen I'd hired to wear a costume to surprise my granddaughter Kat.

"I'll be glad to. It's my favorite restaurant."

"I know. And you'll eat lots of fried frog legs."

"Dozens." My son's laughter poured joy into my heart.

He promised to kiss Kat for me, and then we hung up. I took a moment to experience the happiness of knowing my child who'd been miserable so long was laughing again. And I laughed. And then phoned people I knew even slightly in other places where Gil had restaurants. Lots of people in Vicksburg. Some in Bangor and other cities.

Satisfied, I grabbed the small pile of clothes I'd taken from the dryer and left on the table and carried them toward my room.

The doorbell startled me. I rushed to my room, dropped my dried clothes, and tossed a robe over my nightgown. The bell rang until I opened the front door.

"Delivery from Westell Brothers," said a man possibly in his late fifties. "Where do you want us to come in with the stove? Here or the back door?"

I looked at his delivery truck. *We Haul Everything* plastered on its side. A truck anyone could rent. Westell Brothers probably wasn't large enough to have its own trucks.

"You'll have to drive around to the street behind the house to get to the back door," I said. "I'll go unlock it." I locked the front door and felt apprehensive, probably because I was alone and wearing a nightgown and a strange man would be coming in.

Did I think Stevie would be any help with an intruder? I didn't know but would have felt better if she'd been here. I felt silly for being uneasy now. Darn, I'd ordered a replacement stove for her. But I'd been questioning the trustworthiness of people we took for granted because they came near our houses every day or they wore a uniform like they were representing some place. And this deliveryman looked almost as old as me, too old to be hauling around appliances.

To be on the safe side, I grabbed the bug spray. I held it high and met him outside the back door. "Do you have papers from the store that the stove came from?" I asked.

He looked at the spray. Looked at me. Looked back at his young partner. "Yeah, I'll need you to sign this paper saying we delivered it," he told me, pulling a sheet from his khaki shirt pocket. "But I was going to wait till we actually had it inside."

"I can hold it for you." I put out my hand. He gave me the paper, and I checked the letterhead. "Yes, this is from Westell Brothers."

"Did you think somebody else might send you a stove today?" He raised one eyebrow. They used a dolly to get the boxed stove up the steps and roll it inside. "Somebody got rough with this other stove, huh?" he said, looking on top of the one I had smashed.

"I'll just step out a minute while y'all get it out," I said and hurried to my room. I locked the door. Changed into slacks and a nice shirt. For some reason, I also didn't feel comfortable in my bedroom while strange men were in the house. I still had my bug spray. Would it really cause problems if sprayed directly into a man's eyes? And would I use it? I wasn't sure, so I also carried my hair spray.

The men had already taken the old stove outside. The older man was slitting the new box open. "You use a lot of spray, don't you?" he said, seeing me.

I smiled. Didn't need to answer him.

He and the young guy did rapid work of getting the new stove into place and hooked up. I signed his paper, told them they did a nice job, and locked the back door once they went out.

The stove looked great. Shiny and unused, exactly as I preferred them. I placed the mirror from the old stove on top of the new one, then glanced at the wall clock and cursed. Twelve forty-five. I'd wanted to get to the restaurant early so they would have at least one customer, and Gil might not be too discouraged.

I rushed away from the house.

WE HAVE REOPENED. The large sign outside Cajun Delights could not be missed. Neither could all the cars in its parking lot.

Happiness tickled my ribs. I parked and heard jazz while I went in the front door, the aroma of steak and boiled seafood adding to my pleasure.

Most tables and booths were filled. The combo playing lively music enhanced a cheerful feel. Nobody sat at Gil's table, the only one empty in that area. Father Paul Edward sat in a corner booth near it with two of his female sidekicks, the cousins—and Ish Muller. All of them shared raucous laughter.

"Welcome to Cajun Delights. How many at your table?" a waiter asked me.

"One so far. I'd like to sit at Mr. Thurman's table, please."

A fearful look filled his eyes. "Yes, ma'am." He led me to the table.

People turned their heads and eyed me the whole time I walked. I couldn't let them see how jittery I felt heading there.

Gil's chair had its back to the wall. The chair Fawn had sat in was opposite it.

"I'll sit here," I said to the waiter, pointing to the chair next to Gil's.

He pulled it out for me and gave me a menu.

"If Mr. Thurman is around, please tell him Cealie's here," I said.

He hesitated, but then nodded and took off.

I imagined Gil would join me soon. I had figured his heart would be aching because few people would show up, but the numbers proved I was wrong. I was thrilled.

I peered at customers who still stared at me. I smiled at them, and they all turned away. The priest, group leader, and sex-pot cousins Lois and Sue in a nearby booth didn't look at me.

"Hi, there, Father, Ish, Lois and Sue," I said, leaning toward them to make certain they'd all see me.

"Oh, hello," the priest said.

"Hey, Cealie," the girls chirped.

Ish didn't look pleased.

"This is a good restaurant, isn't it?" I said.

"Uh-huh," one cousin said. "We really like the food. But it would be strange to see somebody fall in their food, don't you think?"

The other girl elbowed her. "That's the table where that woman died," she said in a half whisper.

So that's why so many people had come. Some of them probably knew the dishes were great. Possibly human nature made the majority show up out of curiosity, to see if anyone else at this table would keel over.

Apprehension returned. I feared that same thing myself. I glanced at the spot on the table where Fawn's head had lain in the bowl. I quickly looked away.

Bolstering my courage, I anticipated Gil striding out of his office. His face would light up when we'd see each other. He would kiss my lips and join me.

Eagerness sent heat rushing through my body.

"May I have your attention?" Babs said from the mike on the stage. The band quit playing. "We are happy that all of you joined us today. Please let any of our staff know if there is anything we can do to make your experience at Cajun Delights even better."

She paused, and some people clapped. Me included.

Babs continued, "And now to add to your pleasure, we'll have a joke contest. Please notice that children are here when you consider telling a joke. Any Boudreaux and Thibodaux jokes get extra credit."

"Yes!" I cried. People looked at me. That was fine. They'd learn to love the B and T jokes as much as I did. A Cajun tradition. Gil was part Cajun. I especially liked that part of him.

I felt extra joyful since he must have had those jokes included now for my benefit. I glanced around. Didn't see Gil yet.

A chunky man ran onstage. "Boudreaux and Thibodaux were out fishing, chewing and sipping sweet tea. Boudreaux said, 'Thibodaux, I think I'm gonna divorce Clotilde. She ain't talked to me in three months.' Thibodaux spat, took a sip of tea, and said, 'You better think good before you do it, ole friend. It's hard to find a woman like that.' "

Everyone laughed. Chuckles tickled my ribs.

"Very nice," Babs told the jokester. "You have a distinct Southern accent."

The man pointed to the front of his shirt. A picture of raw oysters. He flipped around to show everyone the back. It read *Cajun Viagra*. He ran off stage.

"Excellent," Babs said. "Anyone else?" She looked around, waiting.

"Cealie," a man standing close to me said.

"Oh, Dr. Wallo. Hi."

"Is it all right if I join you?" He pulled out Fawn's chair. I nodded, and he sat.

Gil walked up.

CHAPTER 30

The corners of Gil's lips looked glued back while he smiled at the handsome doctor seated at my side and me.

"Hello, Gil," Dr. Dan Wallo said to him.

Gil's shoulders appeared tense, his neck stiff as he nodded. "Dan."

"Hi," I told Gil. "I just sat here, and then the doctor came and asked if it was okay to join me."

"How nice," Gil said.

I knew *nice* was not the word he meant about me being with the cutie doc. I also knew that whispering my little recent news about the doctor would have eased Gil's inner suffering.

Ah, but a little jealousy was great for the soul, especially if he was jealous of me.

"Come on. Let's eat together," I told him.

With a grimace, he sat. We all placed our orders. Tension mounted from Gil being silent.

"How's your thigh?" I asked him.

"Terrific."

"You have problems with a thigh?" Dr. Wallo asked Gil.

"Some chairs kind of fell against it," I said.

Gil replied nothing. He glared at me. Uh-oh, he was worried that I was going to ask about his other problem in front of the doctor, the other physical problem I'd created.

"I'd be glad to look at it for you," Dan Wallo said.

I thought Gil's head would fall off, he shook it so hard. "No, it's fine. I'm fine. I don't need a doctor. Thanks. I'm good."

The waiter handed Gil water, and he gulped it. He unwrapped a cracker and chewed.

"Have you learned anything new about that woman's death?" the doctor asked Gil.

"No. Only what you saw in the news."

Dr. Wallo and I received salads and ate. Our entrées came. Few words were spoken. The doctor pulled his wallet out after the meal. Gil insisted he owed nothing. He thanked us for coming. I would have stayed to visit with him, but not with Gil in this mood. I kissed his cheek, walked with the doctor out the door, and drove away.

I went straight to the sheriff's office. Asked for Detective Renwick and soon sat in front of him.

"You have to realize I've been traumatized by tripping over a dead man," I said. "Please tell me something about Pierce Trottier."

He lowered his eyes and apparently considered. He peered at me. "This will be released to the media soon. It seems he victimized some women. Sent them threats. Collected money from them."

Stunned, I couldn't say anything.

"We found evidence in his house. Unsent letters and bank deposits from some women we contacted. One admitted to what happened. Others swore they hadn't paid him anything."

"This was the man who was going to get married soon and become a minister?"

Renwick's eyebrows squeezed closer. "His fiancée was ready to break off the engagement even before she found out about a sexual fling he had right before he died."

"She was, even then? I heard about his apparent wild sexual encounter."

The detective nodded. "Her aunt in Tuscaloosa, Alabama,

recently told her what he was like while he lived there. Her aunt attended services in a church where he'd pass the collection. He'd stretch his arms out to purposely rub his hands against women's breasts. Some women quit attending the church. Others started crossing their arms to block his advances."

I breathed. Tried to think. Found my thoughts blocked. Who in the hell was that man, the good man, Pierce Trottier that I'd once admired?

"Ooh," I blurted and rubbed my aching legs.

"You have problems?" he asked.

"Maybe. Maybe not. Is there anything else you can tell me?"

"Not right now."

I thanked him and left, my legs wobbly from aches and the swooning feeling in my head. How could this be?

I drove to Stevie's house. Went in and sat with elbows on the kitchen table, my hands gripping my head. How could this be? Who—?

The whine of a lawnmower shut down my thoughts. I peeked through the blinds.

April chewed gum and pushed a mower in Stevie's backyard. Cherish sat on the porch, making a mess with puzzles. I went out there. April noticed and shut off the engine.

"Why are you cutting the grass here?" I asked.

"I always do it, but I was real busy and got behind. That's why it grew so long. I'm almost finished."

My confusion built. I smiled at the seated child who frowned at me. "Hey, angel, do you want to come inside?"

Cherish looked scared and shoved up to her feet. She yelled at her mom and pointed at me. "She said my real name."

April was ready to start the mower again. She stood totally still. Then stared at me.

"We need to talk." I walked down to the yard with her.

She glanced around like she was ready to bolt.

"You have a child. You live a lie. You can't keep this up."

She nodded slowly, eyes shifting toward her daughter on the porch.

"You've come into my room at night, haven't you? I found the window partly open and freshly chewed gum under my bed."

The upper part of her body swung back. April nodded. "Stevie sometimes goes into a trance and sleepwalks and opens a window, especially in that room. Probably to let good spirits in." April shook her head. "All that stuff's weird."

"You found the window open?"

"Only a little. I opened it wider to go in and put it lower again when I went out."

"So you came in to my room just to look around? I didn't see anything taken."

Her gaze left mine and then swung back. "I checked for papers. Looked through the drawers and your suitcase. For an old woman, you have nice lingerie."

The old woman comment would have brought out my fighting instinct under other circumstances. Today I had much more important business to consider. "Why, April?" I gripped her hand. "Did you kill that man?"

She yanked her hand back. "No way. We moved here and took new identities but not so I could kill anyone."

"Mamma." Cherish ran out and grabbed onto her mom's legs. She glared at me.

"I'm not hurting your mamma," I said and brushed the hair back from her eyes. "I want to help her."

The girl shoved her hair back down. "Leave us alone."

I looked at April. She stared at the grass. Stared at me.

"I didn't know what he looked like or his real name, but he'd send me threats, saying he'd let my husband know where Cherish—really Angel—and I are. I'd give him money. And you

278

showed up the day he died."

"So that's why you go to garage sales, which you don't really like. You really need to conserve money." Her silence gave me the answer. "You feel you need to protect your child?"

"Yes. I have custody, but she came back from two court-ordered visits with her father and had bruises. He said she fell. Cherish says he's a good daddy. She won't say anything bad about him or me." She bent down and kissed the child. Cherish smiled. April stood. "I also had bruises right before I left him. But I couldn't prove anything about him hurting her. I couldn't trust him to be around her ever again."

Cherish glanced worriedly at her mother.

"So April isn't your name, either," I said.

She shook her head. Didn't offer her real name.

"Where was home for you?" I asked but determined the answer before she spoke.

"Alabama. Tuscaloosa. I know, that's where Mr. Trottier lived. I didn't know it before, but this week Stevie told me. She doesn't know about me and Cherish." April looked at my face. "My husband used to have our taxes done, and maybe by him. I don't know. I had to send cash to a post office box."

"How did he contact you?"

"Notes slipped under the fence. That's why I watched my daughter outside so much." She rubbed her child's shoulder.

"April, why did you get into my room?"

"I thought maybe you were the one blackmailing me."

"*Me?*"

"Stevie always said you were so smart. And then you showed up. I was scared you'd discovered our identities. I wanted to look through your things to see if you had any papers about us."

"Stevie said I was smart?"

"She always said good things about you. Now I need to finish this. I'm cleaning a lady's house tonight."

"April, were you watching me when I went out on the back porch last night?"

She shook her head. "I came in the house through the front door while y'all weren't here one night. I used my key. I checked in your laptop to see if I'd find anything about me." She hung her head. "I'm sorry. My husband makes lots of money. He could have paid you to locate me."

"Why didn't you use your key the first time?"

"Some of our neighbors were talking near the street. I needed to go in the back of Stevie's house. She has a different key for the back door."

I backed away to let her start her mower.

"Get back on the porch," she told her child.

"Do you want me to help you make your puzzle?" I asked, and the girl frowned. She returned to Stevie's porch and sat pouting.

My head spun with new ideas. I walked inside to my bedroom. Tossed myself across my bed and lay on my back, staring at the ceiling. How could all of this be?

The lawnmower buzzed. My thoughts swirled. My eyelids drooped.

I'd slept, I discovered when I awoke to footsteps clunking through the house. Stevie was back from school. The lawnmower noises had stopped.

"You've got to hear this," I said, rushing to her in the living room and blurting everything April told me.

Stevie dropped to the sofa, her face ashen. She stared at a distant vacant spot. Stared at me. "That's why I thought I was going to die," she said. "It's why I wanted you here."

I sat beside her. "I don't understand."

"Somebody shoved a letter under my gate. It warned I'd better follow instructions, or the worst thing I could imagine would happen. I figured that meant I would die. The note warned that more information would follow. Nothing did."

"Did you tell the police?"

"I considered it. But then a friend who lives downtown told me she found a note in her mailbox with the same thing. She was scared—till her kids told her those words are used in a popular video game. We decided some teens must be restless and playing pranks."

"But you were still concerned."

She nodded. Removed her bulky sack of papers from her lap and set it on the floor. "I didn't get another note, but I worried. I'd been feeling too down on myself to call the police and chance looking like a fool in front of them."

"Why down on yourself?"

"Oh, look at me. I've let myself go for so long. My weight. My hair." She ran her fingers through the thin gray stands. "I can't get a boyfriend."

"Stevie, all of those are things you can deal with and improve if you want to. You can go to a beauty shop and get back to exercising. I'll go with you. I've gotten much too chunky and could use lots of help." She really wanted a boyfriend? "We'll see what we can do about a man for you."

A glint of hope touched her eyes. A trace of a grin. "That's why I wanted you here with me. You're my closest relative who could give me advice. Having you with me a while would help me feel protected, at least until I'd gotten over all the fear."

"That note wasn't the only thing that scared you, was it?"

"I found other warnings. My cards." She looked away.

"And I guess your candles and other silliness."

She hung her head. "I am such a failure. I'm not like you, Cealie."

"Like me?"

"You made a go of your business. I know you worked hard for a long time with Freddy, but then you became successful on your own."

I shoved up to my feet. "Stevie, you are a definite success. You have a job you love with children you adore and this nice house."

She scanned the living room. "The house that's half-ass done. It's half-ass Feng Shuied, like I found I used the right colors in the wrong places. I've used half-ass psychic crap. That's how my whole life goes."

I shook my head, unable to believe I was hearing this.

"You know how I go in my inner sanctum, the room with the candles. I've been trying to learn who killed Pierce Trottier, but I'm not getting anywhere."

"That doesn't make you a failure. The police have been trying to find the killer. So have I. None of us have succeeded yet."

"You?" She looked incredulous.

"Every day." My enthusiasm built. I sat close and gripped her hand. "I wasn't sure. I was nosing into everyone's business from your quitters' group, but nothing seemed to fit. But now with what April told me, don't you see? The note you received must have been meant for her. Both of your houses and fences look the same. Pierce Trottier probably put that note under your fence, thinking it was hers, but then realized it was the wrong place. That's why you stopped getting blackmail notes, but she didn't."

Stevie *garrumped*, sounding as though there was a brick caught in her throat. She stared at me. "So what are you saying?"

Compassion filled me for the sometimes-annoying child I now considered in a new light. "The girl needs to be protected."

"You just told me her mother's doing that."

"Yes, the maternal urge to protect our children must be the

strongest drive ever created. And April surely had a reason—more than one—to want that man away from her child. April is wiser than she seems. What if she'd found out who was sending her threats?"

"And—?"

"She'd be terrified that she could lose her daughter."

Stevie snorted, her eyes wide.

My hands felt icy with the thought. "So she had sex with him. And killed him."

Stevie's mouth opened. Her face mottled. "You get the hell out of here."

She'd uttered the words almost as one. I couldn't believe it. "What did you say?"

She rose. Glared down at me. "You get the hell out of my house and leave me and the people I love alone. I mean it, Cealie! Get out of here. And if you tell the police what you *think* you know about the people I love next door, I'll hate you and haunt you the rest of your days!"

I sat, dumbfounded. Then rose. Numbly walked to the bedroom where my things were. Heard a door in the hall slam and lock. I gathered my loose items into my suitcase. Went to the kitchen and got Minnie. I left through the front door.

CHAPTER 31

I drove aimlessly, not knowing where I should go. I would get a room, probably in a downtown motel. And a hot tub. Or I might rent a cabin, I decided after miles of driving without paying attention to anything nearby.

Starting to glance around, I looked for *Vacancy* signs. Didn't see them. Became surprised at the number of motels with *No Vacancy* signs lit.

I stopped at one of the nicer places. Yes, I was told, most rentals were booked now. Didn't I know one of the largest craft shows in the South was taking place this week? I must be the only woman in the country who didn't know.

Da-dunt, da-dunt, da-dunt. I grabbed my phone. "Yes?"

"Ah, yes. A good answer." Gil's light tone lifted my spirits a pinch.

"How are you?" I hated to ask, not needing to deal with more negatives. I'd created his pain. And Stevie's misery.

"I'm much better. Come over, and I'll show you."

I managed a half grin. "Where are you? At the restaurant?"

"No, in my cabin. It's great. You would love it."

"Is it up on a mountainside?"

"Yep, and you can see cliffs and valleys. It's a breathtaking sight."

I did not need temptation. I was woman—able to do my own thing. See my own sights.

I passed cabin rental offices. No *Vacancy* signs yet. "Stevie kicked me out of her house. I need a place to stay."

I heard his excited breath. "Come here. I have plenty of room."

"No thanks. I'll find my own place. I'll call you when I'm settled in."

We hung up. The sky darkened while I drove, going for miles and miles one way, then taking crossroads. Probably retraced many streets. I was lost and stopped at a deli for a tuna and water. The owner said I needed to go back to get near Gatlinburg again. That was where the police wanted me to stay. I inquired about a place to spend the night. He laughed long and hard. Said there would not be one vacant room for me to sleep in.

"Is your offer still good?" I asked when Gil answered my phone call.

His deep-throated laughter gave the answer.

"I can't find a place, and I need a room to sleep in. By myself. I need sleep." *And you can't tempt me. I'm weary.*

"I have three bedrooms and a loft. It's way too large for just me. Pick any bedroom you'd like."

"Do you have a hot tub?"

"I wouldn't do without one here." He gave me directions. His voice sounded so full of cheer I almost called back and told him never mind, I'd sleep in my car.

But then I considered all the dark woods and the bears. Gil's attractive cabin on a mountain cliff sounded better and better. I raced there.

During the last few miles, I drove through a vast dark canopy of trees. I turned to where Gil was staying and gasped.

Set on the edge of a cliff, the cabin was massive, one wall slung against the mountainside. No other cabins visible. I parked and stepped out of my car.

Stars winked through thick boughs. The scent of pine needles and sultry air greeted me. A small animal scurried, making me rush up the stairs to the porch.

"That's probably a squirrel. It won't eat you." Gil smiled and came through the doorway.

"I know. I'm not scared." I glanced into the yard but couldn't see any small creature. Night cloaked all but the valley below, the sunlit sky, this porch, and Gil standing in front of me.

"I feel a slight tremble in your hands," he said, clasping them. And then Gil took a step closer.

I stepped back. Sure, my hands trembled from his nearness and a possible scary creature. "Maybe this isn't a good idea."

He pecked a kiss on my cheek and backed from my space. "I'm glad you're here. I needed to talk to someone. You're my best friend, Cealie. You can give me advice."

"Well, if that's the case. Sure, I'll help you." I walked inside, wondering if I'd truly convinced myself that's why I wanted to stay. The cabin's rustic interior gave off a comfortable feel. "Oh, and you're wounded," I added, supporting the reasons I could safely remain and avoid making love with him.

Gil nodded, and I could have sworn he then started hobbling.

"I know you're sorry about all this," he said, adding a limp.

Guilt flashed, followed by doubt. I didn't think he was bent over or limping when he first came outside, before I mentioned his ailments. But the brightly lit open spaces beneath the vaulted ceiling gave me confidence that I could stay and avoid getting too close to him.

"Can I get your things out of your car?" he asked.

"Let's wait and see. This is a beautiful place. I already ate. So tell me about your problem."

He led me to the posh sofa. Then Gil went off and returned with two glasses of red wine. He gave me one and sat with me, but not too close. "You know I don't complain about employees much, but I've been having a little trouble with my managers."

I took a sip and nodded. "I know the situation."

"Has it been that obvious?"

"Probably not to everyone. But I notice things, especially at your restaurants."

We drank our wine. Gil said, "That's what happened the night Fawn McKenzie died. A waiter wanted to talk to me. I put him off, which is something I seldom do. But you were there at that table. With the doctor." He said that last sentence deeper in his throat. "I wanted to hurry over to see you."

Right, and to make sure I wasn't a couple with that hunk of maleness, the doc—who I certainly won't tell you now is gay.

I lifted my drink. "What did the waiter want to tell you?"

"That my night manager and day manager were quibbling."

"I know how to solve your problem." I took another swallow.

"Let me top these off." Gil tilted the wine bottle to both our glasses. He sat again, this time a little farther from me. "So what can I do about them?"

"You do nothing. I'll do it."

He eyed me long moments. "Part of Babs's anger comes from Jake often running late to replace her."

"Right." I reached out and patted his arm. "And I'll see about it."

We gazed into distant places within ourselves, sorting through the situation. Most likely all Gil knew about the pair was that Babs seemed overly tense when Jake ran late. Gil probably didn't know Babs was scared to drive in the dark. And he most certainly did not notice the attraction between them—especially Jake wanting to date Babs. But matchmaker Cealie did. Ideas raced about when and how I would get them together.

"People might not be afraid to come back to eat," Gil said. "They'll probably keep watching a while to see if anyone else has a problem at my place." He swigged his drink, the pain in his face obvious. A woman had died in his restaurant. He definitely felt at fault.

"They haven't figured out how the pieces of shrimp got in the gumbo bowl?"

"The police are still questioning people at work." Gil sucked in a breath. He swilled his drink. Rose for another.

"That's not like you," I said about his drinking so much.

"Until we resolve this catastrophe, nothing about me feels like myself." His slight limp remained as he went for a new bottle. He poured a little more for both of us.

"Would you like to go outside?" I asked. "I'd like to see the view. And we can get my suitcase and my plant."

We left our glasses behind and went out into the night air. We stood on the section of porch overhanging the mountain's ledge. A slight chill made me shiver. I drank in the sight—the ridge of smoke hanging onto cliffs beyond, the black feathery leaves reaching into the void, the layers of evening sky in soft pastels slipping into the dark. All was silent. I listened to myself and the man at my side breathing.

I looked at him.

Gil looked at me.

We stepped together and kissed, our first kiss since greeting each other tonight. And then we moved apart.

"I need to get Minnie." I stepped down the stairs. Gil walked near me. Our sides bumped. I giggled and nudged him. He laughed, too.

Gil grabbed my suitcase from the trunk of my car. I slid Minnie out of the cup holder in front, smiled, and held her up to Gil. He knew all about her. We walked inside. I set Minnie on the table.

"I'm not going to bed with you," I told Gil.

"I know." He carried my suitcase farther. "There's a loft you can have up there." He pointed up the slender circular stairwell. "Or you can have that bedroom. Or that one. Or the master room."

"The one you're sleeping in? No thanks. I pick that one."

"This one's good. I guess. I haven't looked in it." He flipped on the lights, bathing a lovely white-paneled room with a yellow cast. "It is nice," he said, seeming surprised. Gil set my suitcase on a luggage rack. "Need anything else?"

I shook my head. "Nothing, thanks. And I do appreciate your offer. I couldn't find another place to stay tonight."

"I'm glad I was here." He brushed a kiss on my cheek. Stepped out of the room.

I took in the sumptuous bedroom and bath that balanced the feel of being rugged, yet extravagant. Getting my bath supplies out, I shut my bedroom door and then steeped my body in a long, luxurious shower. With hair still damp, I slipped on my black silk nightgown, turned off the lights, and climbed into bed. Extra comfy. Lots of soft covers.

I lay awake and thought of Gil.

I heard him stirring.

Was he wearing anything?

Not if he was going to bed.

"Gil," I whispered.

"Yes." He answered right outside my door. The door opened, and he walked in. Darkness beyond draped him in deep shadows.

"Were you going to come into my bedroom?" I asked, slipping out from my covers and getting to my feet.

"Not until you asked me to."

"How did you know I would?"

His hand found a spot on my torso that made me smile. Gil's arms came around me, those strong arms I knew so well. We kissed, our bodies moving closer, meshing into a perfect snuggle.

"Would you like to play Twister?" I asked, making my lips stop nibbling his neck.

He smiled. His mouth nuzzled down my chest. "Uh-hm."

I breathed hard, enjoying every minute. "I really wanted a hot tub."

Gil scooped me in his arms and tried to carry me. He limped a few steps, gave me a painful smile, and let me slide down to my feet. We walked out to the porch that wound halfway around his cottage. The door to the screened section of the porch slammed behind us. He stripped me. We slid into the steamy water in the hot tub.

Gil and I twisted together.

Yum.

CHAPTER 32

"Sorry to wake you." Gil stood beside his massive bed. His breath was warm when he leaned down to kiss me. I lay on his rumpled sheets. The scent of strong coffee wafted from the tray he held. His tray also held a coral rose in a vase. "I need to go."

I thrust cobwebs off my brain. "Go. Why?"

He handed me coffee. "I have to be at the restaurant. You know I wouldn't normally, but there are so many questions needing answers right now."

"I'll miss you."

"I hope we'll get together again today. And tomorrow. And the day after that."

And a lifetime, I knew he wanted. I needed more time for discovering myself, for knowing without a doubt what I wanted from the rest of my life.

I kissed Gil. Gave him no promises. Thanked him for the coffee as he went out.

Stretching in bed, I luxuriated in the comfort of sex. We'd made love twice during the night. I felt completely satisfied.

I listened to his truck roaring to life and heard it drive off. My head sank deep into the pillow. I slept until it was almost time for lunch.

Sated, I scrounged through the refrigerator. Bottled water. Slices of cantaloupe. Nothing in the pantry. I drank water and ate half the fruit, then dressed and decided I couldn't hide out here, as much as I wanted to. Stevie might have annoyed me yesterday, but she'd been scared. She feared the young woman and child she loved might be taken from her. April had become like a daughter to my childless cousin. And I had accused April of being a killer. I needed to learn if that was the truth.

Before I left, I went out to the porch deck, wanting to drink in the sight. I viewed mountains and valleys while a warm breeze washed over me.

My soul at peace, I drove back to Stevie's house.

I parked and sat in my car, scanning the street, especially looking for signs of life from April's house. I saw no one.

I let myself in the front door and walked around. Stevie was gone, surely teaching. Her altar room was locked. I'd thought she might unlock it if I wasn't here. Maybe she guessed I'd return.

Nothing looked amiss. My bedroom was exactly as I left it. The window locked. In her kitchen I found sweet rolls on a tray on the new stove and ate two.

On the back porch, I stood. Pondered. Looked around. Yes, definitely a person could see here from the opposite side of the road. I shivered in the heat of the noonday sun, knowing a person had been back there, watching when I put my clothes in to wash. Maybe later when I put them in to dry.

Why, I had no idea.

A dog barked. A man whistled. Down the street came the guy with the bull neck and jogging clothes. He glanced at Stevie's gate. Looked up at me.

Our gazes met, and he spun away. Hurried off down the street.

No, it had not been him watching me. At least, I didn't think so.

Coughing came from the right. April's yard. Her child. What should I call her now?

"Hey, Cherish, are you sick?" I yelled, figuring her mom would respond.

I was right. "She just choked on a piece of ice. She's okay."

"April," I said, "can you come over?"

I thought I heard a smack of disgust. "Okay. Not for long."

A couple of minutes later she swept through Stevie's gate with the child who cast mean eyes at me. "What is it?" April asked, not nicely.

"How did he find out? I understand Mr. Trottier might have done your taxes back in Alabama, but how could he have known you were here?"

"I don't know. The first note said he knew my angry husband was looking for us. I'd need to pay him every month to make sure he wouldn't leak our whereabouts."

"You never went to his office?"

"No, just my husband went. But Mr. Trottier could have seen us together in town back there." She released a sigh. "I don't know. Please don't tell anybody about this."

I bit my tongue, hoping she wasn't a killer that I'd have to tell on. Of course I would tell if I determined she murdered him.

They returned home, and I made phone calls. I checked on a couple of my offices and family members. Nobody seemed to need me right now. Hiring good managers had made my life much easier and my life was usually peaceful. But I missed having Betty Allen run my San Francisco office. She was a major part of my business family. I was going to reinstate her, no matter what.

I realized I'd been so tied up with deaths, I hadn't even called Frank Karney, the CEO of Sterling Bryst.

I got him on the line and apologized.

He was laughing. "Don't worry about it. Everything turned out fine."

"It did?"

"People started e-mailing us, saying our ad was so funny.

They thought it was cute that we'd come up with the idea of saying our sunscreen protected people from fun. All except a handful of people who wrote seemed to think we'd done a clever job."

A *whoosh* of relief left my throat. "I am so glad customers liked it."

"Yes. But we might change the ad next time."

"Whatever makes you happy, Mr. Karney. That's what my company's here for."

We exchanged a few more pleasantries and hung up.

I called my San Francisco office and got Liz, who was taking Betty's place as manager. "Everything's fine here," she said.

"Liz, you're a terrific employee, and I really appreciate the job you're doing there. But I feel the need to have Betty running that office."

"Great. I mean that would be fine, whatever you want. Being manager is a lot tougher than I imagined."

We agreed that she'd resume her previous position. I also gave her a raise since she'd been so willing to take the managerial position.

I got Betty Allen on her cell phone. "Betty, I need help at the office out there. Would you mind going back and taking over?"

She gasped. Didn't answer me.

"Betty," I said, "everything worked out fine with Sterling Bryst."

She sobbed, "Cealie, I'd love to get back to work for you."

"Wonderful. And I'll come out and visit y'all one day."

I hung up, happy. Made another call. I stood in the den, laughing with Bud Denton, manager of my Cape Cod office, and didn't notice the sound of the garage door opening and a car pulling in. Stevie stomped inside with a stuffed school bag. We locked gazes. Her empty hand clenched in a fist.

I got off the phone. "You're back early."

"It's the last week of school. We have half days. We can take papers home to grade." Her words stayed level, along with her hardened stare.

"That's a good thing."

"You aren't supposed to be here anymore."

I breathed. Thought of what came to mind while I was gazing at the mountains. "Our children are but God's precious toys. He loans them to us for a while."

Stevie's face softened. "What did you say?"

"You know those words. Your mother wrote them long ago. They're beautiful and so true."

"You remember them."

"Yes. And April's situation may be that way. She and Cherish are in your life for a while. Who knows how long?"

Looking like she might stumble, Stevie sat. I sat beside her on the sofa. She put down her bag. Gazed at me. "And if I lend you my child, will you love her forever? Keep her safe and always free from pain?"

Tears popped to my eyes. I nodded. My mother, her mom's sister, wrote that.

We traded quotes we recalled from each other's mothers and our own. Some short poems, some longer verses. Each lovely. Each one calling more of our tears to come forth.

Stevie sighed. I clasped her hand. "I couldn't leave you alone. I'm afraid for you." I squeezed her hand. "I hope April's okay and nothing will change for you and her, but I don't know. We need to know the truth."

She appeared to stop breathing. After a long moment, she nodded.

"So I'll stay," I said, "and we'll figure things out. And least I'll feel like you're a little safer with your cousin around, taking care of you."

We both grinned. To lighten her mind even more, I leaned

forward. "Go ahead, for old time's sake, give my hair a tug."

She considered a moment and then lightly tugged. Stevie bent her head toward me. "Now you do mine. Come on, get even."

I pulled a pinch of her hair. The temptation came to grab two big handfuls and pull like crazy. That childish mood only lasted a second, then washed away. "I'm done. Thanks."

Stevie smiled. She lifted her sack of papers. "Want to help me with these?"

We spent much of the afternoon working on averages for her first-grade students, most of them *S* for *Satisfactory*. We recorded notes in her roll book. We laughed often, especially when she spoke of her students, mentioning special things about each one. We shared glances with each other. She might have been thinking the same thing I was—that this was one of the best times we'd ever spent together.

We ate snacks, wonderful homemade brownies with pecans and fudge topping, and tall glasses of milk. I put soapy water in the sink. "Don't you ever leave a few things in here?" I asked, laughing. My phone rang. I answered it.

"You sound happy. That's good," Gil said. "Are you coming back with me tonight?"

"I think I need to be here with my cousin."

"I'll miss you." He quieted. And he said, "Cealie, I love you."

My throat jammed. "I, uh, miss you, too."

We hung up. I stared out the kitchen window. Why couldn't I tell Gil I loved him? Did I?

I tightened my emotions, trying to stop feeling. I did not want to love a man now, did not want to be so in love with him that I felt I needed him to exist. I'd been in that situation too long.

Later in the afternoon, I suggested to Stevie that we go someplace different for dinner.

She took me to a Japanese restaurant. The chefs chopped and sizzled our meal in front of us, steaming greens and noodles on a huge grill. Our chef put on a show, flipping a raw egg off his spatula and into his hat. We chuckled and ate and met nice people sitting around our grill.

Back at Stevie's, we went to bed early since we'd promised each other tonight was the night.

She woke me at two a.m.

I moaned and groaned, and we laughed together, changing into loose clothes we could wear to work out. She drove through the dark to a gym.

"I cannot believe anyone actually does this," I said as we walked into the place. It was small and well lit. Lots of equipment. A sterile smell. None of sweat. "But nobody's here. Maybe we should leave."

A hulk of a balding man stepped out from a rear room. He looked at us. Swerved his head away. He went to work on a machine, adding weights to it, and then sitting, pulling the ropes down and letting them up again. I recognized the jogging suit.

"Stevie," I whispered to her in a far corner, "that's the guy who walks by your house all the time." She glanced at me with no change in expression. "And he has a dog," I said.

She said nothing. I couldn't stay in a place with a large man who might jump us, pretending he wasn't there with us. Stevie stepped up on a treadmill, obviously not ready to leave. I went to the man with the bulldog neck and looked him full in the face. "Hello. I'm Cealie Gunther, and that's my cousin, Stevie Midnight."

He nodded, and I swear, it seemed he blushed. "Mac," he said, yanking the weights down harder. They struck the machine and clinked.

I stepped on a treadmill beside Stevie. We both started a slow walk. In fact, we only sped up our pace for a couple of minutes and then laughed. "No use breaking into a sweat this first time out, right?" I said, and she agreed. We pulled and pushed on a few other machines. Mac stayed on the same one. We didn't get close to him.

"That was fun, but it was time to call it a night," I told Stevie later, when she used her remote to open her garage door and then drove inside.

"Right, and you promised you'll come back there with me."

"Only until you get in the habit again, and I can leave town." My shoulders ached a little. I noticed my legs. No aches in my shins lately. Did that mean they were healing? Or the killer had been caught?

Grateful for either, I shoved into the kitchen door right behind Stevie.

I bumped against her. "Oh, no," she said, sinking backward.

I looked inside.

The back door's window was shattered.

Chapter 33

The police came and checked Stevie's house. Nobody was inside. Someone had gotten in the back door and escaped.

"The perpetrator didn't get anything that you've noticed?" Detective Renwick asked Stevie after she and I went through the house with him and a deputy.

I slumped against the kitchen sink. "He got Minnie."

Renwick came and looked at me, holding the broken Minnie as I'd found her. "Sorry about your plant," he said. "Maybe the perp got in here and then got scared. Could've been a dog barking or some other noise." He faced Stevie. "Let us know if anything happens or you get frightened. Are you sure you're okay with your door like that for now?"

Some men had boarded up the part of the door where the glass had been. The screen door outside it was ripped open. Whoever came here used a hammer or some other strong object to break the window. The police took prints but figured the guilty party wore gloves or held a thick rag or both. Dawn brightened the sky by the time they left.

I held Minnie's broken parts. Soil from her dumped pot trailed across the countertop to the sink. Someone's hand probably bumped against her pot. Possibly accidental. Maybe turning in the dark made that person's hand slide over the countertop. No malice intended toward Minnie, my plant. My plant I'd chosen to come with me during my recent travels. She was a cactus, an adorable two-inch cactus with a pink grafted head of poufs like old sponge rollers on a green stem shaved of thorns.

I heard the front door close. Stevie's footsteps returned. I felt her hand on my shoulder. "I'm so sorry," she said.

I shook my head. "It's okay. She was just a plant." She'd been the living presence accompanying me instead of an animal that might have been more difficult during my travels. "Just a plant," I said, shaking more soapy water off her. She'd been knocked into this water—the water *I* had left in the sink—and was broken into bits. Her head knocked off. Tiny pink poufs came apart.

My arms shook and my eyes burned as I held my cactus, the one I'd spoken to and learned how to keep alive. Until now.

"I want to bury her here," I told Stevie. "And I'm going to get whoever did this."

We went into the backyard. Stevie carried a shovel. I carried Minnie. I chose a sunny spot in the corner near the fence on April's side.

"Do you want to say anything?" Stevie asked once I had Minnie buried.

I stared at the loose dirt. Shook my head. Told Minnie, "You were important."

Stevie called in sick at school. We went to town, and I bought a white trellis. We found a few bright flowers to plant near Minnie's place of rest. Back at Stevie's, we positioned the trellis and plants, creating a memorial.

"You can come and visit anytime you'd like," Stevie said.

I squeezed her hand. "I respect you even more for not laughing at me."

"I haven't heard you laughing when I go in with my candles."

"Do you really believe in all that stuff?"

She sighed with a shrug. "I need something or someone to believe in."

I cut my eyes toward April's house. "You've been afraid to

lose them. You knew everything wasn't as it seemed next door with the way they've lived."

Fear filled her eyes. "Don't hurt them."

"I don't want to. Darn it, I don't want to hurt anyone. I want everybody to be just great! But they're not."

We stared at each other. Parted inside the house and did our separate things. She fiddled with papers. I studied my list, jotting notes next to most names of her quitters' group, pushing my mind to come up with more. Massaged my shins that didn't even hurt.

The newspaper arrived. Fawn's funeral was tomorrow. She had a husband, two children, one brother, three sisters. I cried for her and them and Minnie and myself and Pierce Trottier, who might have had faults but didn't deserve to have anyone take his life.

"Time for lunch." Stevie held her purse.

I sat in my bedroom. "I'm not hungry. I don't want to go anywhere."

"We haven't eaten a thing today. I understand. I'm not real hungry, either, but good food will help us think."

When she said good food, I knew she'd head for Gil's restaurant.

She did, and we joined the dozen or so people inside. It was only 11:15. No Gil visible. If he was inside Cajun Delights, I hoped he wouldn't come out while we were here. Sure, I'd want to share my loss with him, to tell him about Minnie and someone breaking into the house. But he had that other agenda, possibly a heavier one to deal with.

Love.

I didn't want to have to consider my feelings toward him right now. Hatred for whoever was hurting people around us and my plant swelled inside my chest, leaving little room for other emotions. We ordered red beans and rice and smoked sausage and corn bread and iced tea.

The musicians set up on stage. Their presence reminded me of something else I'd said I would take care of. I glanced around.

"Have you seen Babs?" I asked Stevie. "You know, the pretty manager who's here in daytime."

"The one who's scared to drive at night? No."

I spied Babs going toward the restaurant's rear. I wasn't in a mood for trying to get a couple together, but I'd promised Gil I would help him here. I hadn't said how, since he believed people were attracted on their own to find love.

I believed they sometimes needed help. Maybe a nudge would get Babs to really consider Jake a man to date, a man who seemed to like her, but was too shy to ask her out.

I was way past shy. Gil needed more help at this restaurant to get it back on its feet. Getting his managers together so they would no longer argue seemed the best way for me to help.

"I'll only be a minute," I told Stevie. I followed Babs, thinking she'd go into the ladies' room or the lounge. She did go through the empty employees' lounge and continued out the back door.

I smelled cigarette smoke before I opened that door and saw her right inside the fence, lighting up. She dropped her lighter back into her purse.

"You smoke?" I said, surprised. "You don't seem like the type."

"What type of people smoke?" Her voice sounded huskier than I'd noticed before, possibly because tars and nicotine now coated her throat.

"I don't know. People who drink a lot of coffee often smoke. And I don't really know. I'm just surprised at you." I hesitated to speak of dating someone, not certain I was getting off to a good start. But Gil needed help. "Did you think about what I mentioned to you the other day—that Jake seems like a good man?"

I watched her eyes—wide and pale green usually, but now hard and narrowed.

A jolting chill shook me. I feared those eyes had stared at me before.

She held her cigarette high, red lipstick surrounding the filter like a kiss.

My gaze swerved to the ground beside the fence. A few cigarette butts. Two with plum lipstick. My legs numbed. I'd seen her wearing that lipstick before, I now realized. The first time I saw her, that lipstick matched her suit.

"You were with Pierce Trottier before he died, weren't you?" I said, staring at the butts like the one I had found. "And you came outside their stop-smoking session to find out how people would react to his death."

"He was a vicious man." She pointed at me with her long cigarette.

"What you did to him wasn't nice, either." I shifted my purse on my shoulder. Not heavy enough to hurt her. My phone was inside it.

"I don't have to be kind to the people I hate."

Another fear emerged. "Fawn McKenzie? Did you kill her?"

Babs leaned toward me. "She was supposed to be him."

Him numbed my brain.

"Yes, you know who. Your precious man who threatened to fire me if I didn't straighten up and quit arguing in front of customers."

My jaw went slack.

She meant Gil. She'd tried to kill Gil.

I was moving toward her. She drew a pistol out of her purse. Aimed it at my chest.

I kept still. "Were you watching me from across the street of my cousin's house the other night?" I asked, remembering a smoke tendril out there. "You watched when I went on the porch."

"I was deciding. Watching you out there and deciding what I would do. It's a good thing I live only a couple of blocks away and didn't have to drive too far at night."

"So you saw my car out front one day."

"I saw you."

A new chill ran down my arms. "Why would you want to hurt me?"

"I know you're most important to him. I'd hurt him any way I could." She aimed the gun higher, its barrel pointed at my nose. "And I tried last night. I finally made the decision to break in. But you were gone from the house."

So she'd broken in. Moved through the house in the dark. Smashed Minnie along the way. My Minnie.

"There's a gate back here," Babs said. "I want you to go through it. I'll have this gun aimed at your back. I guarantee I'll use it."

I turned toward the rear gate. "What's back there?"

"A garbage vat. You'll climb inside it."

Depravity had guided this woman, making her kill two people that I knew of. And now she believed I'd want to take my chances inside a Dumpster, and possibly she'd miss me with her gun? I faced the gate, slipping my hand inside my purse. I opened my cell phone, ready to press the memory button for Gil. I glimpsed inside my purse. Not one pinch of light. Dammit, was my battery dead? Or maybe it worked, and Gil was about to answer his phone. I'd speak so he'd know where I was and my problem.

"Babs," I said, placing both hands in her view, "do you come here behind Cajun Delights often to smoke? And do you always bring a gun?"

She looked at me curiously. She glanced at my purse, still open. "What are you doing?"

I turned toward her. "I need to know why. I understand you got pissed off at Gil and wanted to hurt him, probably since you'd already killed Pierce Trottier. So what was another dead body, right? But why Trottier?"

"He cheated my mother. They were second cousins, so she trusted him and let him keep the books for her gift shop in Alabama. She thought her funds weren't coming out right, but he promised he'd take care of the problem." Her gaze fell to the ground. Swung to me. "He did. She lost everything."

My heart lightened. "But it's just money."

"My dad always told Mom she was so dumb. She bought that gift shop to prove he was wrong."

"She can still show him. She can get back on her feet."

Green eyes viewing me widened. "She killed herself." Babs straightened her arm, taking aim at my forehead.

"Don't do it," I said, legs shaky. "Your mother wouldn't want you to kill again."

"It's too late." Her knuckles tightened on the gun.

The back door burst open. "There you are." Stevie stood on the top step.

"Squash her!" I yelled.

Stevie's eyes swung toward Babs and widened. She threw herself at Babs.

Striking her side, Stevie made her wobble. The gun went off, the bullet going wide.

I slammed my own body against Babs's opposite side. We all tumbled to the ground.

I scrambled on my knees and grabbed the loose gun. Babs fell on her back.

Stevie plopped down, sitting on her chest.

"Get her off me!" Babs cried. She looked especially frail

under my cousin's wide hips.

Gil came rushing through the gate we'd almost gone through. "What the hell?"

"Long story," I said and kissed his lips. I leaned against Gil's chest for his strength, waiting for my trembles to stop.

Sirens wailed. They came nearer.

I held onto Gil and shook.

CHAPTER 34

"I was pulling up to Cajun Delights when I heard the gun go off and then your yell," Gil told me. "Your voice registered before the gunshot."

Police took Babs away. I answered many of their questions during the afternoon, with Gil and my cousin close by. Stevie seemed shocked that Babs was such a horrid person. Gil hadn't known the terrible things she'd done, but instinct had told him she wasn't a good person. It was one of the reasons he'd threatened to let her go if she didn't straighten up soon. He hadn't hired her. "But soon I'll need to hire someone to replace her."

"My neighbor," Stevie said, standing straighter.

"April?" I said. "She can manage a restaurant?"

"That's what she used to do. She made good money back in Alabama." Stevie leaned to speak into my ear. "And her name's really Molly. Molly MacRae." She grinned.

So she knew.

I smiled back at her. "And her child's Angel," I said, and Stevie smiled wider.

I faced Gil. "You might hire Stevie's neighbor, Molly. She's great. And I know exactly who might keep her child all summer."

Stevie beamed.

The police were finished with us for a while. Gil drove us to Stevie's house.

307

"Stevie," I said, remembering the day I arrived and fell. "What about the dog? Who has a large one that might have come in your yard?"

Her cheeks reddened. "Did you notice the guy at the gym?"

"Mac? Hard to miss him."

"He runs the place at night. He came over a couple of times. With his dog."

Ah, a romance brewing? Or had it blossomed, and my arrival messed it up? Well I would leave soon, and they could catch up where they left off.

Gil stayed with us a while. Stevie admitted that what changed her so much recently was she could no longer deny to herself the signs that April was not who she said she was. Like me, Stevie noted clues over time and figured it out. But she'd come to love her neighbors so much and feared something bad was going to happen and she'd lose them. That was the real reason she'd wanted me here. She'd hoped that together, she and I could figure out the problem and keep her neighbors here.

How sweet that she'd thought so highly of me. And how surprising.

We all determined the threatening note under Stevie's gate had surely been shoved there by Pierce Trottier and meant for her neighbor. He must have gotten confused since their fences were the same.

The police had discovered how Trottier found out where April lived. She'd been cleaning people's homes and offices. He saw her leaving an office with cleaning supplies and later called that office's manager, saying his cleaning lady quit and he needed to hire someone good to clean his office. The manager told him April did an excellent job. She didn't have a phone number listed but said where to locate the house she rented. It seemed the police had been doing an excellent job of trying to find a killer.

We were all exhausted. Gil invited me to join him but understood I wanted to stay with Stevie, especially tonight. At the front door, he and I hugged. I clung.

When my new bout of shaking was over, Gil touched the tip of my nose. "You'll get over this," he said. "We all will."

I nodded. Held onto him. We kissed. Our kiss deepened.

"Are you sure you want me to go?" he asked once our kiss broke. "Or that you don't want to come with me?"

"Uh-uh." I stepped back. Dropped my arms to my sides.

He planted a warm, lingering kiss on my forehead. "Good night. Call if you need me. I love you."

My eyes misted. I bit my tongue. Nodded. Gil went out the door. I locked it. Sighed.

Stevie was down the hall, the door to her candle-room open. She saw me and said, "This room's a bunch of crap."

I considered the ring of candles. The makeshift altar. "There's carpet on that floor. Maybe you could change it into a workout room."

She eyed me.

"*Somebody* could probably give you help," I offered. "Then you could exercise more at home. But you wouldn't have to stop going to the gym, too."

She ran her hands down her hips. "Then one day I might get this figure back the way it was, it seems, not that long ago."

"I understand. If I don't stop eating so much rich food and start exercising, soon my stomach will become a shelf for my boobs."

We laughed. "But this troubles me," I said and led her to my bedroom. I opened a dresser drawer and yanked up the magazines.

"Cealie, that's horrible," she said in disgust, looking away from them.

"Then why do you have them here?"

A moment of hesitation, then, "I have them?" She tapped her forehead. "A young substitute teacher needed a place to stay for a week. I let her stay here. I changed the sheets after she left and checked the closet to make sure she didn't leave anything."

"She left one magazine under a stack of your sweaters. And a bunch more in the drawers."

"Oh, throw them out. That's disgusting."

"Right. Disgusting," I said. We carried all of them out and tossed them in a large trash can.

"You're welcome to stay," Stevie said. "For as long as you like."

"Thanks. I can't. I have a business to run and places to go before my life is done. People to see."

"Where?"

"Who knows? But if I stay around Gil much longer, I probably wouldn't be strong enough to leave again. And I have to. I need to rediscover Cealie."

Stevie squeezed my hands. "I understand."

I went with her to the next Quitters Group meeting. Received harsh stares from most members. I stood and apologized for treating them so poorly. "I didn't mean to hurt you. I was only trying to find out what happened to the people who died. You were the only connection I knew."

"You're forgiven," Jenna said, getting to her feet. "You were only trying to help." She glanced at all the other members. "Right? *Right?*"

"That's right." Father stood and faced me. "I know you came snooping around me and my lady friends, but I believe your intentions were good." He squeezed my hands.

Kern Parfait sat, shaking his head. He looked up at me. "You have no idea what you've done to my business." He got to his feet. "Ever since you came and made all that commotion, my place is filled every day. Mostly older teens, maybe wanting to see if you'll come back. I hope you will."

I hugged him.

Ish cleared his throat behind me. "Detective Renwick came over again. He said he felt so bad for me the night you all came over, and he heard me putting myself down so much. He brought me some books on positive thinking. I've been reading them and perking up about myself. Yesterday I got up the courage to call a woman and ask for a date. She said yes!"

All of us enthused with him.

"One other thing you all need to do," I said to everyone, "is change the name of your group."

Ish nodded. "I'm realizing that now."

"The Quitters Group needs an apostrophe," I said, "but that name also has a negative connotation. How about calling yourselves The New Life Group?"

All of them smiled.

Once Stevie and I were back at her house, I said, "I have another favor to ask before you get rid of all your psychic stuff. I've heard of love potions. How about anti-love ones?"

"Because?"

"I'm trying to remain strong. Oh, and maybe you could also teach me to meditate, especially on pure thoughts."

My cousin grinned and nodded.

A few days later I knew whatever she'd done then had not worked well. When I shielded myself in my mantra, I needed to envision it in all caps. I AM WOMAN. I CAN DO ANYTHING—ALONE!

I had to get away from Gil soon, or it would be too late. We snuggled more than once. Mmm, how much harder it became to stay away from him. I could easily have tried to keep him always in my sight.

To surprise him, one evening when the joke contest started, I ran up. I stood onstage and told everyone my joke. I gave it a twist, making it B and T: "Boudreaux told Thibodaux he'd started a new church with a drive-up confessional. He had put up a sign—Toot and tell, or go to hell."

Everyone laughed. I didn't win the contest but felt fine afterward, glad I'd done it. So was Gil. "I challenge you," he said. "Keep telling them until you win."

I was a winner. I had him at my side.

We still had Molly's problem to contend with. Stevie and I convinced her to use my cell phone to call a friend she trusted back in Tuscaloosa. While she spoke to the woman, hope sprang into her eyes. They were teary when she hung up. "My ex had an accident," she explained. "He broke his back. He'll live in a wheelchair."

"So he can't hurt you or your daughter," Stevie said, and Molly shook her head, tears flooding her cheeks.

"I want to be who I am," she said. "Molly McRae."

"Nice name," I said. "And Angel is an adorable name for an adorable child."

The little girl I'd known as Cherish stood next to her mom, giving me a broad smile.

I phoned Dr. Marie in New England and gave her the details of what had happened. She was surprised to hear that Babs had soaked two packs of cigarettes in water, cooked that mixture down until she had a mega-strong nicotine tea, and injected that into the three nicotine patches she slapped on Pierce Trottier's back. She was not surprised that the ache in my shins was minimal. "It should be totally gone soon," she said. "Take care, and come and see me soon, Cealie." I promised I would.

Molly went to work for Gil, managing Cajun Delights during the day. He also hired the waitresses we suggested: Lark and Clark and Lois and Sue. They all looked attractive in their nonsensual outfits and would soon have opportunities to move up in the business.

I bought a gift certificate to a lingerie shop for Molly and a toy store certificate for Angel. I left them with Stevie, asking her to give them to the pair when the time was right. I handed a wrapped gift to Stevie. "For you."

Looking curious, she peeled the wrappings. Burst out laughing like a hyena. She gasped, and I ran behind her. Got my arms around her, ready to pull off the Heimlich.

"I love them!" she cried, and I backed off. She draped her wrist with the pink plastic bracelets and shoved the matching barrette into her hair. The cheap ring fit her pinkie finger. She wound the metal key on the jewelry box, and a ballerina spun on it.

"You needed your own," I said.

We chuckled and hugged. Stevie gripped my hand. She turned it over. "Oh, no."

"What's wrong?"

"Your life line. It's cut in half."

I gasped, staring in my hand.

"I'm playing," she said with a grin. "Cealie, I'd like to buy you another cactus."

"I might get one later. Not now. Another one wouldn't be the same."

"Are you still going to Acapulco?"

"No. I had looked forward to going with Minnie and maybe finding some others like her. Now I'm not sure where I'll head."

Da-dunt, da-dunt, da-dunt. I kicked my feet and answered, "Hello, Cealie here."

"Hey, Cealie! It's your favorite Jane from high school."

"Jane!" I shrieked. I hadn't seen her since we graduated.

"And I've missed you. So have our other buddies. We've wanted to call you but didn't know how. I just cleaned out a drawer and found the scrap of paper I'd written your cell phone number on."

"I'm glad you did. It's great hearing from you."

"Let's get together. A few of us will spend time catching up on a cruise. Tetter's having major problems we're going to help her with. We have an extra bed. You'll be joining us, right?"

Tetter, super sweetheart. And all of the others I hadn't seen since we were girls. We were so young then. What interests would we share? Who were they now? I had no idea how they'd look.

Surely no relatives of mine would be on that cruise ship. And Gil would not be opening another of his Cajun restaurants on a ship and tempting me.

Would he?

I tightened my grip on the phone. "Count me in."

CAJUN DELIGHTS

Chicken and Sausage Gumbo à la Bob

Ingredients:

3 lbs. chicken
1 lb. smoked sausage
1/3 c. oil
2 lbs. cut okra (frozen)
1 #303 can whole tomatoes (cut up)
1 lg. onion
1/2 lg. bell pepper
1 t. sugar
Salt and pepper to taste
2 qts. water

Step 1—Cut up skinned chicken and season generously with salt and pepper. Bake at 350 degrees until you can easily take the meat off the bone, possibly 45 minutes.

Step 2—While chicken bakes, smother the okra:

In a heavy pot, combine vegetable oil, okra, tomatoes, onions, and bell peppers. Cook over medium heat about 45 minutes or until slime of okra disappears, stirring constantly.

* Cajuns usually cook large amounts and freeze in quart bags for future gumbos.

Step 3—In a large pot combine smothered okra, de-boned chicken, cut-up sausage, sugar and water. Cook over medium heat for approximately 1/2 hour. Serve over cooked rice.

Umm-umm, good!

Bob's Special Lima Beans

1 lg. pkg.. (3 lbs.) frozen small lima beans
1 lg. onion
1/2 bell pepper
1 t. sugar
Salt and pepper to taste
1 lb. cut-up salt pork (optional)

In a heavy pot, sauté onions and bell pepper until onions are clear. Add frozen lima beans and cover with water that extends 1 1/2 inches above beans. Add sugar and cook about an hour, or until beans are soft.

If salt pork is used to enhance the flavor, cut it into small cubes. Wash off to remove some salt and place in a pot of water. Bring it to a boil. Drain water and wash the meat again. Add salt pork to the lima beans while sautéing the onions and bell pepper.

Eat as is or over rice. Enjoy!

FENG SHUI BASICS

Here are a few things Cealie learned from her cousin, Stevie.

Feng Shui is the ancient Chinese art of improving your life by enhancing the harmony and energy flow between you and your physical surroundings. Feng means wind and shui means water.

Wind (or air) and water are natural elements that circulate everywhere on Earth and are basic for human survival.

Following Feng Shui principles in the home and office can help you design working and living environments that allow more energy to flow through your whole being.

Feng Shui should provide comfort, safety, and living with things you love. You can Feng Shui your home, office, and even your desk. Change is good!

Ask yourself these questions about items in your home:

Why do I have this?
Do I need this?
Do I love this?
Does it help me?
If I moved tomorrow, would I take it?

Does each thing in each area feel like the right anchor for a fantastic now for you or an amazing future? Identify things that deplete or drain your energy and those that make you feel happy and alive. Keep only the good things.

Everything in your environment is considered alive. Wind chimes bring in energy. Take them inside. Store nothing just because.

A Feng Shui Octagon divides a floor plan into life areas that hold different energy. Use it with your house or your office. Pay special attention to any area you want to improve: Career is located in the center front. Family is located in the center left. Helpful People in the right front. Knowledge in the left front. Wealth is the back left. Fame or Reputation in the back center. Marriage or Partnership is the back right. Children in the center right. Health in the center of the octagon. Colors and shapes are important in these areas.

As with everything else Cealie learns, she figures she doesn't have to actually *use* her knowledge, especially since she seldom stays home. But if *you* are interested in learning more about Feng Shui, you might try some of these sources: attend conferences on Feng Shui, read *101 Feng Shui Tips for Your Home* by Richard Webster, *Clear Your Clutter with Feng Shui* by Karen Kingston, *Feng Shui for Dummies,* or many other books on the subject. You also might hire a Feng Shui consultant or take an online class with one.

QUITTING SMOKING

Cealie has no idea how hard it is for a smoker to quit.

I do. So do many of you. You probably tried to quit yourself or get someone you love to give up the horrible habit.

I finally quit smoking four years ago! It was terribly difficult. How I wish I had just suffered through the pangs of stopping much sooner. I hope my experiences or things I learned will help someone else, maybe you.

Not starting to smoke is best. I started with teenage friends after school in the graveyard near our house. Fitting place. I coughed like mad and felt weak, but soon tried again. I smoked for decades. Occasionally I'd try to give it up for a day, but that felt uncomfortable and fellow smokers would say it was too hard to quit. How easy it was to give in to that concept.

I eventually tried to quit many times before succeeding. I tried various resources. Some worked for a while; others didn't. What matters is I finally quit! For good. And I'm so much healthier.

There are lots of things people do while quitting smoking. Pray. Call on friends. Hypnosis. Exercise. Walk out the door and go around the block. Dig in your yard; plant flowers or vegetables and watch them grow. Suck on a straw or cinnamon stick or sugarless gum or hard candy.

Support groups are great; many hospitals sponsor them. People use nicotine lozenges or patches or gum. Doctors prescribe medications and do laser treatment. Keep your hands busy. Draw. Color. Do needlepoint. Snap a rubber band on your wrist. Hug and kiss someone. Keep hugging and kissing.

If you smoke, do one thing or a combination of things to help you to quit. Throw away the cigarettes. Don't ever pick up another one. Contrary to what might happen near Cealie, no one ever died from quitting smoking. You might feel uncomfortable for a while, but discomfort passes. You get healthier. You live longer.

Quitting is the greatest gift a smoker can give her or himself and the people who love her or him.

Good luck. You *can* do it! Millions of others quit. I hope you'll tell me about your journey toward regaining your life and your health.

ABOUT THE AUTHOR

Award-winning author **June Shaw** lives along a lazy bayou in south Louisiana, happily surrounded by loved ones, including her large family. She enjoys being with them and reading and dancing and fishing and eating seafood, especially boiled crayfish, and watching L.S.U. and the New Orleans Saints playing football—especially during winning seasons. She hopes you'll enter her contests and write to her at www.juneshaw.com.